I0742946

VENARI

K.N. NGUYEN

Copyright © 2025 DragonScript

All rights reserved.

No part of this publication may be reproduced, distributed, or transmitted in any form or by any means, including photocopying, recording, or other electronic or mechanical methods, without the prior written permission of the publisher, except in the case of brief quotations embodied in critical reviews and certain other noncommercial uses permitted by copyright law.

www.dragonscript.net

Cover design by Brian Flores and Francis Nguyen.

Layouts by Francis Nguyen.

ISBN-13 978-1-949322-21-7

To the many who helped prepare Venari

Thank you for your sharp eyes and claws

Now, let's hunt

I

TWENTY-FIFTH YEAR IN THE REIGN OF AHKASH

THE LAMPS FLICKERED low that night. Slipping through the open passageway, Nefret prayed that none of the guards would notice her. Her bare feet quietly padded on the cool tile ground, the tiny pieces of colored ceramic creating an elaborate mosaic under her feet of the Rise of Ahkash. Symbols of his holy birthright and images of the gods were separated by large fronds incorporated into the tiles. Usually, Nefret would take her time admiring the art, but not tonight. Tonight, she was to meet with Essam.

Her priestess dress rustled around her, constricting her legs whenever she tried to run down the halls. Each time,

Nefret cursed herself for not taking the risk and changing into something a little more free and flowy. In between the large columns lay open sections of the royal palace. A beautiful architectural design during the day, but not Lord Ahkash's best decision when night fell. Despite the tall wall and near-constant patrols throughout her halls, Nefret often felt that leaving so many openings into the royal palace was bound to invite attack. And there, between the columns at the mercy of the winds, the oil lamps flickered. The light they provided was enough to pierce the absolute blackness of night, but the light didn't travel far. It traveled just far enough to illuminate the next column.

The lack of guards unnerved Nefret. She should have encountered someone by now.

Pushing away her unease, she continued on. The golden bands around her arms, her flesh adorned with jasmine oil, slipped a bit as sweat mixed with the oil. Her turquoise scarab pendant bounced against her chest with each step. Grasping it tightly in her hand, Nefret whispered a silent prayer to Heru, asking him to protect her and her husband this night.

On the other side of the palace, a shout rang out.

"Damn!" Nefret hissed.

Weighing her chances at escaping, Nefret darted out from the main passageway and into the darkness of the night. If she stayed in the hall, she could maybe pass for being outside her chambers as her needing a breath of fresh air. Nearby, a jackal howled. More shouts.

Nefret regretted her decision immediately – but she couldn't turn back now.

Her feet sunk into the cold sand with each step. Sparing a glance behind her, Nefret saw the bob of torches moving through the palace. The outline of six palace guards running sent her heart racing. Their torches moved towards the original source of the commotion on the opposite side of the citadel. Something told her to freeze. Stopping in her tracks, Nefret stood perfectly still. She blessed the thick clouds that blocked out the light of the moon, giving her an added layer of protection. With a trembling hand, she grasped her scarab pendant once more and murmured a prayer to Heru.

She prayed that Essam hadn't been noticed and that the two could escape out of the garden walls together. The howl of a jackal rang out once more. Time stood still despite the agonizing pounding of Nefret's heart against her chest. Each beat was like a hammer striking her ribs and brought a gasp to her lips. Throughout it all, Nefret continued to pray.

But her prayers could not help her.

A cry from the palace made Nefret's blood run cold. One of the guards turned towards the dark expanse where she stood hidden. The others followed suit. Nefret's breath caught in her throat, and she let out a strangled gasp. The soft white glow of the moon filtered through the clouds, illuminating the palace grounds just enough that her figure could be seen.

The guards were still too far away from the other group of soldiers. Perhaps she could outrun them.

With the grace of a cat, Nefret spun on her heel and raced towards the outer wall. There was a rock next to one of the sycamore fig trees that dotted the perimeter. Having practiced several times before, Nefret knew she could use the rock and trunk to help her vault over the wall, buying her the few precious minutes she needed to escape. She hoped she would find Essam on the other side.

Nefret's legs pumped until they burned. Her breath came out in ragged gasps. Still, she pushed on, not looking over her shoulder lest she slow herself down. If she had looked behind her, she would have seen that the soldiers were gaining on her.

"Stop!" a man's voice called out.

The words sent chills down Nefret's spine. The voice was much too close.

Another cry, farther away. This time, it was one of pain.

Essam.

She was close. Nefret could see the dark form of the rock she planned to jump off of next to the bent trunk of the sycamore fig. If she pushed herself, she could just make it.

Essam's voice rang out again. His cries of agony chilled Nefret in a way that her pursuers hadn't. They were constant, as though he were being beaten. Or worse.

In a panic, Nefret hoped that with her escape she'd be able to return for her husband in time. The other defectors said that they would be waiting in the slums earlier in the week. Together, they could help her leave the capitol city of Kul El for safety before returning to besiege the palace. Pharaoh Ahkash would rue the day he overthrew the Holy Pharaoh Akhen and bathed Kul El in the blood of the innocent.

Whispering a silent prayer to Heru, Nefret steeled herself to jump onto the rock and launch herself over the wall. Tensing her muscles, Nefret pushed off in a soaring leap. Nimble as a cat, she floated. However, a blow to her back stopped her before her feet reached the stone. Nefret's head slammed into the rock and blinded her instantaneously with a bright white light before she was engulfed in darkness.

***

Nefret cracked open her eyes with a groan. Firelight blazed from the oil lamps surrounding her, their tongues too bright in the otherwise deep darkness of the rooms. She hissed, eyelids fluttering against the glare, every flicker sharpening the pounding in her skull. Her head ached from where it slammed against the stone earlier. Nefret didn't recognize where she was, but the stale air made her wonder if she was in one of the underground chambers. Her hands trembled as she reached up to gingerly touch her head. Rope dug into her wrists, its coarse fibers wrapped tightly around her soft flesh. She paused, her fingers brushing against something rough. A strip of cloth wound around her head, the stiff fabric not helping the throbbing.

Daring to try once more, Nefret opened her eyes just enough that she could see through her thick lashes. A flurry of feet rushed past her and Nefret stilled her breathing, pretending to be unconscious. The soldiers went by without a word, leaving Nefret bound on the ground. Shadows flickered on the walls as people moved about. Men talked about something but in between throbs it all sounded like a bag had been placed over her head.

Being only nineteen seasons, Nefret feared what would happen to her. She'd heard tales of what happened to the young women outside the palace. Yes, Essam was older – as was their custom, he was in his late twenties – but she married older herself. At fourteen, her family worried she wouldn't find a husband. Essam was the reason she had been taken in as a priestess to begin with. If it weren't for his rank as a royal guard, who knows what would have happened to her.

A dark sandaled foot nudged Nefret and she gasped. She regretted the noise as soon as it left her lips.

"She's awake," the guard announced.

The pain in Nefret's head intensified and she let out a strangled yelp as the man grabbed a handful of her hair and lifted her off of the ground. He was a young soldier, younger than Essam when she first met him, with angular cheeks and a sharp nose. He was not particularly handsome.

"Pretty thing, aren't you?" he sneered. "Then again, I haven't seen a priestess I didn't like."

The man threw Nefret to the ground, her body slamming into the carved stone floor. She grunted at the impact, ignoring the tears that sprung to the corners of her eyes as her head felt as though it were split open. She had to be strong and not let him know she was terrified. While glaring at the man, Nefret took a deep breath through her nose to still her trembles. She hoped he didn't notice.

The man met her gaze and stared at her with contempt. A nearby groan caught Nefret's attention, breaking her stare with the soldier. This time, Nefret didn't try to conceal the strained gasp of panic as she saw Essam's bloody body on the stone table in front of her. His arms were tied down with rope to keep him from moving, but they didn't need to do that. He was unconscious.

"Essam," she croaked, her mouth suddenly dry. "Wake up. Essam."

Nefret watched as the soldier in front of her looked from her bound form to her husband. A grin spread from ear to ear as he turned to face her.

"You know him?"

He must be a new soldier. It wasn't exactly a secret in the palace that a priestess married a soldier. The fact that she carried his child was. All priestesses were supposed to remain pure to better commune with the gods.

"Wake him up," the soldier commanded.

Nefret wondered what his rank could be. She'd never seen him before, but the others listened to him as though he had some sort of authority. Another soldier strode over to the table and slapped Essam's face several times. The actions only drew groans from the unconscious man. A second soldier came up and punched the restrained Essam in the gut before throwing a pitcher of water in his face. Essam gasped for air, sputtering for breath between the blow and the unexpected splash.

Without a word, the nearest soldier grabbed Essam's face and turned it towards Nefret. Another gasp, nearly a shriek, escaped her lips. His face was bloodied almost beyond recognition. A large cut above his left eye bled freely, running down his cheek and pooling on the side where his face pressed against it on the stone. His right eye was swollen, and his nose appeared broken. Blood poured from his mouth as well.

Nefret couldn't imagine what the rest of him looked like. Her chest ached as she saw her beloved husband, a man both kind and brave – a man willing to defy the pharaoh to try and restore the order of the gods for the betterment of Ma'Alkin's people. Tears ran down her soft cheeks silently as she grieved his pain. A moment later, she felt a strong hand grasp her face and pull her in.

The sharp-nosed soldier smirked at her, the strength of his hand lifting her off the ground slightly until she could smell his breath. It smelled of anise and arak. Lifting her body and repositioning her when she was parallel to the table, the man straddled over her. His eyes roved over her body hungrily, stopping at her bust that was almost completely exposed by his rough treatment. Nefret felt her face burn hot, but she held his gaze with her own.

"They're on their way," the man who threw the pitcher of water said. "There'll be no trial."

"Excellent," the sharp-nosed soldier replied. "No reason for the traitor to be shown any mercy."

Releasing her face, the man squatted above her, one of his knees resting on the ground. He glanced over to Essam, nodding with his head that she should follow suit. Nefret looked to her husband. His eyes drooped as he appeared to be struggling to remain conscious.

"Should we show him mercy?" he asked.

Nefret's head spun as she looked at the man. Her question died on her lips as she saw his schenti had been removed while she stared at her husband. The man hovered over her, erect, and her chest constricted.

"Should we?"

Wordlessly, she nodded her head, eyes wide. Off to the side, Essam groaned as the other soldiers chuckled. Her hands still bound, Nefret attempted to bring her knees up and wriggle away, but the sharp-nosed man roughly grabbed her tied hands and slammed them over her head onto the ground. Covering them with his forearm, he hitched up her dress with his free hand.

Quick as a flash, he grabbed her hips and lifted them up until her legs wrapped around his waist. A whimper escaped her lips as he forced himself inside her. Once he was deep within her, the sharp-nosed soldier began roughly thrusting, his hand wrapping around her throat. A strangled cry broke free as he moved faster and faster, the friction of his flesh painfully rubbing within her. The man with the pitcher sauntered over, still making sure that she was visible from the table and shoved his erect manhood into Nefret's mouth. She tried to scream, but her cries were muffled and turned into gags as the man tried to get the entire length of his manhood into her mouth over and over.

The two forcefully satisfied themselves with Nefret's body – tears streamed down her face from pain and shame. The sharp-nosed soldier thrusted so hard she felt her body tear. Once the two released their seed within her, they switched spots. The one who had been by Essam came forward and slipped underneath Nefret, entering her from her backside. The remaining five soldiers in the room lined up, their schenti undone and stroking themselves as they waited their turn. One by one they entered her and violently abused her until they could no longer become hard. It felt like hours before it was over.

Finally, they left her be. Their seed poured from her aching, quivering body. Sweat and tears slicked her skin, the top of her dress having been pulled down to expose her breasts. Nefret's body tingled with a pain she would not enjoy. Throughout it all, she stared at Essam, who watched the attack while tied to the table. Tears ran down his face, mixing with his blood. Nefret could see it in his eyes – he blamed himself.

The flames hung low in the oil lamps. Shadows flickered along the walls. Nefret remained on the cold ground, her body trembling as the adrenaline still coursed through her. Tears ran down her cheeks. She didn't bother to fight them at this point, and her body hurt. Essam had stopped making noise a while ago.

Why didn't he protect her?

Nefret knew the thought was ridiculous, yet her heart still ached as she remembered him watching quietly as the men brutalized her.

All she wanted to do was to die. Shame. Anger. Pain. The emotions all swirled around within her, threatening to overwhelm her. Closing her eyes, Nefret said a silent prayer to Asar, begging for release.

***

The sound of talking woke Nefret up. Disappointed, she opened her eyes. The soldiers had now been joined with others. Sem Priest Hori, the high priest of Asar, passed into her field of view.

Why was he here? Hori only came by when people died.

Moving sent a spike of pain through her head. Whoever tackled her as she jumped for the rock was going to pay, but Nefret knew she had to look around. Ushabti and canopic jars lined the periphery of the stone table Essam lay tied to. Nefret's heart froze, her blood running cold. A soft groan from the table sent her heart beating with deep, slow throbs.

Essam was still alive.

Unconsciously, Nefret brought her hands to her body and slowly pushed up into a sitting position. Someone must have untied her while she slept. Her top had been pulled back up too. Men hustled by, oblivious to her awakening. Using the back of her arm, Nefret wiped her mouth. The soldiers had cleaned her up. The bastards.

"O Asar, god of Dū-aat, hear our plea. Take this man. We offer his ba, his ka, and his akh all to you. As a traitor to the almighty pharaoh, we ask that you do not offer him safe passage through Dū-aat. Let his life be a warning to others."

The voice of Sem Priest Hori rang in the room. Nefret quickly glanced around, trying to see if she recognized the room. The oil lamps burned low and the shadows on the walls made it difficult to see any identifying objects or features. Nefret didn't spend much time looking around, however. Her eyes were pulled back to the table.

Hori produced a long silver dagger from the folds of his leopard-skin pelt that covered his linen skirt. A rare beam of light from the dying glow of the lamps flashed off of his shaved head. The blade glimmered, the low-burning radiance casting shadows on part of the steel.

Nefret's breath caught in her throat as the sem priest plunged the dagger into Essam's chest. A gurgling scream tore itself from her husband.

"We offer to you, O Asar," Hori said.

Essam's breaths came out in ragged gasps, his chest barely moving. Without another word, the other group of men, the embalmers, got to work. Their knives cut into Essam's flesh, blood droplets flying as the blades were pulled free from Essam's body.

More gurgles.

One of the apprentices brought over a canopic jar with Imseti's head carved on top. The nearest embalmer dug his hands into Essam's now open body and pulled out his liver. With another slice, the organ was pulled free and placed into the jar. The process was repeated for his intestines and stomach. By now, Essam's breathing was almost non-existent. Globs of blood flew from his mouth as he let out a pitiful cough. Throughout it all, Nefret watched in a daze.

This was not happening.

Nefret struggled to stand, but her head still spun. A stream of pleas flowed from her lips, begging the men to spare her husband despite him being mere minutes away from succumbing to his wounds. Her words came out incoherent as she implored Sem Priest Hori to at least give Essam his holy rites and allow him to return to their world once more. But her cries were ignored, only earning her a swift kick to the stomach from the sharp-nosed bastard.

The last jar was brought forth by the apprentice. Reaching with his blood-soaked hands, the embalmer dipped them into Essam's body once more and brought forth the lungs. Nefret let out an ear-piercing shriek as the lungs were cut out of her husband's body and placed into the canopic jar. Nefret struggled to her feet. She had to reach her husband.

The high priest and embalmers glanced in her direction, Hori's brow rising in a question. Taking a step forward, Nefret's screams turned into cries of agony as the sharp-nosed soldier grabbed her around the waist and held her back.

Why were they stopping her from holding her husband one last time?

"You may continue," the sharp-nosed soldier said.

As Essam's heart was pulled from his body – he had stopped breathing before his lungs were removed – Nefret's knees gave way, and she sank to the ground. Full-bodied wails tore themselves from her breast as she crumbled to the stone floor and wept. Tremors wracked her slim frame, but she no longer cared.

Before he walked away, she heard the sharp-nosed soldier mutter, "Good luck finding him in your next life."

The embalmers worked for many long hours preparing Essam's body for mummification and disposal. Throughout it all, Nefret wept on the floor. Nobody paid her any mind. She was broken.

II

NEFRET WANDERED BLINDLY THROUGH the royal gardens. The high priest decided to grant the illusion of mercy to the rest of the palace servants by allowing the soldiers to return her to her life as a priestess. The story of the poor young priestess, tricked into straying from her holy duties by a deceitful man masquerading as a palace soldier, quickly traveled through the halls. Whether anyone could truly call it mercy, Nefret couldn't say. So much had been stolen from her – her body, her husband, and now her baby. Blood ran down her legs and her stomach clenched in unspeakable agony as her body rejected the last remnants of her former life.

No one spoke of her involvement in the betrayal of the pharaoh. No one acknowledged that she was no longer pure, unfit to continue her holy duties. Instead, they left her to wander the halls, the image of her husband's demise burned into her mind. They knew she would not try to escape again. They knew she would not speak of the horrors she just witnessed. She remained mute, tears falling silently down her cheeks day and night. The palace staff and her fellow priestesses assumed that Nefret felt shame at her naivety and how she had been tricked so easily. The sharp-nosed soldier made it a point to patrol the corridors near the priestess quarters ever since, leering at Nefret whenever they crossed paths.

The gods have forsaken us. The thought ran through her mind ceaselessly, a never-ending mantra that filled her both with despair and anger.

The sem priest will continue manipulate the pharaoh… the fool.

If only they succeeded in their escape. If only they could meet up with the soldiers from the outlying cities and villages to prepare for battle. Essam had been innocent in all of this, trying to stop Nefret from joining those who wanted to avenge the Holy Pharaoh Akhen. If only she had listened to her husband. He would be alive and she would be the one doomed to wander restlessly through Dū-aat for all of eternity, unable to reincarnate so the two could meet up in another life.

In her agony, Nefret couldn't even find it in herself to wish death on the sharp-nosed bastard and his cohorts. The gods had indeed forsaken her, leaving her a shell of her former self.

Nefret made her way to the river that ran into the garden. The tall reeds occasionally hid the unexpected crocodile that managed to sneak far enough upstream. Perhaps one might find her and end her misery.

The cool waters made her dress fan out, the blood on her legs disappearing into the water like small fingers from her flesh. No crocodiles today. Disappointed, Nefret decided to end it herself. Taking one last tear-filled look at her former home and the place that had taken so much from her, Nefret felt her heart jump when she saw a red-headed woman wading into the waters towards her.

"Please stop!" the woman gasped, pulling Nefret into a tight embrace. A slight accent tinged her words. "Please. I can help you."

This simple act of kindness broke Nefret in a way she didn't think possible. Wrapping her arms around the pale woman, Nefret sobbed uncontrollably onto the woman's shoulder. After all she'd been through, Nefret needed someone who cared.

The pale woman untangled Nefret from the reeds, pulling her out of the water and back to safety. Just because they didn't see any crocodiles didn't mean they still weren't there, creeping ever closer for a meal. Once out of the waters, the redheaded woman wrapped her brown head scarf and cream-colored shawl around Nefret's trembling body. The aches of her failed pregnancy still wracking the young priestess' body.

"Where can we go to talk?" the pale woman asked, her wide eyes staring into Nefret's.

With a quivering arm, Nefret pointed weakly towards a door a little way away. The pharaoh's personal library. The two moved slowly, the cramping of Nefret's stomach making it difficult to walk, and slipped into the room, closing the door behind them as softly as humanly possible. Though the halls had been empty, the young priestess worried that someone had seen the them. Nefret went to light a few oil lamps, but the red-headed woman stopped her.

"Be still, my sweet," the woman whispered, her hand running through Nefret's thick wavy hair. "We mustn't be seen."

"How?" Nefret began, but was immediately hushed by the woman.

The woman cupped Nefret's face gently in her hands, staring into her eyes once more. The young priestess found herself crying again at the soft touch. The woman comforted Nefret as her grief spilled forth. By the time she stopped sobbing, Nefret's eyes adjusted to the darkness well enough to see the woman in front of her.

"My sweet, they have taken so much from you," the woman soothed when Nefret finally calmed down. "Let me help you. I can help you right their wrongs. I have resources that these men can't even dream of." Planting a tender kiss on Nefret's lips, the pale woman pulled away to stare into the priestess' soul once more. "Do you trust me?"

Nefret's mouth tingled from where the red-headed woman's lips had just been. She thought she tasted a hint of blood, but quickly pushed the thought away. Her salty tears had poured from her eyes and landed freely on her lips. Silently, tentatively, Nefret nodded. Now that her mind was clearing, she started envisioning all of the horrible ways she could end the sharp-nosed man's life.

She wanted to repay his evil in kind.

The pale woman took Nefret's hands into her own and gave them a squeeze. "Let me help you," she said softly once more. "No man will ever hurt you again, my sweet."

III

FIFTIETH YEAR OF THE AHKASH DYNASTY

THE ARAK FLOWED FREELY in the well-lit tavern. A group of four men played sistrum, cymbals, and ney – the one playing the end-blown flute adding a harmony to the main melody of the song. Soldiers and those in training shared both a laugh and a drink together. His muscles still sore from the day's sparring, Zahir spied his classmates as they waved him over and made his way to their table. The three men who were already seated somehow managed to already be well on their way to drunk judging by the volume of their calls in the crowded tavern. Arak sloshed in their mugs, spilling onto the table that had been darkened from years of heavy drinking, between gulps.

Zahir snorted. Taking the time to speak with their captain may have been a smart idea. If he came home to his wife drunk, she probably would smack him with the pan again. Between her and the hangover, he wouldn't be able to function, and the captain hinted that they would be ramping up the intensity of their training.

"What took so long?" Masud practically yelled, his words slurring, despite Zahir standing so close to him next to the chair tucked under their table. "We thought you forgot so we started without you."

Masud held up his mostly empty mug, the last dregs somehow managing to splash over the lip of the cup and onto the table. Sadiq and his brother Salah snickered behind their own drinks. Their eyes were not nearly as glassy as Masud's. Ready for a bit of levity, Zahir slid into his chair and waved over a serving girl.

"I had to speak with the captain," Zahir replied simply. "He said we should be hearing soon if we will be chosen as part of the Royal Guard or just a lowly City Guard. We need to be the best if we're going to receive such an honor."

"I don't really care," Masud said. "Just want a khopesh and the title. Women love the Guard."

"No, they love the power of the Guard," Sadiq threw out.

"The only ones who love the Guard are the ones who make money off them," Salah added.

"No wonder you're so popular," Zahir said in mock awe.

At that moment, the serving girl returned with a mug of arak. Her gaze lingered on Masud, who threw a coin her way. She caught it with a smile and a wink, retreating into another part of the tavern moments later, leaving Masud looking quite proud of himself.

"You're right," Zahir said. "They really do love you. Best you be with the City Guard then. You can spend more time with the girls."

Salah snorted into his drink and Sadiq broke out into laughter. Masud didn't argue and downed his mug. By the way he tilted his head up at the group, Zahir could tell that he was proud of himself. This was why no one took Masud seriously in their military training.

The musicians struck up a new song, the ney opening it up with a harmonized solo before the sistrum joined in. The smell of opium from the corner of the tavern wafted over. Zahir found himself becoming light-headed after a strenuous day of not eating. Cursing the smokers, Zahir pushed away his drink. He couldn't come home drunk.

The other three began joking around with each other, primarily at Masud's expense – which he took light-heartedly. Zahir leaned back in his chair, his shoulders easing away from the table. The smoke coiled thick around him, clinging to his throat and stinging his eyes. Normally they used better opium, but this poppy must have been really bad with as much as it made Zahir cough and his eyes water. A plate of kebabs slid onto the table, the scent of charred meat mercifully cutting through the haze. The serving girl's grin flashed quick and sly before she vanished into the crowd once more, Masud's coin disappearing into her palm just as quickly fast as she melted into the throng.

Not wanting to stay longer, Zahir excused himself from the table – his arak barely touched. The three bade him good-bye, digging into the kebabs and waving down a serving girl for another round of drinks. Zahir slipped out of the tavern and into the cool night air. It was probably a good thing he left when he did. Masud was well on his way to earning a slap from one of the girls for his wandering hands, and Zahir didn't think he could stand the embarrassment of the man's failed lechery once more.

Stars polka-dotted the heavens, the crisp air helping to clear the opium smoke from his head. Now that he wasn't under the influence of the opium, Zahir wished he'd stayed to finish his drink. Despite not wanting to become drunk, he did want to enjoy his night after a hard day in the barracks.

Allowing himself to wander around aimlessly, Zahir found he retraced his footsteps from earlier that evening, winding up at the palace. The tall sandstone walls stood hovering over him. The entrance lay open, a group of guards standing watch and determining who arrived and departed.

Zahir shared a quick word with the guards, mentioning that he needed to return to his bunk in the barracks to grab his khopesh that needed oiling. The five lowered their wooden-tipped spears and let him pass.

***

Khopesh in hand, Zahir walked briskly through the hall towards the front gate. The weapon hung loosely at his hip, the cool, flat side of the blade slapping against his thigh. Occasionally, he ran into guards roaming the corridor, but the palace was relatively quiet. The light of the torches cast a warm glow. Zahir found himself wishing he were taking a stroll with his wife. Between the flames and the pale moonlight, the ambiance felt very romantic. Perhaps this would be the night he filled her with a child like they had been hoping for the last year. Zahir's daughter had been asking for a sister for so long now.

A bit ahead of him, Zahir noticed someone approaching. His hand moving to the hilt of his blade, Zahir tensed. There shouldn't be anyone unauthorized in the palace, but Zahir's training reminded him to be alert.

"Why so jumpy?" the woman asked as she got nearer.

Dressed in the simple white gown marking her position as a priestess, the woman stopped a few feet away from Zahir. A scarab pendant rested on her chest, the only splash of color in her outfit apart from the smear of brown she'd painted on her lips and the kohl around her eyes. The little bit of color on her mouth accentuated her naturally dark lip and gave them the appearance of being fuller.

"Isn't it a little late for the temple priestesses to be wandering about?"

The bell-like tinkle of a laugh escaped her lips and she closed her eyes in mirth, her hand coming up to her mouth. The reaction released some of the tension Zahir had been holding, causing the stiffness in his face to subside and show off his soft features.

"I suppose you're right," she admitted. "Promise not to say anything?"

Her voice and her face both sounded so young, like a girl who barely stumbled upon womanhood. Zahir found himself strangely drawn to her. He wondered if it was because she reminded him of his own little girl. She would be two in a fortnight.

Zahir assured her that he wouldn't; the young priestesses often struggled with acclimating to their new life in the palace and all the rules that came with serving the gods.

"What about you?" she asked. "I haven't seen you on patrol before. You must be new?" The priestess cocked her head in question and her mouth pursed out, plumping her lips.

"I'm still a recruit," Zahir explained. "I hope to be picked as one of the Royal Guard, then I can move my family out of the slums and protect them better. My daughter deserves a chance at a life instead of being doomed to a prostitute or serving girl stuck performing favors in exchange for additional coin."

The young priestess' brow furrowed, her lips drawing together in a thin line. She hummed in disapproval. "You seek a better life for your family, throwing yourself at the mercy of the Great Pharaoh Ahkash II." Tilting her head to the right, she stared deeply into his eyes, studying him. "That is most honorable. Many do not escape their fate."

The priestess' slim fingers went to her chin, stroking it while deep in thought. Zahir felt an unfamiliar clenching in his stomach. Something about the way she spoke to him, so seriously, tingled his nerves.

"May I offer you something?" she asked abruptly.

"Wha- I... well," Zahir struggled to stammer out an answer. The question caught him off-guard.

"I'm sorry," the priestess said, her demeanor changing instantly as she smiled in embarrassment. "I shouldn't be so serious. No, it's just that you remind me of my father. He sent me here when I was a young girl myself in hopes of at least getting me a better life. He hoped that if I were accepted as a priestess, my other sisters could find sanctuary as well."

Taking a step closer and holding her hands out in front of her as though she wanted to embrace him while still maintaining the distance between them, she added, "I would like to help you. Please, come with me and we can talk about keeping both your daughter and your wife safe."

Hesitating for a heartbeat, Zahir found himself nodding. The sweet, childlike smile she'd flashed before returned. The priestess motioned for her to follow him.

The two walked briskly through the open hallway. After a few twists and turns, a knot tightened in Zahir's stomach. They descended into a dark corridor beneath the palace proper. Torches crowded the walls, their flames flickering and spitting, the light writhing over the sandstone and stretching into long, crooked shadows.

"What are we doing down here?" he asked, his voice strained from the stale air.

"The other priestesses have not been given the liberty to commune with the gods quite like I have," she replied. "During my meditations, I have learned how to harness my own strengths to mete justice out to the evil. Sobakh has sanctioned my efforts to boot the unworthy from the palace, never to return."

Zahir stopped in his tracks, intending to leave, but the priestess' hand shot out and grabbed his arm. Her grip was surprisingly strong for such a petite woman. Zahir struggled to pull free, but the woman's hold wouldn't give.

"Be still," the priestess soothed. "Let Nefret help you achieve the strength you desire. With my help, you will be able to protect your little girl for the rest of your life."

IV

Sixtieth Year of the Ahkash Dynasty

Sobakh's heavy body landed once more on the stone slabs. A guttural hiss filled the room that shook the men to their core. Nefret's mouth turned up. She never tired of hearing the soldiers' discomfort whenever the mighty god entered their mortal realm. The sound of claws scraping against stone broke the rhythmic thumping that filled the room only seconds before. Waving her hand, Nefret allowed the men to leave her chambers. The pounding of their feet in the halls outside sent a wave of elation swelling through her. Despite her failure, Nefret remained upbeat. Today was a special day.

On the stone dais where she had been moments before, Nefret heard a weak whimper, or was it a strangled gargle? It was so hard to tell at this point after completing her ritual. No matter. Sobakh would clean up her mess.

Straightening her dress and rearranging the scarab necklace resting on her bosom, Nefret pulled out a thick tome. Sitting on a little stone outcropping were a collection of faded ushabti and canopic jars. Though the paint peeled, they remained pristine with not a speck of dust befouling the sacred jars or tiny figurines. The papyrus crinkled in a most satisfying way as she flipped through the pages in a way that scrolls could not. Images of Sobakh and Asar that usually would catch her attention no longer gave her pause. In the background, Nefret heard the god's jaws snap close with a crunch. Sobakh had accepted his offering despite her failure.

A low moan came from the opposite side of the room followed by the sound of rattling chains. Ignoring the sound, Nefret continued her search. As if from far away, she heard the sound of Sobakh sliding across the stones once more. Flipping through a few more pages, Nefret came across a small passage in the text.

"The Mother Goddess, most revered for creating Ma'Alkin and all life that the holy land contains, holds the wisdom of countless lifetimes in the lavender chalcedony stone which serves as the centerpiece of her necklace. Known for weaving together the ka, ba, and akh of the mortal realm, her tomb is said to hold the secrets of eternity."

"St-stay back!" a man's voice called out.

Her focus broken, Nefret spun towards the source of the noise. Hanging by his wrists from the chains on the wall, a man dressed in a soldier's uniform with angular cheeks and a sharp nose gazed at the approaching deity with wide eyes. His clothes were ripped and blood-stained from the many beatings he'd received.

"Be quiet," the priestess hissed. "You're disturbing my studies."

"Send him back," the man plead. Tears streamed down his dirty face. Another stream ran down his leg, puddling beneath him. "Please. I've apologized for a thousand lifetimes. Please, release me and I will serve you with my life."

A bell-like laugh escaped Nefret. "Of course you will serve me faithfully. It's the least you could do after I've given you this gift. Now silence."

Returning to the yellowed papyrus pages in front of her, Nefret began to hum. The man started babbling incoherently once more, his words becoming more high-pitched with each scrape of Sobakh's claws. His words reached a fevered pitch at the low rumbling growl from the god.

"I beg of you." His words were barely discernable between his sobs.

With the wave of her hand, Nefret didn't even bother turning to face him once more. "You've served your purpose. As my first follower, you've been invaluable – teaching all of my limitations. For that, I owe you the dignity of your final release." Motioning over her shoulder to the ushabti circle at his feet, she added, "Unfortunately, the fate that you cursed Essam to will soon become your own. Farewell."

The sharp-nosed man's screams picked up in earnest at the priestess' dismissal, piercing her ears and keeping her from her reading. The cries were cut short. A loud snap cracked through the air. The wet grind of bone and cartilage tearing free were nearly lost in the last, frenzied shrieks before his pleas disappeared and were replaced with choked gurgles. Sobakh took his offering quickly. Mercifully. No boat would carry this one through the afterlife into Dū-aat. No wrappings. No rites. The body was gone, and with it, the soul.

And without a soul, just like Nefret's husband, there would be no return for the sharp-nosed man. His crime in life had now been atoned for. His soul was heavier than the feather – at least Nefret judged so.

Having fed, the heaviness in the room vanished. Sobakh returned to his holy realm.

"Oh, Essam," she murmured, alone. "Wait for me. I promise I will find a way to bring you back."

Turning back to the tome, Nefret read a few more pages, not wanting to miss anything. The cries of the soldier as he met his end echoed in her mind. They blended together with the screams of Sem Priest Hori fifty years earlier. Usually, they did not bother her, but now, they made it hard to concentrate. Finally, she closed the book. She would search some more, but at least now she had a place to start. Again. Sixty years Nefret followed every path she could in hopes of bringing her beloved back.

"Neith, Holy Mother Goddess," she muttered. "Don't disappoint me."

V

THREE HUNDRED TWENTY-SEVENTH YEAR OF THE AHKASH DYNASTY

THE GENTLE SYMPHONY OF RAIN falling on the clay tile roof woke Evaline. Stars still sparkled through the clouds as she glanced out her bedroom window at the darkened sky. Despite being woken so early, Evaline found herself smiling as she pulled her covers tighter around her, wiggling under her quilt like a small child. The pitter patter continued, the clouds barely darkening the already black heavens. Moonlight did not filter in through the window, leading Evaline to believe dawn would be in another couple hours.

A sigh escaped her lips. Morning would bring the Venari d'Amore, a celebration that would hopefully see her married to one of the local lords in the area. Or better yet, one of the local boys she'd fancied for the last year.

"Our people have celebrated Venari for centuries," Evaline's mother told her as soon as she came of age. "When the Fraunx invaded Aceatius, their men stole our women and made them their slaves. Venari now gives us a small chance to reclaim our honor and provide for our families. Now, we hunt."

"But what about when the lords choose a bride?" Evaline had asked. "We do not get to hunt then."

Evaline's mother replied with a wink, "Do we not? There is more than one way to hunt. When the time is right, there will be no other who could eclipse your beauty. You will entrap the young lord and claim victory." Emphasizing her words with a childish tap on the nose, her mother turned back to the dishes with a swish of her skirts.

Evaline's mother's words echoed in her head. Wriggling out from under her quilt, Evaline furrowed her brow as the night's chill hit her. Opening her window, she felt the freeze devour her fingertips. Evaline ignored the cold as her arm retreated to the warmth of her quilt.

The rain continued to fall, light as a fairy skipping across the top of her house. The morning would bring with it a magic that filled her with butterflies. A smile crept on Evaline's face as she settled down for a few more hours of sleep. Her lids became heavy as her mind filled with scenes of sweetcakes covered in honey and dancing with her sister around the festival pole. She could almost taste the treats as her body moved between the other young women of the village in time to upbeat music, the colorful silk ribbons twisting into a beautiful rainbow pastel braid. A familiar song of drums, fiddles, flutes and a few spoon players floated in the background, helping her keep time as she danced about. Through it all, a mysterious man loomed in the background, tall and lean, his face never quite coming into focus.

The scene played out in preternatural vibrance, the mouthwatering taste of sweetcakes filling her mouth, as is common for that spot between sleep and daydreaming. It wasn't long before she fell asleep to the gentle pattering of rain on her roof, the water mimicking the beat of the drums in her mind.

The chirping of birds woke Evaline up long before the warmth of the sun did. Birdsong leaked into her room through the open window, the stagnant drips of the night's storm landing on her windowsill, still staining the wood and drawing out the musky aroma of the loamy soil just outside her room. Evaline lay nestled under her quilt, her dreams of a new life slowly fading away as she stared at the ceiling.

As the morning's rays filled her room, Evaline could hear the sound of her mother preparing breakfast in the kitchen. The gentle clinks of utensils against plates and pots created their own chorus apart from that of the birds. Soon, the tantalizing aroma of fresh bread, sausage, and eggs accompanied the music of the tin utensils, the unmistakable sound of sizzling now joining in as sausage links were added to a pan. Evaline's stomach rumbled, and her mouth watered as she took in a deep breath, letting the savory scent fill her nostrils.

Voices began filling the kitchen as those in the house stirred. In the bed next to her, Evaline's younger sister, Amalie, threw off her quilt and leapt out of bed.

"Come on, Eve!" Amalie barked. "It's Venari!"

Racing out of the room, Evaline heard the sound of Amalie's fists on the wooden door of their youngest sisters' room beside theirs. Apolline and Elise's voices could be heard along with the slapping of their bare feet against the worn wooden floor as they ran to the kitchen. The deep voice of their father greeted the girls, quickly becoming drowned out as the youngest squealed in joy, no doubt upon receiving their Venari gifts. Winding her auburn hair into an intricate braid upon her head with a lavender ribbon, Evaline exited her room to join the rest of her family.

With a smile, Marie greeted her eldest. "Good morrow." Flour clung to the sheen of sweat on her brow. She wiped her dainty hands on her apron. "Check the hearth. You might find something to help with the hunt."

Glancing towards the fireplace, Evaline saw a simple dress of brilliant green draped over the closest wooden chair. Nearby, Apolline and Elise played with dolls made of dried grass and flowers while Amalie snapped a bone clip into her thick, blonde hair, pulling her delicate curls off her back. Evaline ran her fingers over the soft fabric of her dress.

"Mama, it's beautiful," she murmured. Turning to face her parents, Evaline felt a twinge of pain. Surely such a beautiful dress cost a hefty price. "You didn't have to do this."

"Nonsense," Émile replied. His chair scraped against the floor as he moved to cup her chin with his fingers, a warm smile filling his face. "Our daughters deserve the best on Venari."

Evaline admired how his eyes sparkled. She knew her father had spent long hours at the smithy the last few months to help them make it through the harsh winter.

"Go and prepare, mon amour," Marie said. "I filled the tub with honeysuckle. Once you're done, I'll help you get ready."

Evaline fought back a tear as well as a smile. A small sob got caught in her throat as she held the delicate fabric in her hands, her fingers gripping it tightly as she brought it to her face. Excited chatter filled the room as Apolline and Elise showed off their dolls to Amalie while their mother poured some eggs and freshly baked scones onto their plates. Their father's gentle baritone could be heard over the girls' as he complimented his wife on her cooking. As she neared the washroom, the commotion disappeared until it was no more than a muffled hum occasionally punctuated by a scream of joy.

The small circular mirror in the washroom was steamed over. In the corner, the small, clawfoot tub sat filled. Honeysuckles floated in slow circles around the bath, filling the room with their sweet aroma. The water warmed her flesh, the cold that she'd grown accustomed to melting away as she slipped deeper into the water until she was covered all the way to the collar bone. A sigh escaped her lips and Evaline closed her eyes. Today was truly a special day.

***

"You'll turn so many heads," Marie whispered, her voice cracking.

Butterflies raced from Evaline's stomach to her chest. She couldn't help but smile as her mother brushed a light streak of red onto her lips, drawing Evaline's eyes away from the freckles that gently dotted her face.

"Oh mother," Evaline mumbled, her voice coming out as an embarrassed moan.

Marie tutted as she gazed proudly at her daughter. "The boys will not know what came over them once they see you. You are beautiful. On top of that, you are smart and hard working. If those aren't desirable qualities, I don't know what are." Pushing Evaline out the door, she finished, "Now go, mon amour. Enjoy your day."

Outside the room, the three younger girls could be heard prattling impatiently. Stealing one last glance at herself in the mirror, Evaline couldn't stop the smile that lit up her face before leading her sisters to the festival.

Amalie's golden curls framed her face, the remainder of her hair twisted up in the bone comb she received for Venari. A blue dress matching the richness of her eyes fit snugly on her slender frame. The elder two Laurent girls turned many heads as they neared the center of town, and with each awestruck look, Evaline felt her smile grow wider. It was nice to be noticed for once.

A crisp chill nipped at Evaline's face despite the sun shining down on her. In the distance, the trilling melody of a flute drew them closer to the festivities. Homes were decorated with bright flower women and ornately carved shields for the holiday. The delicately painted wooden circles all depicted the silhouette of a woman running, some through meadows surrounded by flowers, others of her chasing a butterfly. Always running.

The aroma of meat pies and sweet fruit pies wafted from home windows, making Evaline's mouth water the closer she got to the town square. Apolline and Elise began lamenting that they had to wait until mother made it to the festival before they'd be able to have any sweets. Reaching into a small leather pouch on her hip, Evaline pulled out one of the few copper coins from within and handed them to her younger siblings. With a squeal, the two sped off in search of a snack. Evaline felt a small nudge and turned to find

Amalie shaking her head playfully, a smile plastered on her face.

"It'll give us time to find partners at the pole," Evaline reasoned.

"You mean it'll give you more time to find Henry." Amalie's eyes twinkled with hidden mischief as she was rewarded with Evaline's cheeks flushing brilliantly. "Don't worry, I won't tell."

With a shove, Evaline broke into a jog, her auburn hair streaming behind her between the braids. A short way away, she could hear her sister call out, the sound of her boots against the cobblestones speeding up as Amalie tried to keep pace.

A beautiful melody filled the air as fiddlers and spoon players coaxed young couples into the streets, enticing them to dance. Mothers spun about, their young children shrieking with glee as they held on tightly to their mothers' hands. A few brave young men ventured over to the young women, holding out their hands for a dance. Amalie was quickly approached by a boy barely old enough to grow the beginnings of a beard, and with a nod, joined him.

Their dancing took them closer to the musicians and further from Evaline. With a twinge of jealousy, Evaline watched as the young man's hand rested on her sister's hip, pulling her closer as they danced. She knew her time would come, however. Today felt different to Evaline. It was her time to shine.

Evaline spotted Henry standing with his friends, lounging against a wall and eating a pastry. He glanced her way, catching her eye with his, before turning back to his conversation with a laugh. His chocolate locks seemed to fly slowly as he threw his head back in mirth. Evaline felt her heart skip a beat as she gazed at her Adonis. Before she knew it, Evaline found the gap between the two closing as she strode forward.

"Henry," she heard herself say. His eyes made her heart flutter. "I was wondering if you'd like to join me at the pole later today?"

How did she sound so confident? Butterflies raced around in a panic, and she had a lump in her throat, yet Evaline's words flowed out of her mouth smooth as honey. She even felt her lips turn up in what she assumed was an alluring smile. She could even see some of Henry's friends nudging each other and whispering about her behind his back.

Henry's doe brown eyes gazed back at her through his thick lashes. A chocolate-colored lock fell over his face as Henry cocked his head. Seconds passed by, and Evaline began to worry. The butterflies raced inside her faster and her hands grew clammy. Eternity stretched on in excruciatingly minute detail. She wondered if he'd ever blink again as she lost herself in his eyes. A smile and nod brought her out from her stupor as time returned to normal. Snickers from those behind Henry caused his cheeks to flush the faintest pink.

In the background, the fiddles stopped, and a new song began as the delicate melody of a harp wafted down from one of the windows. The musicians in the square picked up their instruments, joining the harpist with a soft, soothing song. The town's master flutist, Veronique, brought her flute to her lips and began a lilting harmony. Her notes wove between the gentle plucking of the harp as the two women seemed to open their soul to each other and their music became one. The song signaling the beginning of Venari began.

Apolline and Elise stared in awe at their friend's new jeweled butterfly hairclip, their eyes wide in excitement as they jabbered away with the other girls in their group. Like a bouquet of flowers, girls and young women moved through the square, smiles on their faces. Evaline observed as the men gathered around, the gaze of the unmarried men sought that of the young women.

Venari d'Amore, a day where the women of Aceatius remembered those who'd lost it all. Now, they hunted.

VI

CHEERS AND CRIES OF EXCITEMENT filled the air as people danced to an upbeat tune. Fiddles sang between the rousing thumps from the drums and the frenetic clacking of spoons. Women whooped as they moved around the maypole, their lithe figures weaving between each other in their brightly colored dresses. Large swaths of brilliant fabric twisted together, guided by their hands as they moved to encircle the men who danced opposite of them. With each journey around the pole, the length of the men's ribbon shortened, bringing them closer to the women; to those who hunted. The fabric twisted into a gorgeous braid of deep green, vibrant red, and other colors, all expertly dyed by the local clothier. In all of Aceatius, no pole could compare.

Amalie's golden hair, now streaming behind her as the bone comb lay forgotten on a nearby windowsill, shone as it caught the sunlight with each circle. She laughed as she chased the young man she'd been dancing with earlier, her body getting dangerously close to his as their ribbons shortened. Evaline smiled as she saw the flush in his cheeks when her body grazed his.

Henry's wavy hair flew around his face, the sunlight making his eyes sparkle, as he danced in time with Evaline and the others. The orange ribbon in his hand mixed with her cobalt as the two wound together, Evaline chasing her prey. Henry caught her gaze many times, the dimples in his cheeks deepening as he flashed her a boyish grin.

Evaline's heart fluttered as she brushed against Henry's body, her breath catching in her throat as adrenaline coursed through her. His hand grazed her hip, causing her face to flush. Everything was perfection that beautiful morning. Evaline hoped that by the end of the dance she would find the courage once more to admit her feelings to Henry in hopes he would court her. She felt herself prepare to pounce as the ribbon shortened and the music came to an end.

As the song neared its frenzied finale, the women moved in close to their targets, hands often clasping as the two tied the ends of their ribbons together. Henry's fingers caught hers, warm and soft, his brief touch sending a thrill up her arm. Evaline almost didn't notice Amalie leaning in to steal a kiss from her own partner. It wasn't uncommon for the women to steal a kiss during the hunt, but for Amalie to do that surprised her.

A pit formed in Evaline's stomach as she watched her sister pull away, a light flush tinging her already rosy cheeks. Pressure to keep pace with her sister caused Evaline's confidence to falter. In front of her, Henry waited, his big doe eyes pulling her in closer. Evaline felt herself inching towards the young man until her body lightly pressed against his. Henry's head tilted down towards her as Evaline pushed herself up onto her toes.

Their lips brushed together, lightning coursing through her body as they shared a soft kiss. She felt electric, her fingertips reaching for his angular jawline, hoping to feel more of him. At the same time, she felt a longing consume her. Their lips touched for the briefest second before a herald called out, welcoming their Lord Jean Ambrose and his son, Rowan.

Disappointment flooded Evaline as Henry pulled away, his eyes darting to the messenger. It quickly faded as her gaze fell on young lord Rowan. Strawberry blond hair pulled tightly back in a tail, a silk cerulean ribbon that matched his eyes tying it up. Evaline took him in. His cream-colored shirt made of the finest silk paired with dark brown trousers and boots made his simple attire stand out amongst the brightly colored garments of the townsfolk. There was only one reason for the women to hope to be the prey once more – when the local nobility came in search for a bride.

Evaline sucked in her breath as Rowan's gaze swept over her, her heart skipping a beat. Unlike his father, Rowan took in the village with mild curiosity. The young lord's brow twitched up several times, the corners of his lips tugging up as he stopped and looked at some of the other young women. Clearly, the young man was intrigued by what he saw.

Good lord, he's breathtaking! she marveled as she unconsciously pulled away from Henry. As soon as the thought popped into her head, Evaline felt a twinge of guilt. She'd been dreaming of kissing Henry under the pole all year, and for her to forget about it so quickly… Evaline's eyes dropped as the passion she'd felt only moments before returned, dull. The spark she'd felt so strongly was now a distant memory, her body feeling hollow.

"It is time!" the messenger called out, pulling Evaline from her reverie. Instinctively, she moved closer to Henry as the choosing was about to begin. Though he no longer shouted his announcement, the herald's voice maintained its tinny timbre as he ushered the eligible women into a line. "Make haste! His Lordship does not wish to wait."

The eligible women lined up, some reflexively smoothing their skirts or playing with their hair. Evaline found herself standing next to Amalie despite the girl being too young to be chosen. The younger girl's eyes darted from her dance partner to Rowan, chewing her bottom lip in an uncharacteristically nervous fashion. Evaline gave Amalie's hand a squeeze, drawing her sister's gaze to her.

"Everything will be all right," Evaline whispered.

A hasty nod was all she got in return. Amalie's movements were frantic, distracted, as she continued to watch the two men. Before she knew it, Evaline found herself doing the same. Henry had melted back into the crowd, joining up with his friends under the now braided pole. The group observed the line of young women standing in front of Lord Ambrose as he slowly made his way down the line.

One by one, shoulders sagged as Lord Ambrose found fault with each young woman who stood in wait to see if she became the lucky bride. Lord Ambrose's voice carried through the silent town, each word dripping with disdain at the women presented to him. Rowan followed behind, his gaze darkening at each rejection.

"Oh god!" the nasally lord's voice called out. "Surely you can't believe you are worthy? My god, Penningworth. Are there no beautiful women in all of Aceatius?"

The herald raced to the lord as Rowan's voice could be heard hissing and exasperated "Father!"

"My apologies, your Lordship," Penningworth simpered. "I thought there may be a few to choose from who were worthy of your honored name. We broadened your options by including those who have achieved their fifteenth year." The herald's gaze ran down the line, taking in all of the women with a glance. "Here!"

Evaline felt her chest tighten as the three men briskly made their way over. Her cheeks flushed as the butterflies in her stomach from earlier fluttered once more. Rowan's face lit up as he took her in until he was practically beaming. Behind the two, Lord Ambrose's keen eye narrowed. Evaline felt herself break into a broad smile, her head dipping in embarrassment. Amalie squeezed Evaline's hand, her palms sweaty from nerves. Butterflies swirled around within her. Catching Rowan's attention once more, Evaline stood proud.

"Yes," the lord finally said as they stopped in front of Evaline. "She will do." Turning to his son, he asked, "Does this please you?"

"Absolutely, Father."

His voice matched his devastating good looks. Evaline fought back a fit of giggles as several women nearby let out gasps, the one to her right dipping briefly as her knees appeared to buckle. Evaline felt her cheeks burn as she dropped her eyes, gazing at Rowan through her lashes. Her lips turned up in a shy smile on their own accord despite the thrill of adrenaline that coursed through her. Men like him would expect a demure woman, and that is what she would play. For now.

"Then it's settled," Jean Ambrose declared. "Penningworth."

Evaline's head swam as her chest constricted. The butterflies that flew within her exploded with energy, leaving her feeling giddy. Henry's face briefly flashed in her mind, but quickly disappeared as she felt Rowan move closer to her. She'd managed to catch the ultimate prey, and he didn't appear to be horrible at first glance. Her feelings would change, and soon Evaline believed she would feel the same desire for Rowan as she did for Henry.

Their shared kiss only minutes before flashed through Evaline's mind. Sweet. Fleeting. The fact that she'd had her first kiss with Henry made everything feel better. If they'd never had that experience Evaline knew she'd forever wonder what would have been. The thrill of his lips on hers came back, blending in with her excitement.

"The Lord of Aceatius has chosen his bride!" Penningworth's voice rang out.

Opening her eyes, Evaline looked to the young lord. Rowan beamed as he locked eyes with his new bride. Beside her, Amalie let out a shuddering gasp as the young lord grabbed her hand and held it high in the air.

A stunned silence filled the square. Amalie was too young. A polite smattering of applause, one more of shock than excitement, broke out, but Lord Ambrose and his ensemble didn't seem to notice. Roughly grabbing Amalie, Penningworth dragged her out of line and shoved her hand into the young lordling's. Rowan's eyes moved up and down Amalie's body, lingering on her chest and drawing an approving smile. Quiet murmurs could be heard as the pair of lords examined her, oblivious to their surroundings. At a pointed look from Penningworth, the fiddlers broke into a lively tune. Throughout it all, Evaline fought to keep herself upright.

VII

Her world shattered.

Of course it was Amalie who caught the attention of the lord and his son. Though she wouldn't be of age until the autumn, somehow the lord deemed her worthy of marriage. Her heart broke in two. She struggled to accept her sister being torn away so young and that she would not succeed in her hunt for Henry. Out of the corner of her eye, Evaline watched as her sister flashed a nervous smile, one that didn't reach her own eyes. Evaline tried to unclasp her sister's hand, Amalie unwilling to let go as her fingers barely left Evaline's flesh. Hot tears obscured Evaline's vision as Rowan led her sister away, his hand resting on her lower back. Evaline felt her arm tug as Amalie refused to let her go.

Today was supposed to be her day. She was supposed to find her happiness.

"Eve."

Amalie's voice seemed so far away.

A strong pair of hands rested on Evaline's shoulders, but she paid them no mind. In this moment, it didn't matter. Once again, the world showed her that her little sister was the desirable one. She would never catch men's attention; not like Amalie. Disappointed, Evaline turned to find Henry. She spotted him hidden amongst his friends. For some reason, he wouldn't meet her gaze.

Of course, she thought. *There was always someone else.*

As if reading her mind, her childhood friend, Sophie, sidled over to Henry and shot her a timid, apologetic smile as their fingers laced together. Evaline had been so excited that she didn't recall seeing her friend holding the lavender ribbon of the may pole that they both danced around earlier.

How could I have been so foolish? No wonder she never said anything in the weeks leading up to Venari. I wonder how long they have been sweethearts?

Today was supposed to be her chance to conquer her doubts and ensnare Henry with her charm. She'd not even thought about the possibility of a young lord coming. Two rejections in one day didn't seem fair.

Evaline thought back to all of the times when she and her friends would joke about the hunt. Not only about being chosen by a young lord, but who they would dance with under the pole. Every time she had mentioned Henry, Sophie would look away. She'd always assumed her friend was too shy to say anything.

No matter.

"It's time we go, ma petite," her mother's voice could be heard hovering behind her. It sounded so distant. "Tonight will be Amalie's last night before she leaves. I know she will miss you most of all."

"Give me some time, Mama. I need to be alone with my thoughts." Evaline 's voice came out as a hoarse whisper. Though she struggled to keep her voice even, she was surprised that there were no more tears.

A gentle squeeze was her mother's only response.

Blinking furiously for several long seconds, Evaline realized that everyone in line had dispersed throughout the square and the music picked up once more. Laughter and the occasional jealous lament punctuated the festive atmosphere as the dancing resumed. Somehow it all seemed muted. Evelyn found herself wandering away from the center of it all, ignoring both Henry and Sophie's attempts to get her attention. She no longer wanted to play in these silly games of vanity.

Slipping through the now, mainly empty streets, Evaline let her tears fall freely. The tantalizing aroma of sweetcakes and savory treats that engulfed the town square all but disappeared. The beautiful explosion of color from the flowing festival dresses and multitude of flowers adorning the window sills and sides of the homes barely caught her attention, their vibrancy now dulled. With each step, her surroundings became empty. Silent.

She wended her way through the town, not paying attention to where her feet carried her. Here, the houses stood closer together, narrowing the little alley Evaline walked through. The worn cobbles gave way to a simple dirt path, the tiny rocks and dust kicking up and staining her white stockings with a pale, patchy layer of brown. All the while, tears continued to stream down her rosy cheeks.

Why Amalie?

Amalie's face popped into her mind. The two had been sitting by the hearth the night before, Evaline brushing Amalie's hair, the rest of the house having gone to bed long ago. Her soft voice whispered in her ear as clear as it had at Venari Eve.

"I know we both hope to be chosen by someone this Venari," Amalie said, her gaze wistful as she picked at a loose thread on her night gown. "Promise me that whatever happens, you won't leave me."

"What do you mean?" Evaline asked.

Amalie stiffened. "I don't know," she began. "I… I had a dream I lost you."

"Dammit, Amalie!" Evaline muttered, wiping her nose.

A wave of emotion washed over her, overwhelming Evaline. Crouching down, Evaline hugged her knees to her chest, letting her tears fall in earnest. Shame at her disappointment of not being chosen, shame at how she'd been so ready to abandon Henry when she thought she'd been chosen – but most of all, Evaline hated herself for her jealousy. There had been no warning that one of the local lords would be stopping by this Venari to choose a bride. There'd been no reason to believe that her family would be torn apart. Even if Amalie decided to be courted by her dance partner from the afternoon, they wouldn't think about marriage until they at least became of age. Evaline had no reason to suspect Amalie would be leaving so soon.

It should have been me leaving tonight with someone special, Evaline told herself. She was supposed to have been the lucky one. *God, I'm pathetic. She didn't ask for this.*

The quiet of the alley was broken by sniffles as Evaline remained crouched on the ground, hugging herself tightly like her mother would. Gradually, they disappeared until she found herself sitting in silence once more. The shadows around her elongated, blanketing her in semi-darkness. As the sun's rays disappeared, Evaline felt a shiver run down her spine. A light breeze blew a loose strand of hair. It tickled her cheek as goose flesh broke out on her arm. Finally, she looked up.

"Well," Evaline said, straightening up and brushing off the front of her dress. Her voice echoed in the stillness of the empty road. "That's enough of that."

Tucking the loose strand behind her ear, Evaline took a deep breath and wiped her face. A cloud passed over the sun, casting the shadows into an even deeper darkness, bringing more goose flesh to her arms. Evaline rubbed her arms, hoping to create a little warmth.

Tears did not fall as frequently the closer she got to home. It almost felt as though she ran out and could not cry anymore. The sun kissed her freckled face, leaving her pleasantly warm despite moving along the shadows of the brick and clay houses. The sweet scent of honeysuckle caught Evaline's attention. It had been hours since she'd bathed in the honeysuckle infused water.

A sudden movement in the darkness drew Evaline's eye deeper into the small streets between some of the homes. Squinting in the sun, Evaline saw a tall, slim figure approaching her. A startlingly white feather jutted out from the coif, pulling her gaze from the mysterious stranger to its brilliance. The figure paused for a brief moment, noticing her stare and causing Evaline to flush. Underneath the folds of the cloak that hugged their lithe frame, the figure brought a single finger to their lips, motioning for her to keep quiet. Evaline's chest tightened as the person moved out of the shadows and into the light.

Messy sandy hair framed his pale face. Light reflected off his sharp cheeks, illuminating his hazel eyes. Evaline felt herself being drawn closer to the man, her feet taking her several steps towards him before she realized what was happening. His gaze pulled her in, reading her soul. All Evaline wanted to do was learn more about him, to see his essence as he no doubt saw hers.

"Are you lost, ma chérie?"

Smooth as butter, his rich baritone shook her from her trance. Evaline found herself looking around in the narrow alley as though there were someone else standing with her. She pointed to herself. Evaline tried to ask if he spoke to her, but her voice caught in her throat, leaving her only able to mouth the question. Embarrassment overcame her as she remembered that she was the only one there. With a smirk, the man's face softened, taking on a boyish appearance.

"Nobody else." His voice sent shivers down her spine. "I figured everyone would be down celebrating Venari. I never thought I'd see one as beautiful as you out on her own."

The idea that he may be a prowler crossed her mind, but as he moved closer, the thought was quickly pushed from her mind. No one ever called her beautiful, save her parents. Emotions still swirled around her as she acknowledged that her judgement may be clouded from disappointment.

"I needed some time to myself," Evaline managed to choke out. "What are you doing here?"

"I'm looking for my kin's home. She invited me to dinner. Do you know Adrienne? Curly brown hair, green eyes?"

"Oh yes. She lives on the other side of town. By the chandler," she explained, pointing to her left.

"Merde!" he muttered, pulling out a piece of parchment so old and worn that it appeared to be leather.

His eyes scanned the paper, mumbling to himself as he read, what was no doubt, a map. Evaline stood awkwardly, shifting from one foot to the other until the man exclaimed "There!" Feeling her uncertain stare, the man turned his hypnotic gaze to Evaline.

"I'm so sorry, ma chérie. Forgive my rudeness."

Evaline found her breath catch in her throat. How could he be so mesmerizing? She didn't even notice when he closed the gap between the two, standing only feet from her.

"It's all right," she replied breathlessly.

His slender hand grabbed hers, goose flesh rising on her arm once more as an electric thrill went through her just as it had when she'd kissed Henry. His lips brushed gently against the back of her hand, more delicate than a butterfly landing on her, sending a flush through her face once more and making her knees buckle.

"My name is Alexis." His voice melted the chill that had touched her moments before. "I'll see you again, ma chérie."

With another kiss and a wink, Alexis slipped back into the shadows, towards the chandler's shop.

VIII

THE WAY THE FOOLISH GIRL TRAIPSED down the alley after their encounter left Alexis fighting the urge to turn back after her. The way her face lit up with just a simple brush of the lips and a wink. The women here truly were so easy to manipulate. The sound of her boots skipping over the worn cobbles brought a gleam to his eye. Maybe it wouldn't be so bad if he went after her. Chiding himself, Alexis reminded himself that his business with the chandler could wait. It would be foolish to ignore an easy target. Glancing at his pocket watch, he saw it was getting too close to dinner time. He had to go.

With a sense of resignation, Alexis turned and made his way to the chandler's shop. The bright sun somehow managed to stream through the canopy of roofs, illuminating the cooling shadows. Tugging on his hat, Alexis struggled to keep the brilliant light from stinging his eyes after spending so long in the darkness. He'd crossed two roads when he changed his mind. The gnawing sense of hunger that he'd been fighting for weeks pulled at him, clouding his judgement. A little detour wouldn't take too long. Spinning around, he sprinted back the way he came. As he neared their meeting spot, he slowed down. It wouldn't do to scare her. Sniffing the air for the light fragrance she wore, he was able to follow her trail. Winding through the streets, it didn't take long before she came into view. She still had that spring in her step. The sight of her sent a thrill coursing through him.

Keeping close to the houses, Alexis noted how she broke from the main path and made her way up a small knoll. So, she was not part of the town proper. Alexis' face broke into a smile as he turned and headed back into town. If he wanted to see her again, it wouldn't be too difficult. For now, he had business to attend to.

People called out to him, wishing him a happy Venari as he moved through the streets. Women dressed in their finest stopped and gawked as he passed. More than one young lady turned as he went by, earning a disapproving comment from their partner. It seemed like a nice place to settle down in. Alexis made sure to take in the beauty of the town. The homes appeared cozy and people friendly. The shops offered both luxury and practical goods. If the evening went well, he'd have to stop by Bord du Pétale more often.

Down the lane, he noticed a pole with brilliantly colored ribbons wrapped around it. A few musicians remained as the festivities dwindled down. Flowers lay strewn on the ground like colorful gems among a sea of green. By celebrating their past tragedies, Venari helped these people find the beauty within. He'd made sure to learn about their traditions before visiting the town. Doing business in small villages like these required a lot of research; research that would help him build relationships with the locals.

Humming to himself, Alexis turned down a narrow road. The chandler shop should be not much further he told himself. He'd been following Adrienne for a while now, but this would be the first time seeing where she worked. Excitement swirled within him as he spotted her walking a way off. Her dark hair fell to the middle of her back in gentle curls, drawing attention to her tiny waist. Alexis licked his lips in anticipation as he saw her.

He wanted to call out to her, but fear overtook him. It wasn't often that he allowed himself to be so timid when speaking with women. He'd seen time and again that they melted in his presence. Adrienne should be no different.

As she disappeared into her shop, Alexis noted that the building was two stories. She must live above her shop. Perfect. This made things easier. Pulling down his hat, he stepped into the light of the low hanging sun. He greeted a few people as he made his way up the path to Adrienne's home. He hated small talk, but to ignore the locals would bring too much attention to himself. One of these days someone would remember him. It was a problem for another time, however. For now, he needed to blend in.

Knocking lightly on the door, Alexis heard movement inside. The door swung open to a startled Adrienne. Brilliant light nearly blinded his sensitive eyes, and Alexis had to struggle not to recoil from the intensity that the shop filled with candles, lamps, and chandeliers exuded. It was as though the sun resided within her home.

Adrienne immediately took him in, her face softening as a coy smile played on her lips. Every encounter usually went on this way. Forcing his face to relax, Alexis dipped his head into a bow as he waited outside. Leaning on the doorframe, Adrienne took advantage of her ample bust to entice him. Her hip popped out, helping to accentuate her angles as her eyes roved over the slim man.

"Evening, ma chérie," Alexis began. He made sure to lock his gaze with her and flash a dazzling smile. Running his hand through his messy hair, he cocked his head in a boyish fashion. "I hope you can help me. My brother is getting married, and I would like to get him something special. Everyone in town says you're the best there is. Would you mind showing me a little of what you have?"

It was perfect. Adrienne nearly melted as his words flowed over her like honey. Shooting a backwards glance, she held the door open for him and beckoned him inside. Alexis thanked her for her kindness and stepped in.

"It's a bit late, and I would hate for you to have to return to your inn on an empty stomach. The taverns close early on Venari," Adrienne explained. "Would you like to stay for a bite?"

Grabbing her proffered hand, Alexis delicately laced his fingers between hers. He could see the lust in her eyes, as she led him towards the stairwell. Fighting the urge to shy away from the blinding lights, Alexis followed her lead like a lamb to slaughter.

"I would love to."

IX

THE CEREMONY FOR AMALIE'S WEDDING took place at the Ambrose estate outside of their quiet town of Bord du Pétale. A light rain drizzled, the darkened skies threatening to split open and drop a deluge onto the ceremony. Everything felt rushed, but no one said a word. Rowan drank in his new bride with the same intensity as a starving man being handed a winter roast. His were vows nothing more than a pale attempt at hiding his desire for after the ceremony. And all the while, Amalie stood before him, her tiny hands clasped tightly in his, fighting back tears.

It wasn't long until everything moved into the opulent home of the Lord and his family. Statues of elegantly carved deer led up to a fountain in the middle of the courtyard. The figure of a nude woman, her body the epitome of beauty, stood as water spouted around her into a small pool below. Evaline couldn't help but gawk as her family moved past it and into the estate proper.

Her family stood out among the guests, and not in a good way. Their clothes seemed muted compared to the others as they paraded around in their finest, and the distinct lack of gems dripping from their bodies earned them a disapproving glare from more than one. Evaline could have sworn that she heard one woman, not much older than her own mother, refer to them as undesirable as she glided by.

Her mother's voice caught her attention. Turning, Evaline saw Amalie grasping their mother's hands. She was flawless in her gown.

"My baby's a young lady now." Marie's eyes glistened as they rimmed with moisture.

"I'm not ready to leave, Mama," Amalie whispered, her voice hoarse.

Pushing her daughter gently away, Marie flashed a wistful smile. "No more," she said firmly. "You're going to plaster on a happy face. You are being given the opportunity of a lifetime, and I will not have you squander it. Now," she added, her voice softening, "you know your family is always here for you."

There wasn't much room for anything else as Ambrose sauntered over, his face slightly flushed from drink. The young lord slipped his arm around his new bride's waist, pulling her away from Evaline and the others. He ignored her subtle protest and pleading gaze as he led her from the room. The last thing Evaline saw were her eyes, widened in panic.

***

Morning's light streamed through the open windows. The curtains, usually closed at this hour, were left tied back, exposing the sparsely furnished home and filling it with a pleasant warmth. The chickens clucked as they ambled through the front yard as the rooster greeted the day. His raucous cries did not bring out any members of the Laurent family, causing him to crow louder in hopes of having more than insects to eat.

Evaline listened to the birds from under her quilt. The normally comforting blanket felt cold and insubstantial as she stared at the empty side of her small room. Amalie's bed was neatly made, the sheets upturned and ready to be pulled up tight. Evaline sighed, a solitary tear running down her cheek as she pictured the sunlight shining on her sister's golden hair. The house was too quiet. Even Apolline and Elise were still in bed.

"Our first day without you," Evaline whispered as she had so many times before to Amalie. "I miss you already."

The dull thud of shuffling feet caught her attention. Her mother or father must finally have gotten up. It was going to be a long couple of days. The sudden roar of the rooster from under her window caused Evaline to jump, her heart racing in her chest as she steadied her breathing. Damned bird was persistent. A second set of feet, heavier, made its way towards the kitchen.

"Time to get up," Evaline groaned. "Allons-y, Amalie."

***

Birds sang as they flew overhead. Evaline found herself mesmerized by the thin wisps of the clouds as they sailed lazily across the sky. Some pulled apart like cotton, dissipating gradually against the clear blue heavens. Others twisted into different shapes. Evaline found herself lost watching one cloud that changed from a bunny to a candle. The way the ears morphed into a flame, glowing bright before snuffing out left a feeling of unease growing in her stomach.

The ring of hammer on iron heralded their family's smithy followed quickly by a wall of heat. Inside, Evaline could hear her father talking to the other two smiths between the pumps of the bellows and the clanging of the hammer. Before she could settle in and start on some horseshoes, the sound of rapidly approaching feet caught her attention. Henry sped into view, his face pale despite his exertions. Émile brought over a cup of water as Henry worked to regain his breath while hunched over. Through labored breathing, Henry gulped some down before throwing the rest on his sweaty face.

"Adrienne's dead!" Henry blurted out between gasps. "Dead."

"What are you talking about? I saw Adrienne just yesterday before Amalie's marriage," Émile said, moving his hands in front of him as though to stop the youth. "Are you sure?"

"Th-there's blood everywhere," Henry stammered. "The doctor's already been there, but he said she's dead."

"How could this be?" one of the smiths asked. "I've not heard anything unusual. Have you, Pietro?"

"Nothing," the younger smith said with a shake of his head. "I'd even wager that there was even some added protection because of the union."

"The gens d'armes have already arrived and are closing the road," Henry continued. "They're asking everyone to go home and lock their doors."

As the news left Henry's lips, wailing could be heard in the distance followed by shouting. One of the village men spied the group and raced over, yelling at them to go home and not leave until the gens d'armes gave the all clear. Evaline felt her breathing quicken as panic rose in her chest. As her parents, the two smiths, and the third man spoke rapidly to each other, Evaline found herself grabbing Apolline and Elise's hands, their palms just as sweaty as her own. She pulled them closer and gave each a little squeeze, hoping they at least felt some reassurance that things would be all right.

"That's not good, Émile," Evaline heard the man say. She almost thought that there was an undertone of worry. Concern? "I won't say anything for now, but you'll want to talk to someone about this. Can anyone confirm Adrienne was alive after you saw her?"

"I have no idea," her father replied to the gens d'armes. "For God's sake, Gabriel, you know me. She made some beautiful rose scented candles for Amalie's marriage. Tomás helped me craft the silver."

The older of the two smiths nodded his head in agreement. Gabriel's gaze darted from Evaline's father to the remaining men, his brow wrinkled as he fought some internal battle. In what felt like minutes, Gabriel's head dipped ever so slightly, acknowledging Émile's claim of innocence.

"Go home," Gabriel said with finality.

Without another word, the fires in the hearth were extinguished with a whoosh as smoke billowed towards the sky. Evaline and her family rushed from the smithy. As they wove through the frantic bodies clogging the streets, Evaline thought she saw a flash of sandy-colored hair atop a slender, pale frame. Before she could look back into the crowd, it was gone.

X

ADRIENNE'S DEATH was the topic of discussion for weeks. The first few days were a nightmare for Evaline. She huddled with her family in the home, only her father daring to go out and tend to the chickens or harvest their eggs so the family could eat. The pies her mother baked were rationed, the delicious treats losing their sweetness among the paranoia that was growing. Men stopped by the house multiple times a day for the first few days to check on them and bring them any news about poor Adrienne. As time went on, they appeared less and less until they finally stopped coming by.

The days after the gens d'arms stopped their patrol were almost as bad as the first three. Evaline and her family were unsure if it was safe to go out. Émile's trips out of the house began to get longer and longer as he ventured further from their home. Six days after the murder, Émile reported that more people were out and encouraged his family to leave the home. As Evaline made her first journey into town, she noted how the others were walking as though they still feared that the killer was still lurking behind every corner.

She was happy that at least the gens d'arms managed to quash any rumors that her father had a hand in Adrienne's death. One of the women remembered seeing him on her way to get a bottle of milk for her children, having stopped to congratulate him and hope the future brought him many grandchildren. The relief that washed over Evaline when the captain pulled her father aside to tell him that they would not be pursuing him while they continued their investigation hit her like a bucket of cold water. She still wished that her father didn't get those distrusting glances as people walked by.

By the time discussion of Adrienne's death faded away, summer slipped by, and the harvest season fell upon Aceatius. The people of Bord du Pétale began working in earnest to ensure the crops were all harvested. Émile's blacksmith shop experienced a sharp increase as travelers and townsmen alike rushed to get new shoes for their horses. Evaline found herself spending more time in her father's shop holding a pair of tongs as her father shaped the white-hot metal. By the end of the day, the pair were always drenched in sweat and ready for a good meal.

It was a slow day and Émile had sent the two apprentices home early. Evaline and her father began the arduous job of cleaning the smithy. Sweat glistened off her brow and arms, even her hair tied up in a high tail was damp as she stood by the hearth. Though the flames were dying, the heat radiated in the open aired building. It was stifling. Émile put his tools away, humming to himself. The off-key tune brought a smile to Evaline's face. Her father hadn't seemed content since Venari.

"Go on home, Evie," Émile said as he wiped down his hands on a dirty rag. "I'll finish up."

Wiping her brow with a sweaty arm, Evaline slipped out of her apron and stepped out into the street. The cooler air hit her instantly, providing a welcome relief from the heat she'd endured earlier that day. A few boys called out to her as she walked by. The thin, black straps of her top exposing her arms and shoulders and combined with her form-fitting pants stood out from the usual dresses that the women in town wore. She rounded a corner, her spirits still high after the compliments from the boys.

"Careful now, ma chérie."

The voice sent shivers down her spine.

Alexis stood before her, his hazel eyes sparkling mischievously as he took his hands off her shoulders. Evaline's heart raced, her breath catching in her throat. She'd been hoping he would show up, but now that he was in front of her, she didn't know what to say.

"Everything all right?" Alexis asked after a prolonged moment of silence.

"Oh, yes," Evaline replied breathlessly. If only the butterflies in her stomach would settle down. "I... I just wasn't expecting to see you."

I have been thinking about you.

To her amazement, Alexis placed his hands on her shoulders and closing what little gap they had between themselves with a single step. His head cocked ever so slightly to one side, his hazel eyes taking her in. A cool finger tucked a strand of hair behind her ear.

"I didn't think you'd remember a nobody like myself," he murmured.

"How could I not?" she choked out. "You stand out from everyone else in Bord du Pétale."

Alexis' soft exclamation of surprise sent Evaline's blood rushing to her cheeks once more. She thought his eyes flashed in excitement. His slim hands snaked around her waist, causing her to involuntarily move closer. With a moment's hesitation, Evaline placed her hands against his chest and was surprised at how firm his lithe frame actually was. Alexis' head dipped closer, and he took a deep inhale. Evaline silently celebrated her decision to add rose petals to her bath that morning.

They stood together for what felt like an eternity gazing into each other's eyes. At some point, Alexis tipped his chin down and rested his forehead against hers, sending a tingle through her. In the distance a dog barked, startling Evaline and breaking the spell.

"I must go," Alexis whispered, gently pushing her away. "It was a pleasure seeing you again. Perhaps our paths will cross once more."

XI

PARANOIA SPROUTED around Bord du Pétale and the neighboring villages as the harvest season took hold. More tales of sudden, violent deaths popped up throughout Aceatius. The further they were from their hometown, the more absolution Émile received. Where there once had been fearful whispers and nervous glances by the townsfolk, they were now replaced with sheepish smiles as one-by-one, the people of Bord du Pétale apologized to Émile.

With the passing of each month, Alexis noted how the tension lessened until it seemed to finally dissipate. The two younger girls danced more, their singing weaving in with each step and becoming louder by the day. The mother smiled more and even the strain in the father's face lessened.

However, something appeared to be bothering the girl he met in the alley almost a year ago – the one he'd been watching for a year. Though she joined in with her family's happiness, there was a sadness behind her eyes. Something bothered the girl named Evaline.

The fire burned low in the hearth as bedtime drew near. Outside, a frigid wind from the north kicked up. If this was a sign of the months to come, the winter would be harsh and unforgiving. Alexis knew he needed to return home if he was going to survive like the people in the tiny village of Bord du Pétale, but he couldn't pull himself away from Evaline just yet. Licking his lips in the cold, he pressed the tips of his fingers against the glass, his gaze following Evaline as she left the room.

She intrigued him, and soon he would get his claws into her.

***

THREE HUNDRED TWENTY-EIGHTH YEAR OF THE AHKASH DYNASTY

As Venari approached, time slowed until the days dragged by almost to an excruciating halt. Life was quiet, too quiet. In her last letter, Amalie shared that she was with child. Evaline imagined her sister almost daily, her belly swelling as the baby grew within.

Two weeks before the festival, a giant storm hit their little village. Evaline and her sisters had been sitting in front of the hearth and talking about which lord might have an eligible son searching for a bride. Though she didn't say anything, Evaline prayed that it wasn't Lord Boucher. A widower older than her own parents, Evaline found herself cringing at the thought of him choosing one of the local girls to be his bride. She also feared that he may choose one of her sisters. Though Apolline was only twelve, Evaline noticed how some of the men visiting from other towns reacted as she passed. It made her stomach drop each time.

Rain beat the roof to the angry rumble of thunder in the distance. As lightning spidered across the sky, the crack causing Elise to jump, Evaline thought she heard a knock on the door. Their mother and father had gone out for shopping earlier in the day before the rain fell and had not returned. With each angry growl of thunder, Elise scooted closer to her big sister. Evaline grabbed her hand and gave it a squeeze. Another flash of lightning lit up the black sky and Evaline thought she saw the silhouette of a body outside their window. A moment later, it was gone.

It must be her imagination, Evaline reasoned.

The pounding of the rain intensified, and the wind picked up to a howl when another knock, this one more urgent, thumped against their door. They girls shared a confused glance. Who would be out in this weather?

"Did you hear that?" Apolline asked, her voice barely more than a whisper.

"I heard something, too," Elise replied, a tremble making her whisper hard to hear over the crackling of the fire and the roaring of the rain.

"Hush, little ones," Evaline said as she moved her hand to stroke her youngest sister's hair. Though her touch soothed Elise, the younger girl leaned into her older sister, tremors coursing through her body as she sought comfort.

"Are you going to answer?" Apolline asked. "I saw someone outside earlier."

Evaline gulped. So, her sister saw the shadowed figure, too.

"It didn't sound like a tree hitting the house either," Elise added.

With a sigh of resignation, Evaline disentangled herself from her little sister and made her way to the door. A final knock confirmed her fears, and with a trembling hand, Evaline turned the knob. A sudden gust slammed against the door, causing Evaline to grunt as she struggled to push it open. A break in the wind provided the opportunity to shove the door, allowing it to swing back on its hinges. A crack of lightning arced across the heavens, illuminating their darkened surroundings. Evaline's breath caught in her chest. Standing soaked in front of her was Alexis.

***

The fire crackled merrily as the rain continued to pour outside. Apolline and Elise remained on the floor as Alexis sat in a wooden chair holding a steaming cup of tea. His damp hair was matted to his head, his soaked clothes spread out in front of the hearth to dry as Alexis wore a pair of Émile's pants. Evaline couldn't help but gawp at Alexis' slim, shirtless chest. After Evaline ushered him in, she'd tried to find something to keep him warm, but he waved her away saying that the roaring fire would be plenty.

Her eyes traced his barely visible abdomen muscles stopping herself from looking lower as she caught his gaze drifting towards her. The blood rushed to her face as she looked away, but she couldn't help stealing glances at him. She took in the rest of his body, stopping at the thin scar on his collarbone.

Questions raced in her mind as she tried to figure out where he could have gotten the scar. Her thoughts drowned out Apolline's chatter. Evaline noted Alexis' eyes darting to her several times as he listened to Apolline's story, Elise interjecting randomly, but otherwise staring shyly at the stranger. Every time she locked eyes with him, Evaline found herself dropping her gaze.

The flame of the candle on the kitchen table burned low in the wick, a pool of wax filling the holder and providing the only clue for how much time had passed since the rain first started. The shadows elongated on the wall. Evaline couldn't help but shudder as the silhouettes took on sinister shapes in the bright glow of the candle. She found herself wishing her parents would walk through the door, soaked but safe.

Before anyone could speak, the wind howled and the door flew open. Sheets of rain lashed the threshold, and the biting wind whistled inside, nearly extinguishing the hearth. The candle on the kitchen table fluttered wildly, its flame shrinking to a quivering pinprick. Elise's breath hitched into a strangled scream as thunder cracked overhead, shaking the glass in the windows. Evaline and Alexis jumped to their feet, rushing to the door, only to stumble back as two figures burst inside.

"Mama! Papa!" Apolline called out in shock. "You made it."

Émile and Marie stood in the doorway, water pouring off their soaked clothes in rivulets and forming a small puddle at their feet. Their faces were pale, and their dark hair was plastered wildly to their faces. Marie hugged herself, teeth chattering as she shivered. Émile stripped off his coat and shirt, helping his wife slough off her coat as well, and directed the two towards the hearth.

"Thank you for keeping everyone safe," Émile said to Evaline. "It's unbelievable out there. One minute we were talking to Lucas and the next minute it was like God opened the heavens."

Marie stood forlornly at the hearth, staring into the flames. Evaline made her way over and gently grabbed the basket from her mother's hands.

"I'm sorry, girls," Marie said softly. "Papa and I bought you some treats, but…" Marie gestured weakly to the basket, her gaze not leaving the fire.

Evaline and her sisters looked into the basket. Despite their attempts at keeping the rain out with a cloth, the pastries sitting on top of the fruit, vegetables, and other provisions were soggy. Evaline pulled out one of the snacks and couldn't help the disappointment that filled her as it broke into pieces and fell onto the ground.

"It's all right, Mama," Evaline said. To her relief, the forced cheerful tone did not sound as strained as she thought it would. "We still have plenty to enjoy. We're just glad you made it home safe."

"Who are you?" Émile's sudden harsh tone caused the women to jump.

The sound of chair legs scraping on the worn wooden floor and shattering glass was quickly followed by heavy footsteps. Evaline turned to see her father approach Alexis with a glower. His strong hand reaching out for the lithe man's arm, his other hand balled in a fist. Before Evaline could say anything, Alexis slipped out of her father's grasp, his open hands flying up in an attempt to show he was not a threat.

"My apologies, monsieur," Alexis began.

"Papa, wait," Evaline cut in.

"Who are you?" Émile repeated. Without waiting for a response, he closed the gap between himself and Alexis once more.

"I am just a traveler caught in the storm," Alexis said with a nod of his head. As Émile's hands relaxed, his knuckles lost their white color, but his body remained tense. Alexis, however, maintained his composure, as he stood his ground. "I met your daughter," he gestured towards Evaline with a shy smile, "last year during Venari and haven't been able to keep her out of my mind."

Evaline blushed as he glanced her way. There was a glint in his eye as he spoke about her. She couldn't believe he felt the same way about her. Her father's stare never left Alexis, but his muscles relaxed ever so slightly.

"I hoped to speak with you about taking her hand and bringing her to live with me. I don't have much, only my humble estate in Mont Bloom, and my wish that she spend her life with me."

Émile finally tore his gaze from Alexis, but kept his body angled to stay in front of the slim man. Questions raced through his mind, Evaline could see that plainly. She hated how unsure her father must feel at this moment. If it hadn't been Alexis, Evaline knew she would be reacting the same way if a man came for her sisters.

"Evie?" her father asked. He left the rest of the question unasked.

Marie, still standing in front of the hearth, wrapped her arms around Apolline and Elise, the younger girls having sidled up to their mother during the exchange. Evaline found herself facing Alexis and the uncertainty of the future. Would she be able to help her family like Amalie? Would she soon find herself starting her own family? Did she really find someone to spend the rest of her life with? The countless hours of daydreaming were finally coming true. Like her ancestors before her, she succeeded in her hunt.

"Yes," her answer came out in a breathless whisper. "I will."

A palpable silence filled the room, blocking out the rain and angry roars of thunder. No one spoke as the weight of what happened settled in. Even Evaline stood in shock. Did she just say she will marry Alexis, a complete stranger? Glancing at her father, she saw his jaw twitch. Émile did not say anything, however.

"Are you sure, Evie?" Marie asked.

No.

With a gulp, Evaline nodded. She wanted to be wooed and be swept away like the women in her mother's bedtime stories, but this felt wrong. It was all too sudden. Out of the corner of her eye, she thought she saw Alexis' eyes flash in excitement. Émile, though still stiff, held out his hand to Alexis, who took it with a smile. The two men made their way to the kitchen table to discuss when Evaline would leave and other matters. The tension did not dissipate.

"We must celebrate," Marie said, wiping her hands on the front of her damp dress. Her motions almost seemed forced to Evaline. "And we must tell Amalie. She'll be so excited."

Butterflies swirled around in Evaline's chest as the women made their way to the kitchen. Apolline and Elise were uncharacteristically quiet during the whole exchange. The lack of their usual dancing and incoherent singing of happiness left Evaline on edge.

I hope the union ceremony doesn't feel this bad.

XII

THE MORNING OF HER WEDDING dawned bright and crisp. The cheerful chorus of birdsong heralded the day. Dew lay on petals and collected in flowers. Bejeweled hummingbirds and the iridescent wings of honey bees caught the light of the sun as they flit from flower to flower, drinking the sweet nectar. Evaline stood outside in her mother's dress, the white having turned to cream as the fabric aged over time. Still, with the delicate beads Marie had sewn onto the dress all those years ago, it was still a lovely gown. White Fleur de Lys, the special lilies that Evaline's town was famous for, were woven into the braids of her hair. In her hands, a collection of white Lilies of the Valley and white lilac. The simple bouquet did not erase the nervous glow that engulfed her.

Amalie couldn't make the ceremony – it was much too short notice. Afterall, it had only been three days since Alexis asked Evaline's father for her hand. Three days for the storm to clear up and grant them a respite from the heaven's anger.

"So, this is how Amalie felt," Evaline muttered as she stood among the berry bushes. "If only I had been there for her. I have a choice. She must have been terrified."

Evaline's heart ached at her sister's absence. She never realized how intwined her life was with Amalie's.

"Are you ready?" her father asked.

Dressed in his best clothes, there was no familiar sparkle in his eye like when he was happy. There was no warmth to his smile. She knew he didn't approve, but he would never say no if it made Evaline happy. Émile stood stoic, a monolith ready to protect his daughter's peace. As with her sister's ceremony, his excitement was superficial, just enough to not stress his little girls.

Walking through the damp grass surrounded by the glistening berries, Evaline's breath caught in her throat. Before her, Alexis stood in his simple traveler's outfit, his cream blouse matching her dress and the ivory feather in his wide-brimmed hat stood out as both stylish and casual for the occasion. His mouth turned up in a sheepish grin, his hazel eyes twinkling as he focused on her face. Evaline felt her face flush. Rowan hadn't been nearly as tactful as he drank in his bride. His eyes roamed all over her, taking her in. Alexis at least acted the part of a gentleman.

The union ceremony passed in a blur, the words of the officiant barely registering in Evaline's ears. Her eyes were locked onto Alexis'. It came as a surprise when the officiant declared them married and said the lines she had been dreading so far – you may kiss the bride.

Evaline's body trembled, her fingers barely touching his cool hand that crisp morning, as she leaned in for their first kiss. Alexis' lips met hers, soft and pleasantly full, for a brief moment before he pulled away. The boyish smile that played on his face earlier that morning returned, and Evaline couldn't help but reciprocate his shy energy.

I wish Amalie were here, she found herself musing. *She could have given me some pointers for tonight.*

Evaline's family clapped politely as the two turned to face them. A ray of sun broke through the canopy, shining down on Evaline and her new husband. Now that the moment had come, Evaline couldn't help but letting the giddy happiness wash over her. She finally found someone to share her life with. Someone whom she could go on adventures with and explore the world outside of Bord du Pétale with together.

***

Evaline's body rested lightly against Alexis. Even in the cool of the morning air, he could feel the heat of her body as she pressed close to him. She talked animatedly with her family, her mother and sisters sharing in her excitement. Her father, however, his gaze never left Alexis'. Only when he directly addressed his daughter did he finally look away from Alexis.

He doesn't trust me, Alexis noted. *Smart man.*

It had been a long winter and even in Mont Bloom, food had been scarce. Asking for Evaline's hand in marriage had been a surprise, even to him. A surprise that he now had to live with. Cursing himself for letting his emotions override logic, Alexis settled in for married life. At least it would be easier to move forward with Evaline now in his life.

Licking his lips, Alexis found himself smiling and nodding along with whatever the women were babbling about. He couldn't bring himself to focus on anything they were saying. A moment of laughter from Evaline pulled Alexis from his thoughts. The sweet sound, almost like the sound of fairies laughing, sent a jolt through him. Glancing down, he saw the way her face radiated as she spoke with her family. A twinge coursed through Alexis.

It had been a long time since he'd been with family.

XIII

THE CARRIAGE RIDE took longer than Evaline expected. She'd never gone farther than the Ambrose Estate and didn't realize Aceatius' sheer size. Their trip to Mont Bloom spanned several days over the countryside. A few villages dotted along the green expanse, their sheep and cattle adding to the quiet beauty. Inside, Alexis sat with his arms crossed, a smile on his face. Evaline didn't even mind the silence. Seeing the world for the first time left her breathless.

As they rounded a bend, a sprawling home greeted them. Evaline gasped as she saw her new home. The carriage left the dirt path as it transitioned to a pebble-strewn road. The crunch of the wheels sent butterflies flying around her stomach. They passed intricately carved marble statues of young women, their slim forms barely concealed by the clothes cut into the stone. Evaline found herself blushing as she saw the breasts of one of the statues as the carriage drove past.

At last, the carriage stopped in front of a grand door. The onyx horses snorted and stamped their feet as foam slathered their bridles. Evaline shot a final glance at the majestic beasts before turning back to her new home. Alexis waited for her at the first step. Once she was by his side, the pair ascended the steps and entered through the large doors.

A wide crystal chandelier hung overhead, the stones tinkling like a fairy as it delicately swayed. The sound of the doors closing echoed in the massive front room. Evaline stared, her head craning up to take in the immense two-story home as she spun in a slow circle. Her jaw hung open in wonder. Alexis beckoned her to follow him, his footsteps disappearing as he moved deeper into the house.

The rooms were strangely dark as Evaline made her way further inside. She imagined what it would look like to host their wedding, just like Amalie's at the Ambrose estate. Low, dim flames burned in lamps that hung from sconces along the wall. Darkened fabric covered the walls muting the lighter wooden furniture. Other than the lamps, the walls were empty. No pictures adorned the hall. On one of the side tables, a small silver frame sat on a piece of lace. Picking up the frame, Evaline was confused to see a faded image. Holding it up to the light, the pale image of a young woman was etched into some material she couldn't name.

Evaline squinted at the image. The woman's face was gorgeous, her dark eyes seemed to pierce the depths of Evaline soul. The woman's lips turned up in a half smile, but Evaline thought it looked more like a smirk. As she continued to stare at the picture, Evaline thought she saw the smile widen. Bringing it closer, Evaline jumped as a hand grabbed her shoulder.

Turning, she saw Alexis beckoning her to follow him. Seeing that she was holding the silver frame, his expression darkened. Snatching it from her, Alexis placed it back on the table.

"That's my mother," he said simply. "We don't get along."

Evaline stammered out an apology, but Alexis waved it away. They continued on until they reached the main room. An elegant table stood in the middle of the room, a silver candelabra with three glowing candles placed in the center. The remainder of the room was relatively bare. A small shelf filled with books rested against the back wall and a few chairs encircled the long table.

"What do you think?" Alexis asked, bringing Evaline back from her exploration. "It's not much, but it is all mine."

"It's not what I expected," she replied honestly. "But it is humble, like you told Papa. Are you alone?"

"No. I have a friend who stays with me when he's not traveling."

Evaline's fingers drifted over the tabletop, catching on faint ridges where the grain showed through the finish. Smooth, not the kind that comes from decades of use, but from deliberate sanding. Her touch stirred a pale film of dust, rising like smoke in the candlelight before settling down again. Only a few sections had been wiped clean from use.

"You seem displeased," Alexis said. "I've thought about you a lot since our first visit. I was pleased to see you the second time. I didn't think I would run into you again."

His voice was soft, breathy. It sent a shiver down Evaline's spine.

"I couldn't stop thinking about you either," she replied.

Evaline turned her neck to face him. His hazel eyes focused on her. Not wanting him to let her go, Evaline spun around until she was pressed lightly against his body. She wanted him in a way she never thought about another man before. Her head tilted up as she gazed onto his face. His head dipped down and her heart raced. Closing her eyes, she lifted up on her toes to kiss him.

Their lips met softly, sending another thrill through Evaline's body. She wanted to press against him and have him grab her more roughly with his hands, but he did not. His lips moved from her mouth to her cheek before trailing down to her neck. Doing the same, Evaline found a soft spot under his jaw and nipped at his neck. Alexis gave a shuddering breath before returning to her neck. Evaline paused her kissing, getting caught up in his gentle touch. A small pinch under her jaw caught her off-guard. Her surprise quickly turned to confusion as Alexis roughly pushed her away with a gasp and backed up. His eyes bore onto her face, a myriad of emotions evident in his wide eyes. At the forefront, however, lay confusion.

Evaline felt her own surge of emotions swirl within: lust, excitement, happiness, before disappearing. Shame replaced them for a split-second before it was replaced with confusion. That too left, leaving her feeling empty as she stood in front of Alexis.

"I'm sorry," she murmured.

In the flickering light, she thought she saw a small red splotch on his bottom lip. His tongue flickered over his mouth, and he stared at her sheepishly.

"It's all right," he replied. "I – I didn't expect that."

Touching the warm spot on her neck where his mouth had been moments before, Evaline attempted to shake off her embarrassment. The thought that they were both feeling the same awkwardness brought a weak smile to her lips.

"Tell me more about yourself," she said, her voice sounding surprisingly cheerful. "I know we talked a little about how you do a lot of traveling, but you didn't tell me what for."

Alexis cocked his head. "I trade rare and valuable items," he replied with a smirk. "As I explained on the way over, my job takes me all over Aceatius and into other countries. You could almost call me a treasure hunter." He paused as Evaline let out a gasp. "However, I'm looking to settle down and slow my travels."

"Is it dangerous?"

"At times," he admitted. "Anything of value carries an inherent risk. But that's what I love about it. It keeps me on my toes, and I've met some really interesting people."

Taking in the empty home, Evaline asked, "Not to be rude, but why is it so empty here? I would think that your house would at least have furniture and maybe a few high-lights from your adventures."

She felt herself cringe as soon as the words left her mouth. To her surprise, Alexis let out bark of laughter. The unexpected reaction eased her worries.

"I'm never home," he explained. "I bought the estate maybe eight or so years ago, but I don't spend enough time here to find the need to decorate it. I promise, the bedrooms are more like what you're expecting. We won't sleep on the floor."

Reassured by his answer, Evaline began walking around the room, examining her surroundings. The wooden table was a dark mahogany and had vines intricately carved on the sides. She thought she also saw them snaking down the tables legs as well. The few chairs she saw were simple ones made of dark mahogany. The bookshelf on the back wall also appeared to be some sort of dark wood.

"Why are there no pictures?"

Alexis' expression darkened briefly, but Evaline noted the change. She couldn't help but wonder if it had anything to do with his mother. Back home, family had been central to her life. She'd lamented the loss of her grandparents' deaths a few winters ago, wishing that she lived closer to her parents' siblings so she could see her cousins more. The idea that someone would have an issue with their family to this extent startled her.

"Part of why I moved to Mont Bloom was to get away from them," he finally said after a prolonged pause. "I'd heard of an ancient treasure in Bayyum when I was young and used that as an opportunity to finally escape her. It wasn't too hard. My parents always favored my brother, Gabriel, so when I disappeared, they didn't notice it for a long time. After searching for the treasure of Bayyum, I got caught up in the mystery of it all and started looking for new adventures.

"I really enjoyed the people I met. There are few who I would consider family, and they are those I met in my travels. I also enjoyed trying new cuisines. The different flavors of the world caught me by surprise. I'd figured most countries had meals similar to ours.

"If you're second guessing your decision to come with me, you are free to go. However," Alexis met her gaze, freezing her in place and piercing her with his hazel eyes, "I would really like you to stay. There's something about you that intrigues me. Something I can't exactly put my finger on, but from the moment we first met, I knew our destinies were intertwined."

Evaline felt her breath catch in her chest once more. When Alexis spoke, his voice left her mesmerized, pulling her closer to him. Running her hand absentmindedly over the table, Evaline shook her head. The motion was almost imperceptible, but Alexis appeared to have noticed it as his now familiar smile spread across his face.

"Oh, I'm so sorry," Evaline said. "I can't even imagine what it would be like to want to escape from family."

Alexis closed the distance between the two of them once more, and Evaline found herself taking a few steps in his direction as well. Before they could reunite, the bang of the front door slamming shut echoed in the distance. Evaline jumped as heavy footsteps made their way in their direction.

"Don't worry," Alexis told her. "It's just Zahir – the friend I mentioned."

XIV

"I LOST THEM!" a deep bass voice called out with a hint of an accent. The voice reverberated through the halls. "Shit bastards gave me the slip."

A tall man with umber skin and jet-black braids pulled into a low tail froze as he entered the room. His loose crème colored shirt opened at the chest exposing his flesh. Muscled arms poked out from his flowy sleeves, and a brown leather pouch hung from a belt strapped around his slim waist. The man's eyes darted from Alexis to Evaline and back.

"Who is this?"

There was almost a snarl behind his words. Evaline found herself taking a step back from the strange man.

There was an energy about him that left her feeling unsettled. Alexis stepped in between the two.

"Zahir, this is Evaline – the girl I told you about."

Zahir stared Evaline down, taking her in. Evaline found herself feeling defensive as the man dismissed her moments later. A scowl crossed her face, drawing a smirk from the newcomer. Zahir sauntered over to a chair and kicked his feet onto the table. The frustration he must have been feeling earlier appeared to be replaced with a calmer emotion.

"Damn serpents knew I was coming," Zahir said matter-of-factly. Evaline noted that his irritation disappeared. "I managed to speak with a few of the Menes, but most of the influential members slipped out."

"Lose your trade, huh?" Evaline mumbled. "Wonder why."

Zahir's eyes darted to Evaline, narrowing as he sat forward in the chair.

"What do you know about commodities?" Zahir asked slowly.

"Not much," Evaline said, the words bitter in her mouth. For some reason, she did not want to concede anything to this man. "I would assume that you need to at least be pleasant though if you want people to give you their treasures."

A snort from Alexis brought a smile to Evaline's lips. His hazel eyes twinkled as he watched the exchange. Zahir took her in once more. His feet returned to the table, and the front legs of the chair left the ground as he reclined further, rocking slightly.

"I don't think we've lost our chance," Zahir continued. "It's going to be more difficult, though."

"You're sure they have it?" Alexis asked, finally engaging the man.

"Ra's mercy, Ali. Of course. I've seen it. I talked to the Lower Menes and they showed me themselves. If we want to get it, we'll have to move fast. Khufu will have had his priests move to a more secure place for the time being."

"Damn," Alexis muttered.

"Not a concern," Zahir replied with a grin. "It's nothing I won't be able to find."

Evaline couldn't help but take a step forward. Their conversation intrigued her and she wanted to know more. Maybe she could talk Alexis into taking her with him on his next treasure hunt.

"What are you looking for?" she found herself blurting out.

Both men glanced her way, as though they'd forgotten Evaline had been standing there the whole time. She wanted to drop her eyes in embarrassment but fought the urge. If she wanted to join them on their adventures, Evaline knew that she would have to show them she was strong and wouldn't endanger their quest.

"We're looking for two things, actually," Alexis said.

His response drew a cry of indignation from Zahir as he shot up from the chair. "What are you doing? Can we even trust her?"

"I won't say anything," Evaline blurted. "I promise."

"We don't know her," Zahir continued. His gaze seemed to penetrate Alexis, imploring him to keep quiet. To his dismay, it was to no avail.

"There's something about her," Alexis replied. His hazel eyes shot her direction, and he gave her, what Evaline interpreted to be, an approving look. "I don't know how to explain it, but I feel it deep down."

Zahir ignored his chair and took to sitting on the table. Evaline knew she would have to work hard if she wanted him to trust her.

"One is the necklace of Neith," Alexis explained. "Many believe she was an ancient deity and the prime creator of the universe and everything within. She was the goddess of the cosmos, fate, wisdom, water, mothers, childbirth, hunting, and war. Basically, everything needed to keep Ma'Alkin thriving. They even said she was goddess of the rivers that ran through Ma'Alkin's lands.

"I, however, believe that there is much more to her tale. I believe she was also a real person. The true mother, so to speak. There aren't a bunch of modern stories about her nowadays, but centuries ago she was one of the main deities all the priests prayed to. There used to be a temple to Neith as well. It was destroyed a few centuries ago, though, during the Dynastic Wars.

"When I went to find the temple, I found an underground staircase. I didn't get a chance to go down, but if I'm right, that's actually her tomb and all of her earthly possessions will be down there. Getting her necklace would mean everything for me."

A glint flashed in Alexis' eyes as he described the powerful woman. Evaline felt a twinge of jealousy as she imagined his expression once he beheld her final resting place. She didn't know what sort of riches there would be in this tomb, but for someone like Neith, probably enough to last several lifetimes.

"What is the other thing?" Evaline asked in a breathless whisper.

"Vengeance."

Without a word of explanation, Alexis motioned to Zahir and the two walked out of the room, leaving Evaline standing there confused. The way he said the word sent a shiver along her spine. It wasn't spoken with venom, but it dripped with a sweetness like poisoned honey. Even Zahir seemed to share the sentiment, a smirk pulling at the corners of his eyes, but leaving his mouth untouched.

Unsure of what to do, Evaline turned and walked out of the main doorway and back into the dark hallways. Taking a candle from one of the sconces, Evaline wandered the halls, trying to acquaint herself with her new home. The comfort she had been feeling up until that point started to fade, and Evaline told herself that she was just imagining things.

Much like the initial entry hallway, the walls were barren save for a few maps of different parts of the world. Evaline found herself studying them. The thin lines depicting her home of Aceatius were outlined with thicker ones denoting the neighboring kingdoms. Spidering rivers ran through the southern border, reaching up to her own home of Bord du Pétale. Confused, Evaline squinted at the image once more. There were no rivers in Bord du Pétale. Not since before her father's grandfather's time.

Putting it down to a drought or some other natural phenomena, Evaline continued her studies. Reaching up to touch the paper, Evaline was surprised at how delicate and soft the material was - almost like aged leather. Ever so gently, her fingers traced the border of Aceatius once more. The Western Kingdom of the Rose spanned a good portion of the map, much more than Evaline even imagined. Unlike Aceatius and the other nations invaded by the Fraunx, the Kingdom of the Rose did not have their stronghold on the mainland. Instead, it resided on one of the many islands that dotted the coast.

Moving on, she found a map of Ma'Alkin in a silver frame. It was larger than any of the other maps she'd seen, with various segments of the land broken into smaller pieces. Notes and sketches were scribbled in various spots, and several large circles were made on the paper. Turning back to the last map she'd been looking at, Evaline noticed a few smaller circles and notes jotted on that one as well.

One word in particular stood out to her: sourdre du sang.

On the Ma'Alkinian map, she saw a few more scribbles, the scrawl becoming messier. The name Sekhmet also popped up a few times, along with Absalom. In fact, the name Absalom could be seen on the map several times, small x's near the name each time. Evaline found herself going between the two maps, trying to decipher as much as she could. A final name popped up on the map of the Kingdom of the Rose – Estrie. This name was circled along the coastal islands and encompassed the Misty Cay which held the nation's castle.

"There's more to Ma'Alkin than just a necklace," she murmured. Her fingers continued to trace the many lines of the large map.

Turning to continue down the hall, she made a mental note to return to the map wall. A small twinkle of gold caught her eye. Leaning over the smaller image of Men-ne-fer, a light circle around the golden speckle almost hid the faint letters behind it: Neith.

"Neith."

The whispered name sent a shiver through her body. There were too many questions that needed to be answered, but Evaline knew she would find out, and these maps would be her ticket to figuring out the secrets. Whatever lay across the seas and in these other lands, Evaline would prove her worth and discover them. A couple butterflies fluttered in her stomach as she envisioned the adventure before her.

Opening up one of the drawers of the wooden table where she'd seen the etching of the woman, Evaline found something long and thin wrapped up in a bit of brown paper. Pulling the brown string from around the paper, a thin, silver dagger came unwrapped. Glancing around, Evaline picked up the dagger with a trembling hand.

It was a simple thing, just a thin blade and worn leather hilt. Disappointed, Evaline placed in down, now turning her attention to the brown paper. Small, elegant script covered the interior of the page. Holding it up to the candle light, Evaline checked once more to see if she was alone before reading what was on the page.

"The Great Father Absalom was last heard to be in Ma'Alkin. His resting place is still unknown. If he were to waken," Evaline struggled to read the next bit. The writing had smudged at some point. *"Chaos and destruction will reign. She must be stopped. Seek the Menes. They hold many secrets. Find the Bawon San."* More smudging. *"Save the blade for Nefret, and Estrie. – Z."*

Returning the paper to its rightful place, Evaline carefully wrapped it around the dagger. Her hands shook and her ears strained as she listened for the sound of approaching footsteps. She didn't think she would get in trouble for exploring, but something told her that the contents of this drawer were off limits.

"I'll solve this puzzle," she muttered. Her voice rose in determination, the eagerness to piece everything together sending shivers through her body. "I'll earn my keep – maybe even get to truly experience life outside of Bord du Pétale."

Questions swirled in her head, but Evaline couldn't help but feel a sense of excitement and trepidation wash over her all at once. The unknown called to her, just as much as the mystery that stood in front of her. Through it all, Amalie's face flashed in Evaline's mind. She pictured her sister, pregnant and alone despite the many servants that must be housed in the Ambrose estate. Evaline knew how lonely it could be to be surrounded by people and have no one to talk to. The sudden image of her sister tampered down the excitement Evaline had been feeling moments before.

"When I come back, I'll find a way to bring you on the next one, Amalie. Mama can watch the baby, and we'll see the world. Together."

A small ray of hope blossomed in Evaline's chest. She wondered what her new life with Alexis would be like. Obviously, the delicate nature of his work added to his mystique. She hoped that one day the two would be able to enjoy searching for treasure and solving mysteries as a team. She'd show him that her cunning could make up for any head-start he may have on her.

XV

PEERING FROM AROUND the corner of the hallway, Zahir and Alexis watched as Evaline moved back and forth between the maps in the hallway. Her brow furrowed as she squinted at the fine print on the aged leather.

Pressing his lips to Alexis' ear, Zahir spoke so softly that even the winds of the catacombs could not hear him. "Do you really think she will be able to solve this?"

In a barely audible whisper Alexis replied, "I've been watching her for almost a year. She's smarter than the others."

"No matter," Zahir replied. "If not, we can handle it just like the others."

Alexis found an uncomfortable pit drop into his stomach. Unlike the others, he didn't know if he would be able to dispose of her so easily. When he attempted to sate his hunger earlier, he had been greeted with an indescribable sweetness that he couldn't explain. It overwhelmed him, causing him to pull away. He hoped it was just a fluke.

The pair watched Evaline for a while longer. Her auburn hair swished side-to-side as she went back and forth between the maps. She muttered to herself, trying to piece together the various circled cities and random words scribbled on the side. Alexis knew she would struggle to piece together how the gods and the Father tied together. To her, it was just "Fountain of Blood." No doubt they would find her skulking about, trying to eavesdrop on their conversations in an attempt at pulling some morsel of information from their words.

He wondered if she would ask him directly. Alexis almost hoped she would. He wanted to see how her mind worked.

"If she's as eager as you say," Zahir said, startling Alexis as he continued to watch Evaline, "we should take her with us. She'll stand out – that'll buy us some time. Some of their kind have encountered people like her over the years. Letting her wander might draw them out, leaving the tomb unguarded."

Alexis hummed – almost vibrated – in response. He didn't want to leave her to her own devices against Estrie and her minions. Though Evaline was stronger than most of the women he found, he'd seen her working fastidiously in her father's forge helping temper steel and iron, her frail human body was no match for the darkness that lay ahead. Toppling a vampiric empire would be difficult enough for him and Zahir. They would need more than just a little girl to help their cause.

Zahir pulled Alexis away from his sentry. Evaline continued to move back and forth, muttering to herself. Her frustration was almost palpable. No matter how many times she repeated the phrases, she was no closer to solving the mystery.

Alexis hoped his intuition hadn't been wrong.

XVI

DINNER HAD BEEN a quiet affair. Evaline was left to her own devices to scrounge up something from the kitchen. Like a true nomad, Alexis' pantries were all but barren. Still, Evaline managed to find enough to put together a filling meal. She would need to go shopping in the morning. Alexis and Zahir hadn't joined her. Instead, the pair sequestered themselves in one of the rooms, she assumed to have discussions about Neith. The sun set long ago by the time Alexis popped into the dining hall. Zahir was nowhere in sight, but Evaline found that she didn't want to see the man.

"I'm sorry I left you for so long," Alexis apologized. "Zahir and I needed to plan our next course of action, and when he gets excited, he starts speaking in his native tongue. I didn't want you to feel left out."

"You speak Ma'Alkinian?"

"I wouldn't say I'm fluent, but I can manage." Alexis winked at her with a coy smile. "Now, why don't we get ready for bed."

Evaline was completely caught off-guard. Her mind had been trying to piece together all of the information she'd gleaned from the maps, that she forgot that this would be their first night together. Their trip from Bord du Pétale had been non-stop, so they didn't get a quiet moment to themselves at any of the local inns.

"Unless you would rather have your own room for the night."

"Oh no!" Evaline replied, her words spilling out in a rush. "There's just been so much going on, that I kind of forgot about everything. I'm sorry." Evaline dropped her gaze as her face tinged red in shame.

Alexis let out a bark of laughter, the melodic sound turning up the corners of Evaline's lips.

"I think we're both guilty of that, ma chérie. I'm not used to having someone other than Zahir around. This will be good for both of us. Remember, I want to settle down."

Holding out his hand, Alexis beckoned for Evaline to follow him. The familiar butterflies that fluttered within whenever she thought of Alexis returned. Taking his hand, the pair left the dining hall and continued into the dimly lit home.

***

The rooms on the upper floor were beyond Evaline's expectations. Unlike the lower floor, there was a dusty red carpet over the wooden floors. A few scenic paintings in carved mahogany frames lined the walls. The doors and floorboards had white moldings that were surprisingly clean considering the amount of dust in the home.

Three doors from the main stairwell brought the pair to their room. A single bed with tan-colored quilt, a single nightstand, and a desk were the only furniture. Alexis explained that a chest was to be delivered in the next few days for her to put her clothes in. Further down, Evaline was led to the bathroom. As she soaked in the warm tub, Evaline wondered what the night would bring. Once she felt ready, Evaline returned to her room.

Alexis sat at the desk, writing something on a piece of loose paper. Her breath caught in her throat as she beheld his shirtless figure. Though he was slim, Evaline noted that his muscles were fairly well defined. A second scar spidered across his back, this one not as thin as the one by his collarbone.

Clearing her throat, Evaline sat down on the bed and ran her fingers nervously through her hair. She was acutely aware that the white shift she wore was thin enough that he could probably see through it.

Finishing his thought, Alexis put down his quill and turned to face her. His gaze traveled over her body, taking her in. Evaline let out a shuddering breath, fighting the urge to cross her arms over her chest. The springs of the bed groaned as Alexis slid onto it next to her. With his slender fingers, he tucked a strand of hair behind her ear.

Evaline stared into his hazel eyes and found herself leaning closer to him. Alexis' fingers wrapped around hers, his other hand cupping her jaw and bringing her closer to him. As she closed her eyes, Evaline felt the same electric thrill shoot through her as their lips met.

As before, Evaline wanted him to press against her. His lips slowly moved from hers down to her neck. Unlocking his fingers, Alexis' other hand moved down towards her thigh. Evaline flushed as he grazed her flesh, her body burning with desire. Alexis nibbled on the spot under her jaw once more, and Evaline let out a moan. Without warning, Alexis pulled away once more. He eyed her, confusion etched into his face and his mouth slightly agape.

"What's wrong?" Shame filled Evaline's words as wondered what she'd done to displease him. Surely, she hadn't been too loud.

Shaking his head, Alexis mumbled something incoherently before leaving Evaline sitting on the bed just as perplexed as he was.

***

"Why can't I feed?" Alexis muttered after Evaline left. "Why is she different from the others?"

His body ached from hunger, threatening to drive him crazy. Yet, when he'd tasted her, there was something about her that tasted wrong. Not too sweet like children, not too bitter. He couldn't place it, but it was so strong that he couldn't move forward. Just the smallest bit left his body tingling.

"Why?" he asked, his face in his hands. "I'm so close."

***

Evaline waited until the candle in her room had burnt half-way down before giving up hope that Alexis would be returning to their room that night. The first hour or so had been spent quietly sobbing. Was it something she'd done? Amalie didn't seem to have this issue, she thought bitterly several times that night. Now, exhaustion took her as the weight of the last few days came crashing down on her. All Evaline wanted to do at this point was let sleep take her, but her mind wouldn't rest. She needed to speak with Alexis.

Pushing off the bed, Evaline made her way into the hallway. She thanked the thick carpet underfoot for muffling her footsteps. She didn't want to startle Alexis, but she didn't want him to know she was coming for some reason. She wanted to make sure he didn't leave before she could collect her thoughts.

A few rooms down, she found another bed in a sparsely furnished room with only a desk and lamp adorning it. His shoes lay by the desk, leading Evaline to believe that she found the right place. The only thing missing was Alexis. Thinking he must be in Zahir's room, Evaline wandered through the hall once more. A quick search of the remaining rooms told her that neither man was upstairs.

With slow, cautious steps, Evaline descended the staircase. Unlike the upper level, the stairs were just wood, no carpet. As she wound her way down to the lower level, she shivered as a cold breeze hit her. The hearth must be extinguished. Without knowing where to go, Evaline found herself making her way back to the dining hall. Random creaks of the building settling echoed in the near empty home, and with each one, Evaline would pause, hoping she didn't alert them. After several tense minutes, two voices could be heard in the dining room.

"What hold does she have on you?" Zahir asked. From the exasperation in his tone, Evaline could imagine him gesturing pointedly to emphasize his words. "She's just like the rest of them."

"There's something different about her," Alexis replied, weighing every word. "There's something inside her... I can't explain it. She's too sweet."

A snort from Zahir set Evaline's blood boiling. Not even a moment before Alexis' words had touched her, now, she just wanted to snap at his friend.

"Don't let her be the reason we get killed." Zahir's voice carried a note of warning. "If things go wrong, I will have no problem leaving either one of you behind."

Alexis paused once more. "Like you said, she could be a valuable distraction. They won't expect us to involve humans, especially one so obviously different as her. You know what they're like. Let them play themselves."

Evaline's blood ran cold. *Human?* Her stomach lurched, her skin prickling as though unseen eyes watched. What were they if not human? She edged backward, careful, silent, her every nerve screaming at her to flee. The dining room faded behind her, their voices now muffled by the roar of her beating heart. The stairs loomed before her like a lifeline. Evaline darted up them. Blessedly, her cat-like footsteps did not cause any of the stairs to creak. By the time she slumped onto her bed, her heart raced and her body was covered in a cold sweat.

"Oh God," she breathed, her voice ragged from exhaustion and panic. "What is going on?"

Warm tears pricked the corners of her eyes. Swiping them away before they could fall, Evaline locked the door before slipping under the quilt. Now there was one more question to answer. Tomorrow, she would continue to search for answers. Perhaps she would find something. The hours dragged by, and it wasn't until the first rays of dawn broke the horizon that Evaline finally fell asleep.

XVII

SUNLIGHT STREAMED into the room through the closed curtain. Behind the window, birdsong filled the air with their melodic symphony. Evaline groaned and threw her quilt over her head, trying to block everything out by wrapping her pillow over her ears. A low throbbing pressed against her temples thanks to the few hours of fitful sleep she'd gotten. Her body ached from exhaustion. Unable to push away the cheerful light, Evaline groaned once more and pushed herself out of bed.

There were no mirrors in the room other than a silver hand mirror left haphazardly on a little desk in the corner. Wanting to see how horrible she looked, Evaline held it up to her face. Her hair was a tangled mess and dark circles formed under her eyes. Turning her head, Evaline noticed the discoloration on her neck at the base of her jaw where Alexis' lips had been last night. It wasn't the purple blue like a bruise, but there was a faint pink tinge to it, as though a mosquito had bitten her.

Evaline tried to push the evening out of her mind. A thousand questions had plagued her the night before, but she couldn't piece together what the random words she'd seen on the maps meant. The letter she'd read provided no clues either. None that she could decipher, at least. She wanted to explore more of the manor. Perhaps there would be more clues to help her put together the puzzle of what all those strange words meant. Something about how someone as young as Alexis was already a seasoned treasure hunter fluent in Ma'Alkinian was possible given his destitute home caused a part of the back of her mind to tingle. Surely, he could have chosen a smaller cottage in a village instead of this massive estate in the middle of nowhere.

For now, she needed to go into town to buy some food. She would need to ask Alexis for money. Making her way down the carpeted hall, the previous night's conversation played in her head. Zahir's accusatory tones. Alexis saying that they would involve her in their plans. That comment at the end about being human. Surely, she misheard. Being new to this adventurous life would require her to learn the ins and outs of the trade, along with the different terminology that came with it.

It's not like I'm an idiot, she groused. *I'm sure he took a while to learn how to uncover the world's secrets. There's no way he didn't make mistakes. We're only human.*

Evaline's stomach grumbled in annoyance at being empty, distracting her from her musings.

Her heart ached as she remembered the early mornings she had with her sisters, sneaking into the kitchen to grab one of their mother's desserts from the night before. With a heavy heart, Evaline remembered how she turned down her mother's honey cakes before Amalie left after their last dinner on Venari. Her mother hadn't made any cakes since. The delicate sweetness made Evaline's mouth water. Her eyes began to water. The gentle touch of her mother's hand tucking a loose strand of hair behind Evaline's ear startled her. Evaline gasped, her eyes darting about for the phantom of her mother. Instead, she was greeted with the fact that it was her own hand performing the soothing gesture.

Pushing away her emotions, Evaline continued her search for food.

"Alexis?" she asked as she tentatively pushed the door to his room open. "Are you here?"

No light managed to penetrate the room thanks to the thick curtains blocking the windows. As Evaline's eyes adjusted, she tried to discern his body in the bed, but wasn't completely sure if she could make anything out.

"Alexis?"

When she received no response, Evaline pushed the door open further and slipped inside. The room was unnaturally dark. As though he didn't want any light to bother him. Tripping on something solid on the ground, Evaline finally was able to make out the bed. It was empty. Disappointed, she made her way back to the dining room.

A delicious scent greeted her, making her mouth water. Waiting for her, a plate of sausage, eggs, and bread with fresh butter sat lonely in the middle of the great table. Neither of the men were around. Unable to ignore the meal, Evaline sat down and began eating. A moan of contentment escaped Evaline as the savory flavors touched her tongue. It had been a while since she'd had a meal this nice.

"Good morning, ma chérie."

Spinning in her chair, Evaline saw Alexis already dressed. His eyes moved to her outfit, a faint smirk playing on his lips. Evaline was suddenly uncomfortably aware of how revealing her shift was. Her face flushed as she tried to reposition herself.

"I'm sorry about last night," he said. "Everything is happening so fast and all at once. I hope you don't think it's your fault."

Evaline shook her head. "It's been a lot to take in." Pushing her fork around in the food, Evaline couldn't help the awkward silence that stretched. After what felt like an hour, she said, "I heard you and Zahir talking last night."

To his credit, Alexis' face remained impassive.

"Will you leave me if things get dangerous?" Evaline asked, her stomach dropping. "Or does your loyalty lie with Zahir?" A bit of bread hovered by Evaline's mouth, her body moving on its own accord despite the pit nestled in her stomach. She watched him intently.

"Zahir won't leave us behind," he said slowly. "There is a lot on the line, and we work well together. Our goals align, and that necklace holds a lot of missing information I need. To be honest, I don't think you'd be able to leave now if you wanted to. You probably shouldn't have eavesdropped. You know too much and convincing Zahir to let you return home would be difficult."

A palpable silence settled over the room. The piece of bread in her hand crashed on her plate with a crispy crunch. Alexis didn't turn away, maintaining her gaze despite the awkwardness that blanketed them. Evaline struggled to say anything, but her mouth only opened soundlessly like a fish out of water.

I can't leave? Her breath caught in her throat even though her heart started pounding in her chest. *I'll never see my family again. What about the baby?* Evaline's breathing became fast and shallow. The idea of never seeing Amalie or her baby sent Evaline's head spinning. Adventures be damned. Evaline needed to crack the puzzle if she wanted to ever see her home again.

Alexis watched her with mild curiosity as she fought to control her breathing. The seconds dragged by until the adrenaline in her body disappeared and she could breathe normally again.

Does he not care? Or is he testing me – seeing if his gamble will pay off? I need to know what else to expect.

With a slow, steadying breath, Evaline forced herself to take a sip of water from the cup next to her food.

"What, what else could happen? Besides death?" Evaline wasn't sure if she really wanted to hear the answer.

"The slave trade in Ma'Alkin is not exactly a secret. You could either be taken for one of their fertility temples or sold to foreigners. They're not exactly discerning when it comes to selling their captives."

It was almost too much to take in. Evaline found herself playing with her food once more as she processed everything he said. The thought of being taken into the sex trade left a pit in her stomach. She hadn't even experienced her first moment of true intimacy; how would she react to someone forcibly taking it from her?

Leaving Evaline to her thoughts, Alexis turned and busied himself in the kitchen, putting away supplies from what must have been an early morning shopping trip. Cured meats hung in the kitchen and a bowl of fresh fruit now sat on a counter. The loaf of bread Evaline's slice came from rested next to the fruit. There wasn't a lot, Evaline noticed. Just enough for a few days.

As the realization that she was no longer in charge of her own destiny, Evaline forced herself to take a bite. She struggled to swallow, her mouth and throat so dry that the bread threatened to stick to it. It tasted bland, almost like she imagined the color grey to taste, and settled heavily in her stomach like a stone. Whether Zahir left them or not, from this point forward, she was at the mercy of two men that she barely knew, and whatever schemes they concocted to get some damn necklace.

Was this his plan all along? Oh God, what a fool I've been.

Her mind went blank and Evaline found herself staring at her plate, unblinking. A thousand thoughts, questions, and scenarios raced in her mind, jostling for attention, but the chaos only led to a silence that pushed everything else into the background. Time crept by, her bread dangling from limp fingers.

I have to get home.

"When do we leave?" Evaline's voice finally came out, almost as a squeak.

"The boat leaves in three days. Zahir is still in town gathering supplies."

***

Evaline spent the two days leading up to their trip exploring the estate in earnest. Outside, she found a garden that died during the winter, the dried-up stalks and vines provided a grim contrast to the soil. The tall grass surrounding the manor was yellow and crunched under her feet as much as the pebbles on the main drive. Nestled in the grass, Evaline found a sparrow's nest. The egg shell remnants stood out against the dull colors surrounding them.

She'd tried spending some alone time with Alexis, but Zahir always seemed to be nearby. The mysterious Ma'Alkin was never far from his friend, almost as if he were keeping an eye on the two. Evaline noticed a glint that flashed across his face on occasion. She'd seen it mirrored in Alexis as well. On the rare occasion that they managed to steal a few tender moments together away from Zahir's prying gaze and sneak a kiss, things never progressed further. Every time his lips touched her, she felt the same longing. Whenever his lips moved to her neck, he would pull away suddenly as though he received a shock, a look of confusion on his face. After the second time, Evaline resigned herself to never truly becoming his wife – though she wasn't sure if she wanted that to be anymore.

Most of the time Evaline found herself inside. She'd spent a little time exploring the rest of her home, but the bulk of her time was spent memorizing the various maps of Ma'Alkin. She'd never traveled by boat and wanted to familiarize herself with the various ports in case she got separated from Alexis. The key to her survival hinged on her being self-sufficient enough to find a way to return to the docks if things turned bad.

Men-nefer wasn't too far from one of the harbors, so she assumed they would begin their search from there. The area where the tomb rested was next to a river, or so she sur-mised. Its thin line spidered alongside the faint circle mark-ing Neith's resting home. Using some sheets of loose paper she found on the small shelf in the dining room, Evaline be-gan taking notes of what she believed would be important.

At night when Alexis left her, she would pull out the sheets and study them. She was no closer to figuring out what any of the words meant. Playing with the necklace Amalie got her, Evaline tried to figure out the hidden mean-ing behind the words. As the second day came to an end, she realized she would have to ask them before they got on the ship.

***

Heavy footsteps stumbling through the hallway startled Evaline awake. She'd been sleeping lightly, her nerves about traveling to a completely different country gnawing at her. Alexis' door slamming shut with a thud surprised her. She didn't even know he'd left. Slipping into the hall, Evaline made her way to his room, hoping to at least spend the night together with her head resting against his chest.

As her hand touched the knob, a strong hand grabbed her arm. Zahir stood behind her, shaking his head silently. Confused, Evaline tried to enter Alexis' room once more. Again, Zahir blocked her entrance. Getting close enough that their bodies touched, he hissed in her ear.

"Don't go in."

He gave no explanation to his warning. Mission completed, Zahir returned to his room. Alone in the hallway, Evaline contemplated entering Alexis' room, but something about Zahir's message gave her pause. They'd barely spent any time together and exchanged even fewer words.

Evaline found herself standing in front of Zahir's door, waiting. She wasn't sure whether to knock or to just barge in. Steeling herself for whatever happened next, Evaline pushed the door open and stepped into the darkness. She needed to know what exactly was going on.

"I'm glad you listened," Zahir said from the darkness. A hint of amusement tinged his words.

His room, just like Alexis', had heavy curtains blocking out any light that may have accidentally entered his room from outside. Not even a candle flickered.

"What did you mean?"

Blunt and to the point, Evaline did not want to waste her time talking to the man. However, this was something she knew she should listen to. He wouldn't go out of his way to speak with her.

"You have no idea what you've gotten yourself into?"

Evaline could hear the smirk in his voice. It made her blood boil. With a sigh, Zahir moved from somewhere in front of her, his feet shuffling lightly on the carpeted floor, before she heard the groan of the mattress as he sat down.

Evaline wasn't sure if she should move deeper into the room, so remained where she was.

"There is a battle coming, and you've placed yourself right in the middle."

"Then let me go home," she said simply. "I won't say a word."

Zahir clicked his tongue. "You know too much. If we let you go, the others will come after you. They know you are Alexis'. They have eyes everywhere. Your fate is death whether you come with us or you leave."

Evaline's breath caught in her throat. She thought that Zahir would just be stubborn, paranoid even.

"How can things have moved this quickly?" she asked, her voice shaking.

"Fate is funny in how it chooses what paths people take. Sometimes you can do nothing wrong and still be damned."

Something didn't feel right to Evaline. Though his words were blunt, she thought she could almost hear a hint of emotion buried deep inside.

What power does this necklace have? I thought it was just an old wives' tale – a goddess having descended to our mortal plane, but what if there actually are divine powers at play? Am I going up against the gods?

"Why me?" Evaline managed to croak out.

"I don't know," Zahir admitted. "It's getting late. You should return to your room."

The seconds crept by, painstakingly counted with each beat of her heart, yet neither moved. Her resolve began to crack.

"What does this mean for me?" she finally asked. "How can someone like me hope to stand up to God?"

A shiver ran down Evaline's spine, causing gooseflesh to prickle her arms. She could feel Zahir's eyes boring onto her from somewhere in the shadows. Was he still on the bed, or did he get up at some point during their conversation? Her eyes strained as she tried to discern his silhouette in the darkness. Again, time passed at a snail's pace. This time, each heartbeat pulled at Evaline, tearing away the last remnants of confidence she had and letting the anxiety and uncertainty grow until she finally had enough.

"Answer me!" Her voice came out in a strained whisper, begging for him to cut the tension that strangled her.

"If you're as smart as Alexis believes, you will figure it out," he said flatly.

Moving towards her, Zahir placed his hand on her back and escorted Evaline out the door. She tried to resist, placing her heels against the old carpet, but she may as well have been a child struggling against their parent at bedtime. Any effort Evaline made was overpowered by Zahir's surprising strength. If she hadn't been panicking, the reality of her helplessness would have hit her.

The door closed with a firm snap, leaving Evaline alone in the darkened hallway. She glanced towards Alexis' door for a moment before returning to her room.

I am truly alone now, she admitted to herself. *God have mercy on my soul.*

XVIII

CLAW MARKS GAUGED the fabric of the walls. Bits of the bed frame lay splintered on the ground, the unfortunate casualty of uncontrolled rage. The dark curtains covered the windows, blocking light of any kind from entering the room. Curled in a corner, Alexis slept, his head down over his knees. A shelf under the window held several vials. Some were empty, the bottles toppled over and corks unstoppered. The rest were filled. Crimson blood filled the smaller vials, ready to give a quick respite against the gnawing hunger that plagued Alexis through his exiled life. The remainder held a liquid with a faint orange tinge – a special oil he'd discovered with Zahir that allowed for them to spend more time in the sun. One that temporarily blocked the more harmful effects of the sun.

The door opened with a soft click of the knob, waking Alexis from his slumber. His ears perked up, listening to who entered. He'd smelt Evaline come by earlier that night. She almost came in, he could feel it. But something stopped her. Something that saved her life. He'd entered a frenzy when he went to town and feed. Three bodies were left behind. He'd done the same at Evaline's home town with the young couple. Their blood had been especially sweet. The young usually were. If she came in, his blood lust probably would have overcome him, and even her strange taste would not save her.

"She's in her room now," Zahir said, dropping down next to Alexis. "She's a stubborn one."

"Thank you. That could've ended poorly."

"Are you sure? One less human to worry about. More food to keep us full longer. That wouldn't be so bad, would it?"

"I told you," Alexis snapped. "Her blood tastes… off. Not like any blood I've had before. Sure, it'd do the trick, but it wouldn't go down as smoothly."

"Blood is blood."

Alexis gave Zahir a shove as he finally raised his head. He knew Zahir was anxious to get back home and find the tomb. It'd been his life's mission for damn near three centuries. The older vampyre earned his right to be grumpy from time to time. If Alexis ever got that old, he wondered if he would be the same. Alexis knew he wouldn't though. It was much easier to charm people with a smile than a threat of death.

"You got the sailing arrangements figured out?" Alexis asked.

"We sail the *Faded Dawn*. I found a guy who will let us on. Didn't mention the girl. That might be a problem. You know how those seafolk are – even if they are of ill-repute."

"Superstitious bastards," Alexis muttered.

"You're bad enough," Zahir agreed.

Alexis shared a chuckle with his friend.

The two sat in silence until the sun rose. It was like the old times once more. He'd ran into Zahir by chance fifty years ago in Ma'Alkin's capitol, Kul El. He wasn't sure what it was, probably the listlessness that comes with living longer than one would like. There was an apathetic quality mixed in with a sense of searching for purpose. Alexis had been searching for purpose ever since Estrie had cursed him to that endless existence.

There had been distrust in the beginning. Being part of two of the biggest houses didn't mean they were allies. No, Alexis worked hard to gain Zahir's trust. To gain Zahir's loyalty. But he wouldn't change anything. Zahir had been the one gift Alexis received after his life was torn away from him by that bitch of a woman.

Small beams of light fought to get through the dark curtains that smothered the windows. The only way to tell it was now morning was by how the ground turned a slightly lighter shade of hunter green. They would have to leave soon.

"Do you think I'm making a mistake?" Alexis asked.

Without opening his eyes, Zahir mumbled in response. "I do."

"Would you feel more comfortable if I leave her here?"

Zahir waited a beat, weighing his answer before speaking. "No."

"Then what? We can't send her home."

"We continue on," he replied simply. "Plans change; we adapt."

"You want to use her as bait," Alexis said with a smirk.

Zahir let out a snort, not denying the accusation. "She may come in handy," he admitted. "I'm going to head downstairs. Coming?"

Alexis shook his head. "I need some time to think. Last night really gave me some perspective."

Standing up, Zahir made his way to the door. Alexis returned to his curled position, his head resting on his knees once more. There was too much at stake for it to fall apart now. He hoped he didn't make a mistake.

XIX

THE SUN ROSE, its blinding rays creeping across the horizon and into Evaline's room. She groaned as the light burned her closed eyes. She'd stayed up late talking to Zahir before he asked her to leave so he could get some rest. Evaline had asked so many questions her head spun. Zahir provided a wealth of information, most of it baffling her. None if it concerning Alexis or his past. At least, nothing other than their business together.

Evaline desperately wanted to know about both of their pasts. Zahir provided some bread crumbs, but not enough for her to get a feeling for what kind of person he was. She almost wondered if he'd forgotten over the years. One thing she knew, was that both appeared to be waging a war.

By the time Alexis made it downstairs, Evaline had finished her morning meal while Zahir rolled a small golden coin through his fingers. The Ma'Alkinian coin was smaller than what she was used to in Aceatius, but much denser. He assured her that it was not a heavier metal plated.

"Good night?" Zahir asked as Alexis made his way into the room.

"Great. It was a much-needed trip." Turning to Evaline, he added, "I'm sorry I didn't invite you. Next time, I promise."

"She knows," Zahir replied.

Alexis' eyes narrowed, darting from Evaline to Zahir. Evaline almost thought she saw a flash of red in the morning light.

"Have a good talk, did you?" he simply asked, his voice evenly-measured. "What all did you talk about?"

"You mentioned vengeance the day I arrived. How can there be vengeance without a war? She knows that she's tied to us, or should I say you, now," Zahir replied casually.

Alexis swore under his breath, slamming his hand on the table so hard it cracked, sending a chunk of solid wood onto the floor. Evaline yelped. He'd never shown that kind of emotion before. Alexis was always so poised, the perfect gentleman. Taking a moment to smooth back his hair, Alexis let out a small chuckle.

"Dammit, Zahir! This is why I do all the talking."

The way Alexis stared at her made Evaline uncomfortable. His hazel eyes flashed, and a hint of red seemed to tinge them. She found herself rising from her chair and taking a few steps back, not wanting to move too quickly in case it triggered some animalistic hunting instinct.

In his anger, Evaline noticed his canine teeth began to elongate to a sharp point. Combined with his now red eyes, the effect chilled her to the core. She found herself frozen in place as she stared at the monster in front of her. Just as Alexis transformed, Zahir did the same. The two maintained prolonged eye contact, waiting for the other to say something. When neither was going to give, Alexis seemed to disappear before appearing in front of Zahir and landing a massive punch to the man's face. Zahir flew back several feet, somehow managing to keep his feet beneath him.

Evaline jumped, a small shriek escaping her lips at the sudden movement, her feet carrying her to the doorway and nearly out of the room before she could process her body's actions. A thin trickle of blood ran from the corner of Zahir's mouth from where he was struck. Instead of attacking Alexis, Zahir's teeth retracted, his eyes returning to their normal deep brown. However, he did not lower himself like a dog who was submitting to the aggressor.

"You told me yourself that you trusted her and that she was special." Zahir's words came out even and measured. "Was that because you could detach yourself in case she was killed? Or do you not even believe your own words?"

Evaline found she had been holding her breath. Afraid to even breathe, she tried to let it out in a slow, controlled breath. She hoped neither could hear the wild thumping of her heart. She had a suspicion that if they were that strong, they probably had better hearing than someone like her.

"Oh God," she whispered, drawing the men's attention. "You know I heard you the other day. You wanted me to hear you."

As tears of panic rolled freely down her cheeks, Alexis' rage seemed to break. His eyes returned to their normal hazel color and his teeth shrunk back to their previous size. Evaline sunk to the ground, her body giving way to exhaustion once the adrenaline left her. She could feel the cold sweat that now slicked her flesh, matting her hair to the back of her neck.

Alexis turned to Zahir after sparing a moment to catch Evaline's gaze. He mumbled an apology, unable to glance her way any longer.

"We can't change things now," Zahir said. "You brought her into this. She better not get us killed. Get your stuff. We have a ship to catch."

Without another word, Zahir spun on his heel and left the room. Evaline's breath caught in her throat as she stared at the man who she previously thought to be a kind and gentle soul. His eyes, no longer red, were filled with a sorrow so deep she could not explain why it pained her to the depths of her very being. Muttering almost to himself,

Alexis also turned and walked out, leaving Evaline alone in the room to wrestle with her emotions.

***

The ride from Alexis' estate passed slowly in near silence. She hoped they would talk more about their plan or answer some of her questions, but their responses were curt. The small bits of discussion they did have was held in subdued tones so the carriage driver could not hear them. Upon realizing that they did not trust the driver, Evaline resigned herself to watching out the window.

The verdant fields that had enthralled her before, though beautiful, were no longer as awe inspiring. Sheep and cattle still dotted the fields, picturesque villages occasionally sprang up, but the world went by, muted. Even seeing her hometown did not draw excitement from her. Her detachment brought a twinge of sadness. Her life at Bord du Pétale seemed an eternity ago.

Every time they passed a village near their road, Alexis would suggest that they go into town to stretch their legs. Evaline enjoyed those moments, relishing the sun on her face and the mouth-watering aromas of nearby food. Each time, Alexis gave her some coins to buy a warm meal and drink.

The local shops were always a pleasant break from the dreary carriage. Evaline loved looking at the delicately sewn dresses, pristine hats, or fine leather boots in the various shops. Her fingers traced the soft fabrics, moving from the dainty lace accents to the stitching along the sides. They reminded Evaline of what her mother could have done if she had time to create what her heart desired. Memories of their long nights together sewing by candlelight came flooding to her mind. Each time brought a wistful smile to her lips.

After returning to the carriage at the appropriate meeting time, Alexis would be waiting for her, Zahir already inside the carriage. With a wink, he'd help her into the carriage before instructing the driver to speed off. The first few times Evaline assumed that they were just trying to make good time. However, as their stops continued, she realized the true nature of their visits. Everyone was getting a good meal before their long trip.

Two fortnights passed in such a manner.

Just as she had previously, Evaline enjoyed a warm meal and a glass of wine before taking in the scenery. The closer they got to the seaside, the more the fashion and general wares changed. The high-necked dresses with delicate lace evolved into light-weight dresses off the shoulders with short sleeves. Bits of carved bone, and even whale teeth, showed off incredible craftsmanship as they depicted dramatic scenes at sea in the local shops.

Leaving these towns closer to the coast got harder and harder. There was something about the way people lived their lives in these villages that felt right to her. Perhaps she would ask Alexis if she could stay here after they finished their job. Living on the coast would be far enough away that no one could think that she associated with the two men anymore. Maybe she could even get her family to join her. The thought of returning to the dreary, empty estates halls for the rest of her life left her depressed.

Zahir sat in his usual spot in the carriage, arms crossed against his chest and breathing deeply. Somehow, he managed to fall asleep. Evaline wondered how such beauty could be so boring to him. Then again, he'd traveled the world. Zahir must have seen hundreds of breath-taking places. A gentle shaking of the carriage followed by a click heralded Alexis' arrival.

"There you are," he said. "I tried finding you in town but must've just missed you."

"Sorry, I needed some time."

"What's wrong?"

Evaline couldn't help but note the softness of his tone. Could he really be worried about her?

"Oh, nothing," she lied. "I'm just in my head too much."

Grabbing her hand, Alexis shot her a quick smile. "I know that feeling all too well. The mind likes to play cruel games." Addressing Zahir, he asked, "Ready to move on?"

Without opening his eye, Zahir gave them a thumbs up. Clapping his hands together, Alexis stuck his head out of the carriage and shared a word with the driver. The coach lurched forward and they continued on.

XX

GULLS CRIED OVERHEAD as the salty sea spray hit Evaline in the face. The chilly mist was a welcome relief from the heat of the sun as it beat down on her. Aceatius was not known as a hot land, but for some reason her port was blazing. It was different from the pleasant warmth she felt from the nearby towns, this was the full force of the sun upon her.

The cries of sailors and fishermen blended in with the sound of the waves hitting the rocks creating an alluring symphony enticing Evaline towards adventure. Their unabashed use of profanity, including several words and phrases she'd never heard before, intrigued her.

Weaving through the crowd, Evaline bumped into a young woman, barely older than her. Shooting the group a coy wink, the young woman let out an apology. Her mousey voice matched her curly brown hair, but the revealing outfit she wore was at odds with her innocent demeanor. An appreciable amount of cleavage was exposed. After making eye contact with both Alexis and Zahir, she paused, a sly smile crossing her lips.

"What brings you to Brielen?"

Evaline watched as the young woman sidled up to Alexis. Her hand reached out and began rubbing his arm as she met his gaze. The sugar-sweet tone of her voice made Evaline bristle. Alexis returned her coy smile, not removing the young lady's hand.

"We have a ship to catch."

"Oh," she feigned interest. "Are you going on a long voyage? Perhaps you'd like someone who's familiar with the port to show you around."

"How helpful," Zahir chimed in. "Do you know anyone?"

The young lady's head spun as she glowered at Zahir. Evaline noted the amusement on Alexis' face at the young woman's indignation. Fixing her face quicker than Evaline expected, the young lady returned her attention to Alexis.

"As a matter of fact, I am very familiar with most of the captains here. I could find you a fine room on one of the best ships." Giving Alexis' arm a squeeze, she gently tried to guide him away. "Why don't we talk about it?"

"Thank you for your offer, but we already have accommodations," Alexis said. Removing her hand from his arm, he managed to maneuver his way around her and slipped his arm around Evaline's waist. "I will most definitely remember you the next time we're in town though."

Evaline fought the urge to stare at him in shock as the young lady shot him a disappointed glare. Without another words, the young woman turned on her heels and disappeared into the crowd with a swish of her hips.

"You couldn't help yourself?" Alexis asked Zahir with a snort. "You better behave at Tel-Anon. You'll get us killed."

The mousey-voiced young woman was not the only one whose heads turned as the trio walked through the streets. On more than one occasion, one called out to them, inviting them to follow them. Not every woman caught Evaline's eye like the mousey-voiced one, but that didn't stop them from being forward and slightly aggressive in their attempts to get the men alone. Even with Eveline standing between them, woman after woman called out to the two men, promising them a good time. After the third exchange, Zahir mocked Alexis, commenting on how here in Aceatius the sandy-haired man was more popular, but once they reached Ma'Alkin, the roles would be reversed.

As they continued deeper into the town, Evaline admired the outfits of most of the women. They reminded her of the loose dresses worn by the women in the villages leading up to the coast. The local women wore skirts and white blouses that hung off their shoulders. A few even wore brown pants like she wore when she was working in her father's smithy. The simple dress she wore with long, form-fitting sleeves felt out of place against the women and the shirtless, sun-kissed men. If she felt out of place, she couldn't imagine what was going on in the boys' minds. Alexis and Zahir were both dressed in light-weight long-sleeved shirts and simple brown pants. Zahir's braids were tied in a high tail, exposing the back of his neck. A wide-brimmed hat with a white feather, sat lightly on Alexis' sandy hair.

Before leaving, both men rubbed an oil onto their skin. Evaline had asked them what it was for, but all they would say was that it was for protection from the sun. Knowing how painful a burn from the sun could be, Evaline didn't question it, though a part of her wished she'd asked for a little of the oil as well.

Countless flags festooned the port, hanging from buildings, ships, and the occasional wooden stall selling fresh fish or other goods. Her mouth watered at the smell of savory meats cooked in exotic spices as she passed a few taverns, nearing the coast. In the distance, someone played a lute while a stunning tenor accompanied it, floating over the hustle and bustle of the busy coastal town.

Evaline found herself getting lost in the chaos and unnatural beauty of the port. The ships lining the port were massive. They rocked steadily as the waves crashed into them. Evaline admired the strength they portrayed, their thick frames and sturdy masts not appearing to be bothered by the oceans. Topless women or terrifying sea creatures were carved into the bows, the women's hair flowed freely over their chests. Smaller fishing boats capable of holding one or two people, maneuvered between the docked ships. Further out at sea, the smaller boats dotted against the crystal blue sea.

"This way," Zahir's voice called out amidst the throng.

Evaline felt Alexis' slim fingers wrap around her hand as he guided her towards their ship. Calls of fresh fish and strange fruits bombarded them as the local vendors tried to get the trio to buy their wares from old wooden stalls. Gold jewelry sparkled in the sun, while the steel blades of unsheathed daggers tempted those who passed by.

A man walked through the crowd playing a mandora, his fingers plucking lazily on the strings. His voice warbled as he sang a bawdy tune. It must have been a popular one because several of the sailors began singing the chorus with him, laughing when they were done.

At long last, they stood in front of their ship. The *Faded Dawn* was smaller than her counterparts, but still a grand vessel. A beautiful woman was carved onto the bow, a pair of seashells covering her breasts, unlike the others. Her body ended in a fish-like tail with a breaking wave splashing around her. Evaline found herself mesmerized by the beautifully exotic piece or art.

Somewhere nearby, a gruff voice shouted something in a language she did not understand. A gentle tug told her she needed to keep moving. The men working on the ship were different from the others of Brielen. Their tanned skin glistened in the sun underneath their light, white shirts. Their dark hair was either short cut or hung around their shoulders in braids. A few had their braids in a tail like Zahir.

Approaching one of the men, Zahir began talking quickly in his native language. The man eyed Alexis and Evaline with an untrusting eye. Evaline noted how Zahir slipped the man a small red gem. She was surprised at how the man pocketed it quicker than she could blink. Turning his back, the man gave a nod and motioned them aboard.

"What was that about?" Alexis asked as they made their way to the side of the boat.

"Superstitious bunch," Zahir replied. "Said a woman on the boat is bad luck. I had to convince him to let her join us. Let's just hope the captain doesn't kick us off in the middle of the sea."

Evaline gulped at the thought. Were all sailors superstitious like he was? Why would she bring bad luck?

"Don't worry," Zahir said, no doubt noticing her concern. "As long as the seas are calm, we should be fine."

"Would they really kick us off?" she asked.

"They'd try, but let's just say it'll be better for everyone if they don't." The way Zahir responded so casually to the threat of drowning chilled Evaline. The implication that he'd handle things left no doubt in her mind.

By the time they found the ship's entrance, a strong wind kicked up. The ocean spray left her shaking as the freezing water splashed her leg. Her mind went back to the threat of being tossed over the side of the ship, and the thought of being drenched in water so cold sent another shiver down her spine. Forget the fact that she couldn't swim well, flailing in the sea petrified her. Making her way up the gangplank, Evaline looked down. Below her, a wave slammed into the dock, its foam spray breaking and splashing everywhere. Suddenly, she found her knees threatening to give way beneath her.

"It's so high," she managed to squeak out.

Alexis gave her hand a reassuring squeeze. "You'll get used to it. For now, just stare straight ahead."

Clenching her jaw, she nodded. Mimicking his gesture, Evaline clutched his hand in hers as they finished their ascent into the boat. Once aboard, the bustle of the crew distracted Evaline. Men raced about, ensuring everything would be ready when the captain gave his orders. The ropes whipped about as hands frantically tied the loose ends into complicated knots. A few men crashed into her, send her staggering several steps as they carried provisions below deck for storage.

"Let's find our room," Zahir called over the noise.

The wind picked up as they followed the men who bumped into Evaline down below deck. Strong gusts slammed into Evaline's back, lurching her forward just as she reached the entrance. Once out of the elements, the air seemed unnaturally calm. She could hear it howling overhead, but down here, it was quiet, eerie.

Men bustled about below deck as well. Final inventories were taken, crates stacked, and barrels organized by a handful of men, the results being tallied in a small leather book. They spoke to each other low and quick in a foreign tongue. Evaline resigned herself to being left in the dark for most of the trip. She made a mental note to ask Zahir to teach her a few basics so she wouldn't be completely lost.

Ahead, Zahir spoke to a member of the crew, his hands emphasizing whatever point he was trying to make. The two shared an affectionate shoulder clap before Zahir motioned for them to follow him. Evaline realized at that moment that she didn't know where Alexis was. A second of panic filled her before she found him observing some of the crates and talking to another crewman. The man seemed amused to find out a foreigner spoke his language. The two gestured as they talked, Alexis leaning casually on the large wooden box, his dazzling smile flashing in the darkened room.

By the time Alexis noticed Zahir waving him over, the man gave a final nod before walking off to complete his duties. Taking his time, Alexis pushed off the crate and sauntered over to the other two.

"What was -?" Evaline began.

Almost immediately, Alexis wrapped his arm around her shoulder. "Quiet," he hissed into her ear.

Leading the way, Zahir managed to find his way through the weaving, rocking ship, passed the crew's quarters, and to a small room that was usually used for storage. It was dark and dank, but Evaline was happy to find that they'd at least been left with candles and a lantern that were already lit. Nets were stretched out from the frame, creating the strangest looking bed Evaline had ever seen.

Inspecting the ropes, she muttered, "I wonder if it'll even support us?"

A series of loud thumps shattered the silence, so violent she jolted as though struck. She turned to face the pair, dumping their meager luggage into a pile in the middle of the floor. Alexis sat on a crate off to the side of the room while Zahir lounged in his swinging rope bed. Evaline couldn't imagine how he could look so comfortable, but as the ship continued to rock, Zahir's bed swayed, and a contented smile filled his face.

"So, what were you and that man talking about?" Zahir asked.

Alexis brought a knee to his chest, wrapping his arms around his leg as he leaned back on the crate. His eyes were closed as he recalled the conversation.

"He has family near the tomb. There's been movement at night. We're on the right track."

"Well, we have to be careful," Zahir replied. "The Menes are on the move."

Alexis sat up, his eyes popping open. "Have they started moving out from the temple?"

"No. He has family who is part of the Menes. I wouldn't be surprised though if they're expecting something to happen. I didn't leave on the best circumstances. I could've been seen. Nefret remembers all her children."

Who is Nefret? And what are the Menes? Evaline wondered. Her musings were cut short as Alexis cursed. She made a mental note to ask Alexis for more information when they got a moment.

"Damn!" Alexis hissed. "Then we're on the right ship. The *Dawn* could hold a lot of answers for us."

"We can't," Zahir replied. "One, we have her," he motioned to Evaline. "And two, there's talk of some of the crew not acting right. I think the Menes may have sent soldiers out to look for suspicious people. Us. We need to lay low."

"I'll stay inside as much as possible. Zahir, you'll have to be careful. We'll need to come up with an escape plan in case you see someone you recognize." Alexis nodded to his friend, his expression stoic.

"Unless there's a Menes onboard, we can handle it. I know enough about sailing that we can make our way to land." Propping his head on his arms like a pillow, Zahir closed his eyes once more. "Get some sleep. I'll go out and check out things on deck once the ship sets sail. Alexis, you keep watch at night."

And like that, the discussion was over. Evaline glanced from one to the other in shock as the duo got comfortable and fell asleep. She couldn't believe it. Her mind raced and these two didn't have a care in the world. She didn't want to sleep. She couldn't if she tried right now. It seemed like moments before they were breathing steadily. Now was her chance to explore.

Careful not to kick something or knock something over, Evaline made her way to the door. As her hand turned the knob, she felt a strong hand on her arm. Alexis stood behind her, boring into her with his stare. She hadn't heard him make a sound.

"Go to bed," he instructed.

Without another word, Evaline clambered into the strange net swing and tried to get comfortable. She gripped the edges in a death grip, her knuckles a stark white color, as the thing rocked side to side, threatening to dump her onto the ground. A string of soft curses poured from her lips as she fought to remain upright. The muffled snort of laughter sounded from Zahir's direction, or did she imagine it?

XXI

THEIR TIME ON the *Faded Dawn* blended together in one long, dark nightmare. Evaline found herself praying every night as the ship lurched with every swell, the boards groaning all around her. Her stomach did summersaults, keeping her in a constant state of discomfort and preventing Evaline from getting a proper night's sleep. Above deck the dread loosened, a little. Wind wiped her hair, cool against her clammy skin. The waves looked smaller from here, almost harmless, though every so often the sea gave the ship a playful shove, reminding Evaline of the true power of the vast waters. Still, the sound of the sea left her craving adventure.

Evaline took advantage of the limited space of the ship and tried to get to know Alexis. Trying to disguise her questions as innocent prattle, Evaline worked to pick up any information she could about Alexis and his adventures. To her delight, Alexis humored her, regaling her with tales of his trips to various countries in search of gems, necklaces, and even an ancient dagger. Evaline felt the familiar sense of wanderlust she'd experienced as a child grow within her after each story. Growing up, she never imagined her life would be anything but simplicity in Bord du Pétale.

To her disappointment, Alexis carefully stayed away from topics like the words she found on the maps. There was no discussion of what Absalom, the Menes, or Estrie were. At night, Evaline pretended to sleep, hoping to lure Alexis and Zahir into a conversation about their trip, but neither seemed keen on talking about Neith or any new information they'd uncovered. Undaunted, Evaline continued to press Alexis, hoping he would one day slip up and reveal something to her that she could use to uncover a piece of information to solve her mystery. Despite the nausea that overwhelmed her, Evaline woke up most mornings exhausted, but with a smile on her face.

A loud commotion woke her one morning, causing her to sit up suddenly and slam her head into the ship's wooden frame. Stars exploded in her eyes and a dull ache immediately pounded as she rubbed her head with a groan.

"What's going on?" Zahir asked groggily.

"I hit my head," Evaline moaned.

"No. Outside."

"Let's check it out," Alexis suggested. "We should be arriving soon. Maybe we're early."

"We can't be," Zahir protested. "The last few days all the crew could talk about is how poor the weather's been. Calm waters, and barely a breath of air for the sails. They've been rowing for at least two days now."

"Damn. Hope they don't expect us to row," Alexis said. Shooting a glance Evaline's way, she saw the worry etched into his face in the way his brow crinkled. "They might want us to row."

Hopping out of his rope bed, Zahir, threw on his shirt, covering his slim frame. Doing her best to ignore the pain, Evaline rolled out of her bed and slipped on her shoes. If they wanted her to row, she might as well be ready.

***

The salty air refreshed Evaline. The combination of warm sun on her flesh and the cool sea breeze felt like heaven. How she'd missed the daytime. On the deck, men spoke in small groups, their conversations hurried and muffled. As Evaline and her companions searched for an open spot on deck, more than one pair of eyes following them. The waves broke against the side of the ship, the sound having faded to background noise long ago, the spray lightly misting those aboard. More than one pocket of sailors fell silent as the three settled into a little corner, their backs not against the side of the ship at Zahir's suggestion.

It wasn't long until the captain clambered up from below deck, silencing everyone above. Evaline had seen him on several occasions, though fleetingly. A strong man with wild, unkempt hair tied back, the captain gave off an aura of supreme authority. One of his eyes was forever closed, a long, thin scar running down the middle. The sun had beaten his face mercilessly, leaving it weathered and aged.

"Captain Hasani," Zahir whispered to the pair. "Although, undecidedly not," he added with a chuckle.

Evaline stared at the man, nonplussed as he enjoyed his own joke.

"Hasani means handsome," Alexis explained.

"Oh," she let out in a long, slow whisper.

A thin sword hung on Hasani's hip, and he walked with a pronounced limp. His one good eye scanned each group as he made his way around the deck. With each heavy thump of his boot on the wood, Evaline felt herself flinch. There was an energy about him, one she did not like.

With a gruff bark, the man began speaking slowly, deliberately.

"All right, you shits!" Zahir translated quietly. "Yamm is not pleased with us."

Hasani's gaze continued to rove the deck. Evaline was surprised at how thoroughly he commanded his crew. Not a sound could be heard, not a body shuffled. Even the gulls overhead fell silent as his boots thumped lopsidedly on the deck.

"The sea is for those who know her temperamental ways," Zahir continued as Hasani's lecture carried on. "And Yamm does not tolerate insolence. So!"

At this, Hasani's attention was drawn directly at Evaline and her companions. The captain's pace picked up as he closed the distance between them. When he was close enough to spit on them, the grizzled man's hand shot out so quickly that Evaline could barely react before he grabbed her by the collar of her dress. Readjusting his grip in the blink of an eye, Evaline's heart began to race as she struggled to breath. His thick, calloused hand yanked her forward as he squeezed her neck.

Beside her, Alexis and Zahir made startled noises but held their ground. Evaline tried to whimper, but only a gurgle came out. Her lungs burned for air and her wide eyes watered as they met his unblinking gaze. Hasani roared out a question, spittle flying in her face by the end of it.

Uncomfortable murmurings from the crew could be heard in the now palpable silence that hung over the ship. Evaline wondered why Alexis and Zahir didn't do anything. Her nails dug into his hand, but he didn't seem to notice her futile attempts to break free. She tried reaching for his face, but Hasani just slapped her hard. Tears rolled down her cheeks as her heart continued to pound in her chest.

Zahir let out a low growl, his words barely distinguishable from the animalistic sound. Hasani spat at Zahir, a vein throbbing in his temple and his eyes blazing. Zahir ran his hand over his forearm, his gaze dropping uncomfortably for a moment.

Why aren't they stopping this man? Why won't they save me? God, they said I would die. Am I going to die?

"Help." Evaline's plea came out as a weak whisper.

Hasani smirked, pulling her close. His eyes roved her body, taking her in completely. He muttered something low, a slight lilt at the end of his sentence as he stared hungrily at Evaline. An instant later, he met Zahir's gaze and motioned with his head towards the edge of the ship. Evaline gulped at the thought of him throwing her over. A second hand reached for her skirts and Evaline's blood ran cold. She felt the fabric bunching between her legs. She tried to squeak out a protest, her legs kicking feebly, but no sound came out.

Zahir let out another growl, his tone carried a deadly threat that Evaline hoped the man wouldn't ignore. To her relief, Hasani stopped for a moment, turning to face Zahir. The captain sneered at Zahir, motioning towards the edge of the ship. Behind him, a few of the crewmen pulled daggers from their waistbands.

"We're almost to Tel-Anon," Alexis cut in, speaking so Evaline could understand him. "Leave us to our room. We can provide you with an offering to Yamm in the form of gold. Perhaps that will appease him?"

Hasani's gaze turned to Alexis as Zahir translated his words. A hungry smile twisted on his grizzled face, and he licked his lips. Evaline's vision started to darken as she fought to remain conscious. She felt her skirts drop as Hasani reached for his waist. She felt the hilt of his sword lightly scrape her thigh.

"We'll take your gold as payment for your deceit," Hasani said in broken Aceatian. "But that won't sate Yamm. No, you'll still die."

Blackness moved from her periphery and seeped to the center of her vision.

A sudden jolt brought a pained yelp from her lips. As the pressure around her neck disappeared, Evaline took a large gulp of air as she gasped for breath. Her vision cleared until it was preternaturally clear. Above her, there was a flurry of movement followed by several startled cries. Evaline sat on the deck taking in greedy lungfuls of air. Her hand touched her neck delicately. With as tender as it was, it probably would bruise.

A strangled shout caught her attention. Her vision still unnaturally clear, Evaline saw Zahir lifting Hasani in the air with one hand. Like Evaline, Hasani's hands clawed at Zahir's hand as he squeezed the grizzled captain's throat. She thought she saw a glint of red in his eyes in the morning light.

How strong are these two? she wondered as flashbacks of Alexis striking Zahir back in Mont Bloom played in her mind.

The second in command, as well as several others, raced forward several steps to help their captain before Alexis stepped in between them and Zahir. Evaline watched as these muscular men balked at approaching the slender man, unsure of any hidden strength he might have.

Hasani choked out a command. The men, however, hesitated. Alexis rubbed his hands together before holding them out in an open, non-threatening manner.

"Gentlemen," Alexis began. "Clearly there has been a misunderstanding. The seas have not been violent. I have seen Yamm's wrath, and this is nothing. Just a calm patch. There is no reason to let fear rule you."

Hasani tried to reply, but Zahir must have readjusted his grip on the man's neck, because it was quickly cut off with a high-pitched yelp. Nodding to Alexis, the sandy-haired man took that as his cue to continue.

"We are not far from shore. Either give us a boat and we will leave you or let us stay the remainder of the trip. We have caused you no trouble thus far. Let us keep it that way."

"And if we don't?" one man asked, his words coming out stilted as he stumbled on the language. His hand went to his hip to emphasize his point.

The glint of steel reflecting the sun's light caught Evaline's eye. She found herself on her feet, not being conscious of the action. Several others appeared to take courage from their comrade as they too started pulling out their swords. Dangerous curved blades of polished steel sparkled in the light. Evaline had never seen any like it. She wasn't sure if she was more scared of the swords, or the desperation gleaming in their eyes.

"I don't think we want to consider the other options," Alexis said flatly.

The crew gasped and many took a step back. Whispers broke out amongst the men that neither Alexis nor Zahir translated for Evaline. From the way men hesitated to grab their swords, Evaline wondered what could be causing the sudden change in their attitude. Cries of Sekhmet or some other curse rang out. Men stumbled over each other to put distance between themselves and the two men, leaving Hasani forgotten. Abandoned. Suddenly, she felt powerful.

What's happening? Evaline wondered.

Somewhere in the back of her mind, Evaline recalled her father talking about how the right expression can change the outcome of a dangerous situation. *"Some people have crazy eyes, and that will keep them safe from attack. No one wants to rob a man who might give them more trouble than the few coins are worth."*

Of course, as travelers, they've probably run into many dangerous situations, and a language barrier would only exasperate that. They must have found a way to look more intimidating. I'll have to ask them to teach me how to do crazy eyes.

Alexis and Zahir stood still, Hasani still dangling in the air, his mouth open as he gasped for air. His hands dropped to his sides, no longer clawing at the hand that held him. The deck became quiet once more as the scrambling stopped. Men watched the pair warily having completely forgotten Evaline's existence. It felt like an eternity. The only way to tell the passage of time was Hasani's wheezing gasps. Finally, two men took tentative steps forward.

They look familiar, Evaline said to herself. *Where have I seen them before?*

"Please," one begged. "We showed you kindness. Please return the favor."

A single red gem slid across the ship as the other man straightened up once more. The two men kept their hands held out in front of them, open and begging for mercy.

"You were the one who let us on the ship," Evaline blurted out. "And you were talking to us the first day."

A strangled gasp came from Hasani and Evaline gasped. Did she get these men in trouble? Surely, they wouldn't face any consequences for this. Alexis and Zahir shared a glance. Without another word, they nodded to each other. Hasani's body plummeted to the deck with a thump, his body crumpling under the weight of his bad leg, gasping for breath. Alexis motioned for the two to follow them to their room. Zahir bent over and picked up the gem, the sun catching in its facets and sparkling in his hand like droplets of blood. He pocketed the jewel with a smile.

"If we row, we can reach Tel-Anon in two days," the gem man said.

"Two days," Alexis confirmed.

As they descended into the heart of the ship, Evaline turned and watched as several members of the crew rushed to help their captain. The two men to had begged for forgiveness stood motionless as the others moved around them. Evaline wasn't sure if those two would make it to Tel-Anon.

XXII

SHOUTS FROM ABOVE WOKE Evaline, providing a poor start to the day. This time, she made sure not to bolt up in bed. Another day of near-constant headaches did not appeal to Evaline. Alexis stood in the corner checking their food rations and other supplies, while Zahir was nowhere to be found. The gentle sway of the ship was a pleasant relief after the turmoil of the last few days. Evaline watched as he poured a bit of clear liquid into his hand and began rubbing his body wherever his flesh was exposed.

"We must be at Tel-Anon," she said.

"Yes."

"Where is Zahir?"

"He's getting some final supplies and should be back shortly." Alexis turned to face Evaline. "Would you like to go above deck to take in the port?"

Images of Hasani and his angry crew flashed in her mind. She hadn't gotten over what he was about to do to her; what he was going to allow the crew to do to her. The idea of going anywhere by herself on this ship left her feeling terrified.

"I think I'll stay here," she said.

"I don't think you should," Alexis replied, his tone hard.

"But –"

Before she could finish, her protestation was interrupted as Zahir came in. Behind him, an unconscious man dragged on the floor. Evaline's heart jumped to her throat.

"What are you doing?" she asked.

Propping the man onto one of the crates, Zahir ignored the question and bit down on the man's neck. With a yelp, Evaline watched, mortified, as the two clamped their mouths on the unconscious man. She didn't understand what was happening. The man remained unconscious, letting out only a grunt as they remained latched onto his neck on both sides like a pair of animals. Though they didn't tear at the man's flesh, the two stayed locked onto his neck for several long minutes, the man's skin turning an ashen grey with each passing second.

Evaline felt her stomach turn in a way the tumultuous sea couldn't manage, the tight clenching in her gut and the taste of bile threatening to come up. Evaline had never seen something so unnatural. Try as she might, Evaline couldn't tear her eyes from the scene. The man's head began lulling to the side as the two feasted. That was the only way to describe what they were doing. Finally, his head slipped back as he slumped to the floor, only propped up by the two men's hands. A soft exhale stole the breath from the man before his body went completely limp. Zahir ripped open the lid of a crate before stuffing the man's now lifeless body into it before replacing the top. Blood coated his teeth – had they been longer a moment before?

"Better they not find out until after we're gone," he explained causally, ignoring Evaline's frightened expression. "Come, let's go. We don't want trouble."

"What's going on?" Evaline squeaked, her hand motioning to the crate now housing the dead man. "What the hell are you?"

Flashing Evaline a quick smile, Alexis wiped his face before answering. "The damned."

***

Grey clouds hung in the air, obscuring the sun. Despite the gloomy coverage, Evaline thought it a blessing as it was already sweltering. Without the clouds, Evaline didn't doubt that the heat would be blistering. Men rushed about on deck tying off ropes and securing the sails to the masts. No one moved to stop the three as they walked across the deck. No one made direct eye contact with them since the incident a few days ago.

"I never realized how much goes into sea travel," Evaline mumbled, trying to push the image of Alexis and Zahir drinking blood from her mind. It wouldn't be an easy thing to forget.

Just another reminder of the dangers of what I've gotten myself into, she thought with a shake of her head.

"It's actually quite relaxing, assuming the sea cooperates," Alexis replied. His arm wrapped around her shoulder, pulling her into a side hug. Evaline felt her body tense at his touch, but the unexpected coolness of his body against the heat of hers distracted her enough that she relaxed, letting her body melt into his and enjoy the change in temperature. "There's a reason why these people believe in the tyrannical Yamm. The waters are fickle, and the winds can be life-changing if not in your favor."

A loud thump announced their arrival. Zahir motioned for the group to quickly follow him, cautioning them to hold on to the rope guiderail. Evaline remembered her first experience with the gangplank and kept her head level, staring ahead at the bustling port. She quickly found that it wasn't difficult to ignore the sea.

Tel-Anon was a beautiful gem hidden in a sea of tan and golden sand. The ocean transitioned into a sparkling sapphire river, no doubt bringing life to the rest of Ma'Alkin.

Small wooden stalls covered in brightly colored clothes to protect them from the sun dotted the ground, and people weaved around in an intricate dance to get to their destination without bumping into those around them.

The journey down the plank was bumpy and slow, but Evaline didn't mind. She enjoyed the cries of the vendors and the new aromas the greeted her. She even heard a lute playing in the distance, the faint jingling of coins or cymbals accompanying it. A small group of Ma'Alkinians seemed to head towards the music.

I hope we have time to stop there.

"Watch yourself," Zahir warned as they neared the end of the thin wooden ramp. "Be on guard. The children here are not here to sell you goods, and they're not lost. They are your biggest threat right now."

"What?"

"Pickpockets, thieves, and slave traders use children to lure young women and provide a false sense of security. Much like the thieves who portray themselves as wandering travelers or holy women in Aceatius," Alexis explained.

Evaline found herself gripping the guide rope tighter as she processed the news. What monster would use children to deceive those who wanted to help? She made sure to keep the information in the back of her mind, hoping to not fall prey to their evil tactics. The irony of her traveling across the world with a pair of otherworldly beings of her own was not lost on Evaline.

"I could never imagine Apolline or Elise asking for help but having malicious intentions," she muttered.

"They use younger ones," Alexis replied. "Between three and ten, I want to say."

"Sounds about right," Zahir said, almost absentmindedly. "They're young."

The scent of incense hung heavy in the air, masking the salt of the sea and the smell of fish. The women passed by, their eyes lined with thick, dark kohl and their hair clasped together with gold wraps. Most men did not have long hair like Zahir, but those who did also kept it in braids. People glanced their way as they got off but continued about their day. Stepping onto dry land left Evaline feeling confused. Her body rocked as it had on the boat, as if she were still experiencing the waves on solid ground. Stumbling forward, Evaline managed to crash into Zahir's back, helping her maintain her balance.

"It's strange," Alexis said with a grin. "Takes some getting used to for sure."

Wrapping her arm around his, Alexis helped Evaline straighten up. Zahir disappeared into the crowd. Fear welled in Evaline as she realized for the first time how different she was from the rest of the people around her. Her only hope at returning home was Alexis, and he stood out as much as she did with his sandy hair.

"Walk confidently," he whispered, untangling his arm from hers and sliding it around her waist. "Thieves can smell uncertainty. It'll make us all easy targets."

The pair strolled through the throng, dipping left and right to avoid running into those who hurried past them. Evaline fought the urge to jog through the crowd, her body full of adrenaline and wanting to get somewhere where she could regain her composure. The lilting melody of the pierced lute sounded to their right.

"Over there," she said, pointing to the crowd. It had grown bigger since she last saw it.

Guiding Alexis, Evaline lead the way towards the music. As they approached, the clinging sound of finger cymbals grew louder, keeping time with the fevered plucking of the pierced lute. Evaline marveled at the long-necked instrument, noticing the tortoiseshell that made the bowl of the instrument. It wasn't a peaceful song, but one of strength and excitement. The steady beat of hand drums completed the song. Squeezing their way between a couple of men, Evaline gasped in delight as she saw a group of young women, no older than herself, dancing to the music in colorful clothes.

Their mahogany skin contrasted beautifully against their costumes of the most exquisite red, orange, yellow, and turquoise. Around their hips, a cloth with coins sewed in jingled with each swish. Their long dark hair played around their back, fanning out as they spun in time with the song.

"They're beautiful," she breathed.

Evaline found herself getting caught up in the song. Her body bounced as the dancers moved about. Even the musicians danced, their bodies swaying as they played. Sweat glistened off their exposed skin in the heat. Soon, a fine layer of perspiration formed on Evaline as well. She couldn't imagine how hot the dancers felt.

The song ended with a spirited round of applause. People began to disperse, some remaining to watch the next dance as the musicians struck up another lively tune. Evaline wanted to stay, but Alexis gently pulled her away. There was still work to be done. As they made their way back to where the *Faded Dawn* had been, a man called to them from his stall.

"What's that?" Evaline asked, craning her neck.

"Leave it," Alexis said. "Best not to get drawn in."

"But everything is so amazing," she begged.

With a resigned sigh, Alexis allowed himself to be steered towards the man. As they neared, the man began calling out to them excitedly. His fast speech sounded like one continuous word to Evaline, but she smiled as she approached the display.

"Politeness is universal," she said as she nodded to the man as his hands waved around his wares.

Small trinkets of burnished silver glittered in the sun. Alexis pulled back a bit as Evaline leaned forward. The man picked up a turtle shaped hair pin with a turquoise stone for its shell and held it out to her. Evaline took the proffered pin and held it up to the light, letting its angles shine. The man continued to babble happily to the pair.

When there was a break in the sales pitch, Alexis responded. The look of absolute surprise on the man's face disappeared in an instant as a huge smile broke out. He spoke rapidly to Alexis, pleased that, to his knowledge, the pair could understand him. Alexis held up his hand to politely decline, but the man was persistent. He pushed Evaline's hands back as she tried to place the pin down on the cloth with the other baubles.

The sound of children's laughter rang out nearby. Evaline thought she felt something brush against her backside, but when she turned around, it was just someone walking past her. Returning to the display, she saw Alexis and the man reaching an agreement. A pair of silver coins exchanged hands, and the man hummed as he walked around the stand to place the hair pin in Evaline's hair.

Once the transaction was over, Alexis pulled Evaline away. This time, he was more forceful. Children ran in the streets, but Evaline didn't pay them much mind. It wasn't until a pair of children, no older than five, bumped into her and fell down crying that she noticed them. Their wails filled the streets, somehow managing to sound over the general din of everyday life. Evaline froze, unsure of what to do. A couple of older women were approaching them, scowling as they spoke quickly.

"What do we do?" Evaline squeaked out in panic. "Everyone is looking."

Alexis called out to the women, while at the same time pulling Evaline in closer. The children stood up and were inching closer to the pair. Evaline looked around, frantic to find an escape. Behind them, a pair of men neared. Evaline yelped as soon as she saw the daggers hanging from their hips. The men noticed they'd been spotted and split up, disappearing into the crowd. The angry women were now arguing with Alexis and more children circled them. Evaline twisted and turned, trying to find a way out, but Alexis' arm pulled her into him.

Evaline spotted one of the two men coming out of the crowd and let out a strangled noise.

"They're here!" she gasped.

A loud voice barked at the group, causing Evaline to jump. Zahir wove through the group, shouting at the two women who quickly backed up, startled, by the arrival of the newcomer. The children around Alexis and Evaline also disappeared so that by the time Zahir arrived, there was plenty of space between the two parties. Zahir shouted at the ladies who tried to defend themselves but ended up slinking away. They glared at Evaline and Alexis as they melted back into the crowd. The two men who Evaline saw earlier must have decided better of it, because Evaline couldn't even tell if they were there.

The merchant who sold Alexis the hair pin spoke quickly to Zahir, his hands gesturing for emphasis. A pair of men stood behind Zahir. There was something about them that intrigued Evaline. They looked familiar.

"Ah, dammit!" Zahir cursed once everything settled down. He ran his hands over his braided tail as he turned to the pair. "I leave you two alone for five minutes and you almost get robbed and kidnapped. What the hell?"

"It wasn't our fault," Evaline protested. "If those ladies hadn't started yelling at us –"

"The vendor was a distraction," Alexis cut in. "He wasn't involved, per se, but it's not unusual for thieves to seize an opening like that. I told you, best not to be drawn in. My gods that was close."

Evaline's attention shifted to the two men behind Zahir. The pair were not much taller than Evaline, but their frames were muscular. Again, she had the distinct impression that she'd seen them somewhere before.

"Akiiki and Hapu," Zahir said, motioning to each man in turn. "They were the ones on the ship who begged for leniency."

"Why aren't you translating for them like you did for me?" she asked.

"Until we decide what we want to do with them, best to leave them in the dark."

"Makes sense," Evaline replied.

Turning to Alexis, Zahir continued. "Their captain put a price on their heads. They had to sneak off the ship as soon as she docked. I would bet they need to lay low for a while until they can find a new ship to work on, assuming they can even return to the sea. Their kind aren't exactly forgiving, or forgetful."

"Having a larger group would make it easier to get near the temple," Alexis conceded. "We can always leave them. They'll have no loyalty towards us. Do you trust them?"

"I don't know. Hapu mentioned he has kin further inland who could loan us something to ride. We could probably find a few places to rest and recover too. I always forget how damned sunny it is here."

"Liar," Alexis said with a snort. Returning to the two men, he hummed as he thought. "I think a bigger party will afford us more coverage. If things have gone bad after your last visit, more people will allow for us to sneak off, leaving the group behind."

Turning to Evaline, Alexis whispered, "It's best not to mention why we're here. You never know where the ears are."

Evaline bristled at the insinuation that she wouldn't know to keep quiet.

Why are they bringing them anyway? she fumed. *If I'm so much trouble, why are they not leaving these two to deal with their own?*

Opening her mouth to retort, Evaline noticed that Alexis' attention was focused on Akiiki and Hapu, but when Evaline looked closely, she noticed how tense his body was. Almost as if he was straining to hear some far away sound.

Furrowing her brow, Evaline observed Alexis and the others with renewed intensity. Recalling the maps in Alexis' estate, she pictured Ma'Alkin. It was a large country with the capitol deep in the heart of the land. Rivers snaked along, coming together at what she now rationed might be the royal palace. Zahir and Alexis would be familiar with the land, having been there before, but why the two men?

Are they pawns like me? I wonder if they got too involved and are now in danger too? What kinds of artifacts are they dealing in besides the necklace?

"It's settled then," Zahir said. Motioning for the group to follow, Zahir led the way through the bustling throng.

Evaline made sure to stay close to Alexis. Something about their little group left the hairs on her arms on end. Evaline racked her brain, trying to remember anything from their trip. A faded memory from when they first boarded the ship wriggled its way to the forefront of her mind.

They have family by the tomb… and something about movement nearby. The revelation filled her with an emotion she couldn't name, but it released the tension that had welled inside her. *I wonder how many pawns there are in this game?*

XXIII

BEHIND THEM, Tel-Anon's port shrank along with the last cries of the harried crowds. The farther they walked, the quieter the world grew, until only the lap of the river kept them company. Evaline brushed her fingers along the tall grasses at the water's edge, their blades glittering like citrine jewels next to the sapphire that was the river. By midday, the clouds had burned away, leaving the sky an unforgiving blue. Sweat gathered at the nape of her neck, the blistering heat stinging her skin.

Evaline marveled at the wildlife she passed. Long-necked herons stood in the river, catching bejeweled fish in their bills. On several occasions, she saw a large lizard sunning itself on the bank of the river. Sharp teeth could be seen as their mouths gaped open. Small huts began to dot the river and further out. People could be seen leading cattle to the waters to drink or washing their clothes in the slow-moving current. Several of them called out to Akiiki or Hapu, waving cheerfully at the group. The men would wave in return, calling out to them.

The group left the bank of the river and moved through the dried grasses. It didn't take long before a ring of huts appeared. An old man more wrinkles than skin flashed them a toothless grin. He led a long-horned creature unlike any Evaline had ever seen. Children darted between the huts as women laid clothes out to dry on a reed mat. Hapu and Akiiki broke away, each picking up a child and wrapping them in a tight embrace.

The scene reminded Evaline of her little sisters. Smiling, she turned to Alexis. To her surprise, his eyes turned down. She'd never seen anything close to sadness from him. Reaching out, she gently grabbed his hand and gave it a light squeeze. His attention snapped up to her, a soft smile playing on his lips. He returned the gesture, wrapping his fingers around hers as they continued into the village.

"When all this is over," he said, "I will let you go." Dropping his voice and glancing at Zahir, he added, "Estrie, the woman in the picture you saw back at Mont Bloom, who cursed me to this life, has spies everywhere. Once it is safe, I'll help you disappear and find safety for you and your family."

"Who is Estrie?" Evaline asked. The name sounded familiar, like she'd heard it long ago.

Leaning in close until his lips tickled her ear, Alexis whispered, "She is the queen of the damned, and my mother, so to speak. Zahir and I are what you call vampyres, and a war is about to start."

***

Sitting inside one of the huts, Evaline plastered on a false smile as she enjoyed the respite from the sun. Despite it barely crossing the horizon, she struggled to remain cool in her new heavy clothes. As promised, Alexis disappeared to try and find her some new clothes. Evaline wondered how hot it would be to wear a cowl under the sun's beating rays.

Vampyres... what did Mama say about them? Predators. Her mind raced with countless thoughts and ideas pulling it in different directions. *They eat humans,* she thought, remembering how they drained the sailor of his life essence. *But how? Mama said they steal your soul. I don't understand.*

Evaline's brow furrowed. The men continued to talk about whatever they thought important, ignoring Evaline for the most part. Alexis occasionally shot a glance her way, his own brow twitching up as if in question, but he didn't say anything.

How do I get home? Evaline continued. Right after the thought, she felt her stomach drop. *This is what they meant by I'm too involved. Aligning myself with one of these monsters has put my life, and my family's in danger. This really is a death sentence.*

With an internal sigh, Evaline deflated, her shoulders drooping. A cool spot formed on her back, causing Evaline to jump. Alexis sat quietly beside her, rubbing the spot between her shoulders as he continued to listen to the other men.

Why? she wondered. *There's no reason for him to treat me with any kindness. Their kind aren't compassionate.*

At least, that's what her mother had said.

Vowing to keep her wits about her, Evaline excused herself to Alexis with a whisper, saying that she was tired. Cuddled under the thin blanket, Evaline strained to listen to the conversation as it continued on for hours.

If I have any hope of escaping, I need to be ready to do anything. I'll need some of their gems to secure payment on a ship. Her eyes finally drooping, Evaline made one more note to her list of tasks to do. *I need to remember the way back.*

***

The journey to Kul-El passed quickly once they'd left Abukhar's small village. Abukhar and Hapu managed to secure the group a few horses, much to Evaline's relief. Her new clothes also proved to be a blessing, keeping her cool and her face from further burning. Not worrying about the heat had a second benefit – she could focus on their route, trying to remember any landmarks that she could on the flat, barren land. A gnarled tree, a large rock, anything.

After nine days in the grueling heat, the group crested a small hill. Below spanned a large, flat valley covered in golden sand. Tall palms dotted the city of Kul-El, providing a little respite from the blistering sun. Clusters of mudbrick buildings with wooden roofs created small living districts. Farther away, a majestic building, undoubtedly the pharaoh's home, sprawled about. The sapphire river sparkled in the sun as it wended its way around the palace. A few smaller buildings sat near the palace, both the pharaoh's home and the nearby buildings a pristine white, contrasting against the dull brown of the mudbrick homes.

Pointing north of the palace, Alexis shook his head solemnly as Zahir covered his mouth. It took a moment for Evaline to locate what Alexis was looking at. The sands continued on behind the majestic building, and behind it, a pyramid was under construction. The golden sand transitioned into black, and unlike the part of Kul-El she saw from her vantage point, the trees were felled, the fronds blackened as well.

"What?" she whispered to Alexis.

"Khemit," he replied. While Zahir and Abukhar spoke rapidly, Alexis explained. "Black land. It wasn't like this when I was last here. This reeks of death."

Hapu laced his fingers together, as if in prayer, his eyes closed as he mumbled a prayer to the gods. "What can we do?" he finally asked in broken Aceatian.

Both he and Abukhar made an effort to speak the language so that Evaline could understand as well. Their command of it, however, was so broken, it sounded like a three-year-old was speaking sometimes.

"What of our pharaoh? Menkhe'n and our priests must be protected," Abukhar said. "They are our connection to the gods. Without them, Ma'Alkin is in danger."

"Do you think the pharaoh is involved?" Alexis asked, his brows disappearing into his sandy bangs.

"I don't know," Zahir replied. "I don't think so, but I don't even know the extent of the Menes' control. Nefret could easily have slipped someone into the pharaoh's inner circle."

Alexis hummed, rubbing his temple.

"Alexis," Evaline broached tentatively. "What are the Menes, and who is Nefret?"

Glancing towards the two grieving men, Alexis gently guided her out of earshot. "The Menes are the Ma'Alkin eternal family – the royal vampyric bloodline. Every great dynasty has a dark secret, someone behind the curtain pulling the strings. The Ahkash Dynasty is a sham. The Menes manipulate the pharaoh into doing their bidding, and Nefret is the head of the Menes. She is responsible for bringing vampyres to Ma'Alkin."

Evaline's breath caught in her throat. Her head spun in Zahir's direction.

"Did she?"

"Yes," Alexis replied. "Like Estrie did to me." Sighing, Alexis added, "There's no reason to hide it now. There is a good chance you will die here. The war is between the dynastic leaders like Nefret and Estrie, and those of us who are unhappy with their ways. Those of us who resent being turned into the damned and doomed to eternal life. We are few, but we are determined. We don't expect to survive for long, but Zahir and I want vengeance on Nefret and Estrie."

Evaline's voice caught in her throat as she watched Alexis' eyes change from their normal hazel to crimson. He didn't appear to notice the change. His focus on the darkened land was intense, his face a mask. In the distance, large sandstone blocks moved as if on their own. Evaline imagined that large numbers of men were required to move just one of the stones, but from her vantage, they weren't even visible.

"We need to find a place to hide," Alexis said loudly.

His words caught the attention of the other Ma'Alkin's. Hapu and Abukhar watched Alexis intently. Hapu clasped his hands together, rocking in silent prayer once more.

"Let's go," Zahir agreed. "I'll take her," he added, motioning to Evaline. "We need to find some way to disguise her further. Maybe some spices to rub onto her skin. She'll give us away the moment she speaks, but if we can at least travel through Kul-El unnoticed, it's a start. I have a safe house on the eastern side."

Alexis paused for a moment. Grabbing a length of cloth from the bags, he bound Evaline's wrists together before tying the other end to Zahir's mount. Evaline sputtered in confusion, panic welling in her breast.

"You'll need to play the part of a captured slave," Alexis explained, cinching the cloth tighter around her wrists until she winced. "You can't exactly walk in without and expect to not draw attention." To Zahir, he added, "I'll meet you there."

***

The streets wound through the capitol in a zig-zag motion, making it difficult to follow the turns as they made their way to the Eastern District. Evaline's stomach rumbled as she saw a man selling small chunks of meat on a stick, kebabs, she thought Zahir had called them. The kebabs smelled of cumin and saffron, spices she enjoyed maybe once in her life. A small groan escaped her lips as she remembered the special treat she'd had long ago.

Hapu and Abukhar turned to see what was happening. Noticing the stumbling Evaline, Abukhar said something to Zahir who just glowered at her before snapping back at him. A man at a nearby stall sauntered over to the men, talking calmly. This scared her more than the ones who grabbed at her. The way he casually spoke to the three, shooting her a few sidelong glances before beckoning them to follow, put her hackles up. This man was dangerous.

His dark hair was slicked back and hung freely around his shoulders. A gold earring hung from his left ear, but it was the two-inch scar on his left cheek that caught Evaline's attention. The man spoke to Zahir and the brothers, his face lit up in a good-natured smile. He must have told a joke because all, but Zahir laughed.

He patted his side, jostling the scimitar on his hip under his long tan-colored shirt. Next to the hilt, Evaline saw a bulging leather pouch that clinked as the coins inside moved. His fingers inched towards the pouch as he flashed a smile. Zahir shook his head. The man's previously charming smile now faltered as anger flashed in his eyes, but Zahir held his ground. Motioning to Evaline, Zahir told the man something, pointing back at her before pointing off ahead. He clapped the man on the shoulder, his voice more sympathetic. The man nodded and shook Zahir's hand, his other one covering the hilt of his curved sword.

Did he threaten us, or was I imagining it? Evaline squinted at the man as he returned to the stall and began browsing wares on the cream cloth covering the surface. The vendor and man began quietly conversing, the merchant following Evaline and her companions as they passed. A shudder went down her spine as she thought she saw the man slip the vendor a coin from his pouch.

***

The merchant's bazaars gradually vanished as Evaline found herself deeper into the inner city. The tall mudbrick buildings crammed almost on top of each other and providing a welcome respite from the sun. The streets narrowed from the main roads, and many disappeared into the shadows. There weren't many people wandering about, but those who did were furtive in their movements, preferring to stay hidden. Even the dogs seemed tentative as they slunk through the streets looking for scraps to eat. It was eerily quiet.

A young woman slipped out from one of the buildings and approached the group. Unlike her surroundings, she was clean, and her clothes were pristine. Her eyes were rimmed with dark kohl and a fragrant scent followed her as she moved. Without sparing a glance at Evaline, she walked up to Zahir and began speaking to him in a soft manner, rubbing his bicep as she maintained eye contact. Her lips turned up in a coy smile as she spoke.

To Evaline's surprise, Zahir returned the smile, his face softening as he placed his hand over hers. Hapu and Abukhar scoffed, trying to turn the young woman's attention to them. Evaline almost thought she saw Abukhar flexing subtly in the shadows. This drew a bell-like chuckle from the young woman. Her hand never left Zahir though. After many long minutes, Zahir gently removed her hand from his arm, slipping his own around her waist. She returned the gesture, and leaned into him, placing her free hand on his chest.

Evaline's mouth dropped as he gave a small tug on his horse's rope, continuing their trek towards his home. Abukhar grumbled as Hapu elbowed him in the side, but neither complained to Zahir. The five wended their way through an even tighter alley, the sides of the mudbrick homes crumbling from disrepair. Leading the group to an especially derelict building, Zahir instructed the others to take the horses to the nearest stable. With Evaline's bindings clenched tightly in his fist, Zahir, the young woman, and Evaline entered the dilapidated home.

***

Stale air greeted Evaline, the musty aroma reminding her of death once more. Dust layered almost every surface so thickly that it muffled their footsteps. Tying Evaline to one of the table legs, Zahir took off her boots to match his own bare feet before pushing her down to the ground. Evaline let out a gasp as he smirked at her. Next to him, the young woman cocked her head as though she were trying to solve a puzzle. The two spoke for a brief moment before Zahir led the woman through the darkened home and into a separate room.

Alone with her thoughts, Evaline waited for her eyes to adjust. Like Alexis' manor, the home was barren. They'd taken stairs so old that she was amazed when the wooden boards didn't break and send them plummeting to their doom. On the third floor, there were more stairs leading to higher levels.

Unlike the main streets of Kul-El, the Eastern District seemed empty apart from the few children and beggars she saw. In another part of the building, Evaline heard a baby crying. It struck her that she didn't see any women other than the one with Zahir. She hoped the baby had someone to comfort it. Soon, the cries subsided and were replaced with the breathy moans of the young woman in the other room. The loneliness she'd been feeling returned, pulling a tear from her eye as she curled as best she could into a ball on the floor.

I miss you, Amalie.

***

Evaline startled awake. The heavy thump of boots on the decrepit wooden stairs announced a new arrival. The noise got louder as the person approached. Evaline wondered if they would continue up the stairs or if it was Hapu and Abukhar. Or was it Alexis? It had been hours since she'd last seen him. Had he made it through the city safely? Evaline's concern over Alexis' well-being surprised her. She didn't think after all she'd discovered she would care for someone like him.

The door to the home opened and Abukhar and his brother wandered in. Before they could say anything, the men provided an update to Zahir as they dropped into the other chairs surrounding the table.

"It was damn hard to find a stable to take the horses," Abukhar said. Evaline felt a wave of relief that he spoke in his broken Aceatian. "Something's happened, and they don't trust outsiders."

The way Abukhar said "outsiders" and not foreigners really said a lot. Though they were from Tel Anon, they did not belong to Kul-El. They were not welcome anymore. Zahir leaned forward in his chair, his hands on his knees. Evaline struggled to a sitting position on the floor, noting that the young woman was beginning to look uncomfortable. Her arms crossed tight across her chest and her mouth sucked in to a thin line.

"It's because of the Sons of Anubis are turning our people to akh," Zahir replied. Tipping his head in the girl's direction, he explained, "They started patrolling the Eastern District not two months ago, and then people started being found dead in the streets. It seems that no one travels alone very much anymore.

"Akh?" Hapu asked. "Ghosts?"

The young woman, Safira, nodded. Looking from the brothers to Evaline. As she landed on Evaline, her eyes narrowed, and she bit her lip. She glanced at Zahir, her eyes widening as if asking a question. He nodded, taking hold of her hand like Alexis took Evaline's.

"They cannot die," she said softly, her words stilted as her tongue tripped over the strange words.

XXIV

"CANNOT DIE?" Hapu asked, his eyes wide in disbelief. "Don't exaggerate."

"It's no lie," Safira spat. Her voice was earnest, almost as though she begged them to believe her. "I've seen it with my own eyes. In the beginning, we fought back. We killed one. I watched his blood soak the sand with my own eyes. He was strong, killing many. But once the sun left Dū-aat, he was back. Red eyes... like a monster."

Safira hung her head as a tear rolled down her cheek. Her hands clenched the fabric of her dress, balling it up in her pain.

"Where they're building the pyramid?" Zahir thought out loud. "How are they related?"

Evaline's mind began to wander as Hapu and Abukhar talked amongst themselves, speculating about where the Sons of Anubis could be. Zahir sat with his chin on his knuckles, trying to piece together some unknown puzzle, while Safira remained with her arms across her chest, chewing the inner corner of her mouth. Evaline thought she heard a soft thump but chalked it up to one of the brothers scooting their chairs. Zahir, however, shot up, his body tense.

"Quiet!" Zahir hissed.

Abukhar and Hapu fell silent, their ears straining to hear whatever noise caught his attention. Evaline thought she saw something slither into the room, but as it was becoming dark out, it was harder to see since they hadn't lit any candles yet. In the wan light, Evaline caught a glint of redfrom where Zahir was seating. She hoped Safira didn't notice.

"Next time announce yourself, you shit," Zahir swore, his body relaxing as he leaned back in his chair. "Damn Aceatian bastard."

The change in the room's atmosphere was palpable. It went from heavy and frightened to almost sighing in relief. Hapu and his brother returned to lounging in their chairs as Alexis brought out some candles. One by one, their flames popped into life, filling the darkened room with their warm glow. There was no hearth, Evaline noted, a little disappointed that the Ma'Alkinian chill would seep into her bones once more.

Alexis held his hand up once the last candle had been lit. "My apologies, my friend," he said. "I didn't want to draw attention to myself. I might have been followed, so I needed to double back a few times. I think I managed to give him the slip though."

"I get the feeling many in Kul-El are now involved," Zahir replied. "We also ran into someone."

When he did, the tension in the room shifted once more. Safira and the others watched the three warily as they spoke, Safira's gaze always returning to Evaline.

"The man following me had hair about as long as yours and a scar on his left cheek," Alexis said.

"The man from the bazaar!" Evaline exclaimed.

All eyes went to Evaline as she sat on the floor still bound with her cloth bindings. She felt her face flush at the sudden attention and dropped her head. She didn't know why, she remembered the man well. His expression was one of superiority, and anger at being turned down by Zahir. He was a hunter, no doubt.

"You met him?" Alexis asked. Rubbing his chin, Alexis hummed in concentration. "This is not good. We've already been noticed by one of their men. Did you speak?"

"Yes," Zahir said. "He wanted to buy the girl." He nodded to Evaline, who balked at being referred to as "the girl." "I said she wasn't for sale, that she was my trophy from my journeys at sea. They confirmed my story," he said, jutting his chin towards Hapu and Abukhar. "He didn't take it too well. I wouldn't doubt he's already told someone about us."

"Damn," Alexis muttered. "And you had to bring her here?" He motioned to Safira who, to her credit, held his gaze. "Couldn't you wait until later to bring a working girl to our safe house?"

"And be killed in her den by some corrupt soldier or den boss? If we need to, she's gone."

So, they can die, Evaline noted. *But how?*

Alexis and Zahir continued to talk, their words sounding muffled in the background as her mind worked to solve the puzzle.

The answer hit her like a wave slamming into the side of the *Faded Dawn.*

"The Sons of Anubis..." Evaline breathed. "They're vampyres."

"And they're turning people into some of their own," Zahir added.

Hapu and Abukhar exchanged a glance. Evaline noted that they didn't seem to fully understand what was being said. She hoped, for their sake, that they didn't figure it out until after they'd left Kul-El.

"How? I thought only a sourdre du sang could create new vampyres?" Alexis wondered aloud.

"What if Absalom has awakened?" Zahir asked. The slight quiver to his voice alarmed Evaline. "He has the power. He may know how to share it."

The question sent Evaline's head wheeling. There were so many questions that even those two didn't understand. How would she figure anything out? Once more, her mind went back to the maps that she studied, trying to remember as much as she could. The name seemed familiar, and sourdre du sang had definitely been on there, whatever that meant. At this point, it was a question for another occasion. But Absalom, that sounded more pressing.

I think I saw his name on the map by Estrie, she thought. *Maybe he's like Estrie. Maybe he's someone who can create new vampyres. Oh God, how many of these monsters are there?*

Alexis, finally noticing Evaline was still bound, made his way over and untied her wrists.

Hoping Zahir wouldn't notice, Evaline leaned forward, as though she needed to relieve the pressure on her wrists. Once her body was as close to Alexis as she could get, she whispered into his ear, her lips brushing against his flesh:

"Who is Absalom?"

Alexis didn't answer. He continued to untie her wrists. Once free, Evaline rotated her wrists. Disappointment settled into her stomach, a heavy stone against the swirling waves of emotion. Her eyes tracked Alexis, trying to discern whatever she could from the mask that now covered his face. Darkness fell on Kul-El and the pale light of the full moon poured into the small window along the wall. Evaline sat in silence, pondering the information, wishing the pair had included her in more of their conversations.

The stones in her jewelry rested lightly against her skin. They felt warm. Touching the pendant lightly with the tips of her fingers, she confirmed that they indeed felt warm. Not just from the contact with her flesh, but like it radiated its own heat.

There were too many unanswered questions, and Evaline couldn't spend time worrying on something like why the stones were warm when she had more pressing matters to deal with, like a who army of undead monsters that sucked the very life out of people.

"Perhaps they've found a way," Alexis admitted. "Damn! If Absalom is awake, we're in deep shit."

Zahir got out of his chair and began pacing. A steady stream of curse both in Ma'Alkinian and Aceatian flowed for several long minutes. Safira and the brothers shot the three uneasy glances. After a few moments, Safira made to leave. Quicker than the beat of her heart, Evaline watched as Alexis moved to block the young woman. The two shared a hurried conversation, the name "Lateef" coming up several times. When Alexis made no effort to move, and Zahir didn't come to her aid, Safira sat down once more. She made one more remark, motioning to Evaline casually.

This caught both Alexis and Zahir's attention. The brothers, sensing something was up straightened in their seats as well. Hapu said something to his brother under his breath, but Evaline was sure the Alexis and Zahir caught it. Their hearing seemed to be better than most.

"What did she say?" Evaline asked when no one said anything further.

"Her boss, Lateef, isn't happy," Alexis explained. "He wanted to buy you as an offering to the high priestess to continue his operations. Apparently, he is familiar with the Menes."

XXV

IT FELT LIKE A SET UP to Evaline. How could this woman find them and know that she would be able to seduce Zahir so easily? Did that mean that Lateef had spies watching them as they made their way to the Eastern District? Did they know where they were now? Evaline couldn't fathom how deep everything went. In the distance, a baby began to cry. Zahir led Safira back to his room. Abukhar and Hapu followed, taking the empty room next to Zahir's.

At last, Evaline allowed herself to release the tension in her body. She slumped into a nearby chair with a sigh, closing her eyes as she let her body to melt into the aged wood. The loneliness and uncertainty she'd felt all afternoon from the moment Alexis left her weighed on her like one of her father's steel anvils. Exhaustion consumed her, but she couldn't allow herself to rest.

Beside her, Alexis leaned against the wall. In the pale moonlight, his features appeared gaunt. Exhaustion must be gripping him as well. She wondered what exactly he needed to do to ensure his safety in Kul-El.

They remained where they were for a long time. At one point in the night, they heard the breathy moans of Safira once more and Evaline felt a twinge of jealousy that she quickly shoved away. Though they were wed, she knew they would never be one and had to force herself to accept that fact. The flames burned low in the candles, melting the fat and eating the wicks. Evaline's eyes felt heavy, and her head began to droop onto the table. The light from the moon completely filled the room, better than the sun had. Evaline found herself thinking of her sister, and her family. Amalie would have had her baby by now.

I have to make it back to meet her baby, Evaline told herself.

"You know," Alexis' voice broke the silence. He spoke in a low tone so as not to wake the others. "I knew this would be a difficult heist to pull."

His body slid down the wall until he was curled up on the floor. As the moon shone on his face, his red eyes sparkled like the stones in her necklace. The weight of the world sat on his shoulders, and it was etched in his visage. Alexis heaved a sigh, pulling his knees to his chest.

"I didn't realize it would go sideways so quickly. I fear I've brought you all into something that you can't escape from. If the Great Father Absalom has awakened, my search for Neith is pointless."

Anguish dripped from his words as he closed his eyes in defeat. Evaline could not bear to see him so dejected and scooted closer to him. Taking his hands, she gazed into his face. When he did not open his eyes, Evaline gently grabbed his chin and turned Alexis to face her. This caught his attention and he opened his eyes once more.

"We all went into this knowing there would be risks," she soothed. Somehow, the lie flowed easily from her lips.

With a sigh, Alexis shook his head. "No. You had no choice. Death here, death back in Aceatius, your fate was sealed once you agreed to marry me that rainy night back in Bord du Pétale. The others, they're here because things have now been placed into motion. They've fallen into a river and can't grasp the branch to help pull them out. I would do it again, if it meant there is a chance at killing Estrie."

The two sat in silence for a bit.

"You asked who Absalom is," he said finally, breaking the quiet. "He is the Great Father, the first of our kind. The stories say that once there was a child born from the flesh of a mortal woman. When the women who helped deliver the baby prepared the child for his mother, they noticed that he had not cried since leaving the womb. They listened, and noted there was no heartbeat. And yet, he stared at them with eyes ringed red.

"Believing the baby to be cursed, the child and his mother were exiled from their town and sent to live in the wild. It is said that the mother was killed by a lion, leaving the babe alone in a patch of tall grass before he was found by an old man hunting. The man took him into his home with his wife, children, and grandchildren, and when the baby was old enough, he consumed the entire household."

Disgust filled Evaline. Her body recoiled at the news, but Alexis didn't notice. His eyes remained downcast as he spoke.

"I told you, we fight demons and the damned. I have done you a disservice involving you in all of this. I only thought of myself, the hunger I faced at the time, and not you. You are stronger than I believed. I owe you an apology." Lifting his head until his gaze met hers, Alexis stared deep into her eyes, touching her soul.

"I'm sorry."

His words brought tears to her eyes. His sincerity nearly broke her heart. Evaline could feel that a part of Alexis broke at that moment, a part that she found herself suddenly wanting desperately to fix.

Scooting around until she was facing Alexis, Evaline grabbed his hands in both of hers. Something inside him must have broken. His face softened and his eyes looked truly human even though they were still red. He reminded Evaline of the charming young man with a boyish grin that she saw last Venari. She wondered if this was the first time he'd allowed himself to feel vulnerable since he was cursed to living an eternity in solitude.

Following her instinct, Evaline leaned forward and kissed him on the lips. It was tender, not the fevered ones she'd shared with him back at his estate. Her hand rested gently on his cheek as she inched closer. To her surprise, Alexis did not pull away. Evaline felt his hands slip around her waist and bring her towards him. When she opened her eyes, she saw his twinkling back at her.

Even though she now knew what he was, he still mes-merized her. Her heart skipped a beat, thumping rapidly in her chest as she allowed for him to direct her. After all these years, he knew what he was doing. Alexis guided Evaline onto his lap, her legs straddling him as they continued to kiss. His hands traveled up her body, one hand placed on her chest and the other lightly gripping the back of her head, his fingers becoming entwined in her hair. A heat welled up in Evaline and she struggled to not push him too far. In some far corner in the back of her mind, she wondered if this was an animal instinct triggered by being around some-one like him – a vampyre. As a compromise to herself, she pushed her body against his, her hips rubbing against his groin in the process. She heard his breath catch in his throat, his hand leaving the back of her head and moving to her back to press her closer.

The desire she'd tried to hold back welled up within her. She wanted more but was afraid to push. Her heart hammered as his tongue found hers. The two shared a passionate kiss, still tender, but building. Evaline wanted to melt into him and have their bodies become one as Alexis ran his thumb gently over her nipple on top of her dress. The touch sent an unexpected thrill through her. A soft, nervous giggle escaped her, and she rested her forehead against his, teasing him as she ran her hands over his chest in a slow, deliberate motion.

Keeping her pressed to him, Evaline felt his other hand leave her breast and slip up the bottom of her dress. She felt his fingers search underneath the folds of the fabric, finding her and eliciting a gasp as he began rubbing her tender spot. Their lips pulled apart, and she met his gaze once more. The boyish smile returned. He focused his attentions on her, enjoying the slight shiver he got from her after a few minutes of teasing. A moan escaped her lips, and it was as if that was his cue. Evaline felt his finger enter her completely.

It was a strange feeling, but it felt good at the same time. Her body twitched as he continued to pleasure her, taking his time and sharing a deep kiss with her. As he ramped up the intensity, Evaline felt her body tingle in ecstasy and longing. Another moan slipped through her lips, and she pressed herself closer to him. His hands left her and un-buckled his belt. Everything was preternaturally clear as he slid his pants down to his ankles with her still on his lap.

The sudden sensation of him entering her sent a wave of panic through Evaline. Things moved quickly between them now that she had given in to lust. Her body attempted to clench, but it felt different now that he was inside her, but in a good way. They fit together perfectly like a key in a lock.

He was patient, his hands gently guiding her up and down in the beginning as they finally solidified their mar-riage. With each movement, Evaline felt more comfortable with him within her. Their passions rose, the tingling re-turning once more as the head of his manhood hit the right spot. Her body began to heave, and she gasped in pleasure. Alexis nipped her neck just under the jaw, his hands pulling her closer to him and following her rhythm. Sweat beaded on their bodies and their breaths came in unison. With a groan, Evaline felt him stiffen as his seed filled her. When they finally broke apart, Evaline knew things would never be the same again.

***

Weak sunlight streamed in through the small window in the gloomy mudbrick building. The candles burnt out long ago, the stubs of the wicks hidden by the now hardened fat from the butt of the candles. Evaline lay curled on the ground wrapped in Alexis' arms. The night proved too short, and the two fell asleep in the early hours of dawn. The room heated up quickly as the sun inched towards its mid-day position. As the light hit her eyes, Evaline stirred.

"Wake up," Zahir said, nudging Evaline with his boot.

A groan escaped her lips as she rubbed the sleep from her eyes. Zahir and the rest of the household were in the small room they'd stayed in the other day. The brothers sat in their chairs, unabashed grins plastered on their faces as they leered at Evaline and her hitched up dress. Blood rushed to her face as she hastily smoothed down the fabric and thanking her luck that nothing was exposed.

"Up!" Zahir repeated, this time with more urgency. Without waiting for a response, he grabbed Evaline's arm and yanked her to her feet, eliciting a yelp of pain. "Let's go," he said as he slipped his arm around Alexis' waist and lifted him up. "The heat's gotten to you."

Rubbing her arm, Evaline noticed that Alexis looked particularly pale in the light, his arms and bare chest turning a bright pink before her eyes. Leading his friend to the back room, Zahir quietly scolded the sandy-haired man for something Evaline didn't catch.

"Oh God," Evaline muttered. "What happened?"

Safira said something Evaline did not understand, but judging from the smirk on her face, it wasn't pleasant. Hapu and Abukhar snickered as they got up and found their boots, lacing them up after plopping back into their chairs. Abukhar said something to the group and the others replied in what appeared to be the affirmative. Zahir exited the darkened room, Alexis following albeit unsteady.

"You," he said to Evaline. "Come."

Unsure of what she did, Evaline followed him, noting how he gently directed Alexis back into the room. Once her eyes adjusted, Evaline saw their bags sitting in a corner, their contents splayed on a table. A bottle of the oil the two shared sat on the corner.

"Did the sun burn him?" she asked.

"This is your fault," Zahir hissed as Alexis slumped onto the thin mattress on the floor. "If you hadn't kept him in the sun, he wouldn't be this weak. Today was to be crucial for gathering information. By the gods, girl!"

"Zahir, calm down," Alexis begged. "It's my fault. I should have made sure I wouldn't be exposed like that without my protective oil. She didn't know."

"Know what?" Evaline asked.

"Still! If you were to get in trouble it would be impossible to get out unscathed." Zahir paced around the room as he spoke.

"If Absalom is involved, it will be almost impossible to avoid injury."

"Lateef is one of them," Zahir blurted out, sinking onto the bed next to his friend.

Evaline felt her chest tighten as the silence was instantaneous. A palpable tension filled the room as the weight of the words hit them. Lateef wasn't just trying to curry favor from the High Priestess Nefret, he *was* one of them. A Son of Anubis.

"Are you sure?" Alexis asked softly, rubbing his temples.

"Safira told me last night. She's afraid to go back to him, but even more terrified of not returning. Alexis, we're completely fucked if we don't go about this the right way. Nefret has silver, she will torture us for fortnights before she kills us. Until we give her everything we know. We can't get captured or it's all over."

"What is Safira to you?" Alexis asked slowly.

"I don't know," he replied. "She reminds me of my wife. It's as though Khepri was reincarnated and found me once more."

"Then we have much to do. Send Abukhar out to gather information on Lateef. If you can get Safira to stay by him in the shadows, we can make sure people don't follow them back. Can she do that?"

"People in the Eastern District are good at staying hidden," Zahir said. "She's seen much. I think she should be able to avoid detection."

"Good." Turning to Evaline, Alexis dropped his gaze, unable to meet hers. "I have a favor to ask you."

Evaline nodded, wondering what he could need from her. Zahir packed one of the oil bottles in his pouch and prepared the other one for Alexis. Alexis waited until he was finished and left the room before turning to Evaline.

"My kind are hurt by the sun. There are not many ways to hurt or kill the undead but exposing us to the sun or using silver blades are two ways. That is why we use the oil; it lets us go out into the sun without being injured. But it wears off. This morning, I was careless and did not protect myself. I need, I mean, would you help me recover?"

Evaline hesitated. What could she offer an undead being to help him heal?

"What can I do?" she asked, her eyes narrowing. Evaline hated how distrusting her voice sounded after the night they had together, yet she couldn't shake the feeling that she was in danger.

"When I found you, I was weak and needed to renew my strength by feeding. I haven't fed on you since shortly after Zahir arrived in Aceatius. Would you let me have some of you now?"

Her breath caught in her throat. Alexis did not look at her as she made her decision, but Evaline thought she could see the pain in his eyes. He'd given up so much, given so much to her, that if felt wrong to deny him. Could she live with herself if he was captured and tortured because she wouldn't help him? And again, there was last night. She felt so close to him then.

"Yes." Her reply came out as a small, quivering squeak.

"Thank you." The gratitude was clear in his voice.

"Will it hurt?" she asked.

"I will be gentle," he assured her.

Scooting closer, Evaline felt her body tense as she waited for him to bite into her. Instead of feeling his fangs tear into her flesh, she felt his fingers trail along her face. His touch was gentle, caring. His fingers continued down her face, tracing her jawline until he reached the hollow of her neck. Evaline gulped as his fingers rested on a spot underneath her jaw. Last night, he'd covered that spot with soft kisses, but now...

Evaline felt her body tensing. As his lips made contact, she felt a small pinch. She waited for the pain but was surprised when she felt none. His fingers linked between her own as he sat next to her on the bed sipping on her blood.

This feels weird, she thought. *Maybe it's not so bad.*

A moment later, a wave of dizziness washed over her and she almost swooned. Her vision swam and her body went limp, but he was ready to catch her. A second later, she blacked out. When she woke up, she saw his hazel eyes watching her with concern. His fingers ran through her hair, wiping off the cold sweat that dotted her brow.

"Are you all right?" he asked.

Sitting up, Evaline almost blacked out once more, but she managed to grumble out an answer while he held her. A cup of cool water pressed against her lips and Evaline sipped. The refreshing liquid helped clear some of the haze, but her body still felt weak. She thought she heard him mumble a "thank you" before placing her on top of the mattress. A few seconds later, the door shut, leaving her in total darkness.

A cold chill washed over Evaline, and she felt her stomach clench angrily. Barely aware of her surroundings, Evaline shot up and staggered over to the window as fast as she could. A thick cloth blocked the window, but she shoved it out of the way and stuck her head out of the window seconds before emptying the meager contents of her stomach. It twisted and tightened as she struggled to cough up bile.

Alexis returned a few seconds later and guided her back to the mattress. His hands felt cold even in her clammy ones. A groan escaped her lips as she toppled onto the mattress only to be caught and slowly lowered onto it by Alexis. He offered her the cup once more, insisting that she drink.

"We need to get you something to eat," he explained. "Abukhar and Hapu have gone into the bazaar to find you something. Rest until they return."

"What about Zahir?" she mumbled, her words slurring together as though she'd had too much to drink. "And Safira? She doesn't trust me."

"Safira is making sure that she's seen, but Zahir is watching her closely. We can't have her going back to Lateef."

Evaline babbled incoherently, her mind still reeling as she struggled to sit upright. Alexis smoothed out the hair on her sweaty brow, tucking a loose strand behind her ear. The world spun and darkness engulfed her. In the distance, Alexis could be heard calling her name.

XXVI

F RESH MEAT SEASONED TO ABSOLUTE PERFECTION waited
for Evaline when she woke up. A plate with three kebabs, their juices dripping onto it, sat on the small table. Pieces of onion were interspersed between the meat,
adding to the aroma. Tentatively, Evaline sat up. Her head
no longer spun, but her body felt a little shaky. Giving herself a moment, she took a deep breath and made her way to
the table. Her stomach clenched and rumbled in hunger, and
Evaline gave a small word of thanks that the smell didn't up-
set her further.

Back on the mattress with her food, Evaline dug in. The
riot of flavors that exploded in her mouth made Evaline's
mouth water. An array of exotic spices gave the kebabs and
onions an extra layer of savoriness. The food was gone in

minutes, leaving Evaline dejected and wishing she had more. A clay cup sat on the table as well. The cool water she'd had before she'd blacked out waited for her to wash down her meal.

A soft conversation could be heard outside the room. Evaline thought she heard both male and female. Zahir and Safira must be back. Making her way out of the room on uncertain legs, Evaline slipped into the closest chair and closed her eyes to stop the room from spinning.

"I'm surprised that worked," Zahir's voice sounded unnaturally loud to Evaline. A dull thud grew behind her temples. "I've never had to do it before."

"Me neither," Alexis' voice replied.

Cracking open her eye, Evaline saw that all but the brothers were back. Worry stirred in her breast. Were they all right? The thought slipped away as quickly as it came. Her heavy lids fell shut again. Every muscle felt drained, and her head pounded so loud she could hear the blood in her ears.

"At least we know it's an option now," Alexis added. "Although, a final resort."

"Just say she's off limits," Zahir said. "I don't want to have to think about how much I'm consuming if I'm inches from death."

Their words sounded far away, muffled as though her head was in a bubble. It reminded her of when she had too much after Venari. Her body ached, her vision swam, and her head hurt. A small groan escaped her.

"I feel horrible." Even Evaline's own voice hurt.

Safira cut in, her hurried question creating a palpable tension in the room. Her and Zahir shared a rapid exchange, the young woman's body clearly showing her agitation with her stiff, sharp movements. Alexis watched closely, still recovering from the effects of the sun.

"So, Lateef has begun searching," Alexis said so Evaline could understand. "If she goes back, he'll probably kill her." Glancing at Safira, Alexis tilted his head as if calculating something.

"Send her back to the streets," Evaline said, surprising everyone as their heads snapped her direction.

"Why?" Zahir asked, his brow arching.

At the same time that Zahir spoke, Alexis interjected with an emphatic, "No!"

Safira watched their exchange with curiosity, the strain in her body not releasing. She asked Zahir something to which he brusquely replied. Evaline noted how Safira's hand reached out and gently touched his forearm, her big doe eyes widening like a child's. A strong sense of motherhood rushed through Evaline. She couldn't protect Amalie from being taken too soon, but she could at least try to keep this poor girl alive.

Ignoring Alexis' outburst, Evaline took Safira's hand in hers and inhaled deeply. She'd made her decision. Though her time with Alexis had been nice last night, it was time for her to leave Kul-El and go home. If she could convince them to let her go out on her own, Evaline could slip away and find a way out of the city and back to her family.

"You need a distraction," she said slowly. "I can't speak Ma'Alkinian, but I can at least try and help her. Death awaits her, and I can't sit idly by."

"So you'll give your life for nothing?" Zahir asked as Alexis fought to cover a gasp.

"No, for my sister. She would want me to help any way I can." With a deep breath, Evaline added, "If I can help her see that she isn't a slave, maybe she can help the other girls find safety. I don't know, it doesn't make sense, but my sister was basically taken against her will." Her voice quivered as her resolve threatened to break. "I see a lot of her in Safira. I have to try."

Silence filled the room following her statement. Alexis pinched the bridge of his nose and Zahir turned away, while Safira crossed her arms uncomfortably across her chest.

"It's a dangerous gamble, one I don't think will pay off," he said, looking pointedly at her. His eyes searched hers. Evaline imagined he was trying to find a reason for her to go. After a pause, he added, "But if that's what you want, I won't stop you," Alexis finally said. "Your odds of survival aren't much better if you stick with us. You might as well do something you think will help."

Evaline turned to the young woman. Fear rose in her chest, and she tried to smother it lest it envelop her in a blind panic. If her emotions kept her from remaining level-headed, she would be doomed.

I have to trust her, Evaline told herself forcefully. Hearing the thought echo in her mind helped Evaline push down the fear. It didn't disappear, but she managed to beat it back a bit.

Evaline folded her arms across her chest, mimicking Safira's body language. The reality of what she was about to do truly sank in, and she didn't want to break. Could she handle another man roughly taking her? Could she handle the abuse? She'd seen it happen before when her family took the rare trip out of town, and they ran across a battered young mother. At the time, Evaline thought the woman had been weak. Maybe she was wrong. Women like Safira were probably stronger than she could ever be.

Abukhar and Hapu still hadn't returned by the time Evaline and Safira were ready to leave. As Zahir spent a private moment with Safira once more, Evaline sat at the table trying to keep her breathing steady. Her breaths wanted to come out in short gasps, but Evaline forced herself to be deliberate and make them slow and deep. A cold sweat left her hands feeling clammy and she wiped her palms on her dress multiple times.

"They will probably hit you," Alexis warned. "But if you try and follow their directions as best you can, perhaps it won't be too bad. People like Lateef thrive on fear and control."

"What do I do if he is like you?"

"Give him no reason to notice you. Stay to the shadows with your head down. Don't act out of place, don't anger those who have been there longer. The girls who have been around will expect you to fall into place. Don't be shocked if they slap you or pull your hair. Even if it's Safira. No matter what happens, be meek and subservient."

Blowing out a deep breath, Evaline nodded. Safira's moans provided her with a welcome break from her uncertain thoughts. She wondered if this offered the young woman a respite from her fears as well. Perhaps falling back on something familiar helped her cope. Evaline couldn't help but remember the terror in her eyes whenever Safira thought about Lateef.

If she can be brave, so can I, Evaline told herself.

***

Zahir laid on the mattress as Safira got dressed once more. His undead heart didn't flutter, his breathing didn't get heavy during the feverish moment of passion. Instead, he leaned back and felt a pang of anguish as he stared at her backside. Safira reminded him so much of his wife that it hurt. Closing his eyes, Zahir brought forward memories he buried under lifetimes of pain.

A darkened room, hundreds of candles burning, the scent of incense hanging heavily in the air – multiple voices chanting in unison, the deep timbre echoing off the walls. His wrists and ankles were tied to a thick slab of stone, preventing him from moving. Zahir pulled against the bonds but gave up soon after. His eyes struggled to adjust, but whether it was the incense or the many flickering flames, he found he could not see much. Hovering over him, Nefret stood wearing a crimson dress, her breasts spilling out from the deep slit that went down to her navel. A gold chain encircled her waist, a delicate contrast to the thick bangles that wrapped around her arms and wrists. The outfit stood out to Zahir as he'd never seen the high priestess dressed so immodestly before.

Her lips were stained a deep red, the color also tinging the tips of her teeth. An unfamiliar look flashed through her eyes, one Zahir now knew to be hunger and anticipation. Behind her, a young man began singing a song Zahir could not understand, his high voice giving away his loss of his manhood. As the man continued to sing, the words taking on a fevered pitch, Nefret pulled out a dagger of pure silver. A bead of sweat ran down Zahir's back as she started chanting.

Again, the words were unfamiliar to Zahir, but the tone and intensity of the speech sent a shiver down his spine. Deep in his soul, he knew that whatever she was saying was not of Ra. Black tendrils clouded his periphery as the two voices intertwined. The flames of the candles flickered and he thought he heard a thump, as if something heavy hit the ground. Nefret gave a passionate cry, her eyes closing as she clutched the dagger to her chest.

Silence.

It was deafening.

Zahir's heart raced, its frantic pounding echoing in the very room where he lay tied to the stone. A collective tension built in the room, as if they too could hear his heart beat. A smile filled Nefret's face, her teeth standing out in the darkness, accentuating her elongated canines, the tips still stained red. Were they always that pronounced?

Leaning over Zahir until her breasts gently brushed against his bare chest, Nefret whispered in his ear: "It'll all be over soon, my pet." Her lips tickled his ear. Tracing a line down his chest, Nefret climbed atop him, straddling him. Goose flesh prickled his skin as her touch electrified him in a way he did not want. Still pressed against him, the fabric of her dress no longer able to contain her, Nefret's hips began to move up and down, arousing him against his wishes. A pair of hands slipped his linen wrap from his waist, and to his dismay, he felt Nefret position herself atop him.

Her movements became stronger as she rode him. Her breathing quickened, soft moans escaping her as she closed her eyes, savoring the pleasure of both Zahir and his discomfort. Despite himself, Zahir found himself moaning as she continued. Soft chanting could be heard in the background along with the still echoing beat of his heart. As the beating grew louder, Nefret's motions became rougher. He could feel her body clench around him, and his own responding. Before he could release the tension, he felt a sharp pain blossom in his chest. Moments later, something pierced his neck.

A groan escaped his lips once more. Nefret was latched onto his neck, her tongue licking the side as she continued to bite him. Lifting his head off the stone as much as he could while Nefret held him down, he spied a silver handle sticking out from his chest, the blade buried deep into his flesh. He felt a warm liquid run out of the corners of his mouth, the coppery tang of his blood filling it and nearly choking him. His vision blurred, yet the thumping of his heart resonated in the room. Through a hazy fog, Nefret sat up, a trail of red running down her chin and a satisfied smile on her face.

His heart's beats slowed, until it no longer echoed in the room. The chanting had ended. All that remained was the ghostly flickering of the candles and the heavy scent of incense before the darkness took him.

After waking up from Nefret's ceremony – it wasn't a ceremony he'd told himself countless times, it was murder – Zahir struggled to understand what happened to him. The way adrenaline coursed through his body, and at the same time his heart did not race, terrified him. His chest moved as though he drew breath, but his lungs never inflated. He didn't even feel lightheaded after holding his breath for long periods of time. A dull ache ran through his entire body, masked by the adrenaline. He also felt strength and energy fill him. Something had happened during the ceremony, but it changed him beyond his mortal wrappings.

Safira's mutterings brought Zahir's thoughts back to the present. Now fully dressed, she stared at him in earnest having had asked a question he hadn't heard.

"You'll keep me safe from him?" she asked again, her voice barely more than a whisper.

She was a child, nothing more. Zahir could only imagine what his wife went through after learning of his demise. He couldn't save her. How could he save Safira?

"Yes," he heard himself say.

Liar.

XXVII

PULLING HER COWL OVER her hair, Evaline followed Safira through the narrow alleys of the Eastern District. They snaked through the streets, barely a soul to be found in the impoverished area, without saying a word to each other. Even the strays clung to the shadows, their eyes flashing momentarily as the two women passed. The sheer emptiness of her surroundings left Evaline feeling on edge. Her skin prickled with each step, the silence creeping into her every pore and squeezing her soul, causing her stomach to clench.

Evaline kept her eyes peeled, looking for a chance to slip away unnoticed. She could no longer stay with Alexis and the others. She had to go home, and this was her only chance to escape without putting him in danger.

Safira whispered something Evaline couldn't understand, but Evaline didn't know if that was an attempt at communication. The young woman never seemed too keen on her, but Evaline wondered if it was just because they couldn't understand each other. Then again, Safira did not seem to trust many.

"You know," Evaline said softly, trying to comfort the young woman. "We could find a place for you to hide. A way to escape."

Safira did not respond. Evaline wasn't sure if it was because the young woman didn't understand her, or she didn't believe her. Evaline wondered if she would believe herself if she were in Safira's place. The two continued on. Evaline's gaze darted all over, trying to see where Safira led her.

Stay unnoticed, she told herself. It had been her mantra since she left the safe house. *That's how we survive.*

A light squeeze on her wrist nearly caused her to yelp. In front of her, Safira froze, her eyes darting around as she appeared to be straining to hear something. She whispered something once more, finally meeting Evaline's gaze. Tears rimmed her deep brown eyes, and she trembled slightly. She gave Evaline's hand a squeeze before saying something softly.

Evaline nodded, attempting to swallow her fear. It was time.

"Take care," Evaline whispered returning the young woman's gesture. She hoped Safira could at least understand her tone.

A shadow moved ahead of them, catching Evaline's attention. Her body tensed and her heart began to race. She'd hoped that they wouldn't run into someone so quickly – that she'd find the right moment to slip away. Instead, a woman with a tan silk cloth covering her head approached the pair. Evaline squinted at the stranger as she moved from the darkness. She'd expected a man, specifically, the one she'd seen when she first arrived in Kul-El – Lateef.

What's going on?

Evaline could now see that the woman was around her mother's age judging by the small wrinkles around the corners of her eyes and the hard lines by her mouth, spoke quickly to Safira, glancing over at Evaline several times with a furrowed brow. Her voice snapped harshly at the younger woman, who replied demurely with eyes cast down. Evaline struggled to follow the conversation, hoping she could maybe guess its direction by the tone. Her efforts were stopped when the older woman slapped Safira across the face. The smack echoed in the empty streets.

Risking a look at Safira, Evaline noted how her hand covered her cheek as she stared at the ground. A fire in the young woman's eyes blazed. This relationship wasn't as hierarchical as Safira played on. The older woman snapped at Safira some more, gesturing towards Evaline this time.

Safira mumbled something back, composing herself before lifting her head to address the woman. The two shared an uneven exchange, the older woman dominating the conversation, before Evaline's head covering was ripped off.

"Asenath!" Safira exclaimed as Evaline's hands flew to her head, grasping at the cloth that was no longer there.

Asenath gawked at Evaline, taking her in with a slow, trailing gaze. A wide smile crept onto her face as she let out a soft exclamation, her eyes sparkling. Evaline felt her body tense at the expression. It reminded her of the pirates who took her to Ma'Alkin and the greedy way they observed her before they disembarked.

Barking a command at Safira, Asenath grabbed Evaline's arm and yanked her forward. Evaline almost stumbled, but the woman's firm grip and momentum somehow kept her on her feet. Safira followed behind the two as they weaved through the streets and out of the shadows.

Slowly, the busy streets of Kul-El appeared, leaving the dreary Eastern District, and Evaline's only sense of safety, behind. Chickens pecked at tiny stones and bread crumbs as they meandered through stalls where vendors sold their produce and fresh meat. Children's laughter could be heard once more, the sound almost deafening after the stifling silence from before. More than one head turned as Asenath led the two women to wherever she was taking them. A few of the women gave slight nods of deference. Possibly colleagues of hers trying to earn a few coins in the early morning.

Abukhar's absence left Evaline feeling completely exposed. Those two had been her last form of defense. To prevent herself from drowning in her helplessness, Evaline tried to memorize as much of Kul-El as she could. With each step, she found herself looking for distinguishing characteristics to the whitened clay buildings, wooden vendor stalls, and even the people themselves.

She wondered several times if she should run, but Asenath would occasionally tug her forward as if to throw Evaline off-balance. Each time, Evaline would stumble, but correct herself. The last time this happened, Amalie's necklace slipped out from under her dress. The bright crimson stone caught the light of the sun momentarily before Evaline hastily shoved it back under her clothes.

She began trying to focus on the stone. With each step, it shifted against her flesh, the sun's warmth causing it to heat the little bit of skin it rested upon. Evaline could almost imagine that the stone thumped like the beating of a heart, and that it was her special connection to her sister giving her strength for what was about to come.

The jeers from men on the streets faded into the background as Evaline focused on her family. She pictured their smiles, the tight embrace of her mother, and the excitement they all shared every Venari and yuletide. Each image filled her with warmth, loosening the pit that had settled into her stomach. Alexis and her final moments with him ran through her mind unexpectedly. Before she could reminisce on their passionate experience, the maps from his estate flashed by one-by-one.

I'll sneak out later tonight, she told herself. *This was a bad idea. I'll just head back to Alexis' home and leave Kul-El in the morning.* A small twinge in her stomach gave her pause. Alexis' face flashed before her eyes. Images from last night, the way that his lips trembled against her flesh as she rode him, gave her pause. *Why do I feel guilty for leaving him?*

The pain of nails digging into her flesh followed by a sharp tug pulled Evaline from her thoughts. Asenath spat something out at Evaline, to which she could only shake her head with wide-eyed confusion. The woman gave an exasperated sigh and shoved Evaline forward. Sudden darkness engulfed her and the heavy scent of incense filled her nostrils. She hadn't even realized that they arrived at their destination.

Low lanterns with flickering lights lined the walls. Men sat on cushions along the wall smoking, while a few sat at the small, round tables and played cards. Women in form-fitting dresses moved about, offering drinks and tobacco to the men. Evaline didn't have much time to take everything in before she was ushered to a backroom that was even more dimly lit. Safira followed and broke away once the door behind them closed.

The building was bigger than Evaline imagined. Several doors lined the walls, leading to many rooms. She could hear moaning through the wooden walls. Evaline wondered just how big the place was. To her right, a group of women slipped into the room eyeing Evaline and her bright auburn hair as they passed. One said something to Asenath, to which she responded with a hungry grin, that greedy sparkle returning to her eye once more.

Asenath said something to Evaline. When Evaline didn't move, she rolled her eyes and began pulling at Evaline's clothes. Evaline let out a cry as she gripped the fabric close to her body, only to be slapped by Asenath and reprimanded harshly. After more struggling, the dress lay on the floor, Evaline's arms crossed over the simple shift she wore underneath. Her face flushed as she stood before the older woman.

"Mmm… very nice," a deep voice said from behind.

Evaline jumped, letting out a yelp as well, as she felt a man's hands trace the small of her back and move lower. Her head whipped to her left and her breath caught in her throat. Standing beside her was the scar-faced man from Kul-El. Lateef.

It took her a moment before she realized that he spoke the same language as she did. Evaline's heart began to race.

"How do you know my language?" she stammered.

The same greedy grin she'd seen from Asenath spread across his face. Around his eye, the scar crinkled, giving his face a more sinister expression. Cupping Evaline's chin, Lateef pulled her in close and yanking her head up at a painful angle. She could smell the strong odor of spirits on his breath.

"I can get by," he said with a stilted accent. Emphasis was placed on certain syllables, further accentuating his foreign tongue. "My girls can please all."

Lateef then snapped a command to the other women who lingered in the room. Evaline caught sight of Safira as she left once more. When the two were finally left alone, Lateef took a step back to better admire Evaline. In only her shift, Evaline wrapped her arms tighter around herself. The heat from the lamps and the stifling scent of the incense left her feeling sticky.

"What is going through your mind, Hedj?"

"Hedj?" Evaline asked.

"White," he explained. "It also means purity or simplicity. Although," he paused and closed the gap between the two. "Perhaps purity would not be the best soon."

Evaline took a step back, wanting to put distance between herself and Lateef as he continued to approach her. Wrapping his arm around her waist, he brought her in to him. A moment later, she felt his fingers enter her. Not wanting to give him any sense of power, she tried to keep her expression as passive as possible, but when he inserted another finger, Evaline let out a small grunt.

"Shame, not pure. I won't get nearly enough."

The way Lateef said the last line almost dropped her jaw.

"Are you going to sell me?" Evaline wished her voice didn't quiver as much as it did.

A bout of smothered laughter broke free from the man. "I wouldn't let go of you that easily, Hedj." The way his tone mocked her would've made her blood boil, but she couldn't summon the rage. "Men will pay a pretty price for you. I can probably trick them into thinking you're pure."

Pulling her close to him once more, Evaline tried to brace herself against his chest and push away. That only seemed to amuse the man more. His lips brushed her neck, sending a shiver of disgust through her. The heat of his breath on her flesh made her want to scrub herself – everything about this man made her skin crawl.

"I like to sample my wares," he whispered. "Can you please me?"

Evaline attempted to break free from his grasp, her palms straining to push through his arms that still held her pressed against him. Her heart pounded in her chest and her breath came out in strangled gasps. Lateef let out a soft chuckle, his eyes flashing red for the briefest of moments. In that instant, her heart froze.

He's like Alexis.

With every fiber of her being, Evaline forced herself to calm down. He probably was like an animal and could smell her panic. She couldn't let him know that he was in charge any more than he was. She would not let him break her. After a few tense seconds, Lateef released Evaline and stooped down, throwing her dress at her as he straightened up.

"Door on the right," he commanded. "You listen to Asenath."

XXVIII

EVALINE'S FIGURE DISAPPEARED into the glaring sunlight of Kul-El's streets. Alexis pressed deeper into the shadows. His legs trembled from the sun's power, but her blood lingered in him, giving him the strength to follow. He'd made sure to cover himself in his special oil before leaving, giving him that added layer of protection. Soon he would be back to full strength. He drew his cowl tight, scanning the bustle of the crowd for a ragged beggar or a fertility temple courtesan that could easily disappear without raising concern. He would be ready if any unlucky soul crossed his path. He needed to be at his best.

Zahir had left with Abukhar and his brother right after the girls, leaving Alexis to his own devices. His instinct was to follow Evaline and locate Lateef's lair, but he knew that would have to wait. They wouldn't kill Evaline, not before they could earn a few coins from her. He hoped she wouldn't do anything stupid, but he had to trust her. For now, Alexis had to focus. Neith called him.

The streets of Kul-El were bustling, as usual. Though he kept his head covered, he could feel the blistering sun beating down on him. The heat was unbearable. The rough shove of a body bumping into Alexis distracted him. A young boy muttered a hurried apology before running away. Alexis noted how a few other boys his age, all malnourished by the way their clothes hung to their skeletal frames, joined the first. He thought he saw the muted brown of a coin pouch. Reaching down to pat his hip, Alexis confirmed that the boy did steal his pouch. Pity it was only filled with a few stones.

They get younger and younger, he thought with a shake of his head. *It's a shame that Kul-El has become such a shit hole. She used to be so beautiful.*

A shout in the distance caught his attention. The kids must have found out they only got pebbles and not silver or gold. One yelped before they rounded the corner, trying to blend in with the rest of the crowd. The one who bumped into Alexis had a small trail of blood running down the corner of his mouth. Their boss wasn't too pleased by the looks of it. Alexis watched as they disappeared amongst the people of Kul-El, their dirty clothes providing the perfect camouflage against the browns of their surroundings.

The further he got from the Eastern District, the more pronounced the change in scenery became. Where the streets had been dusty and full of people struggling to survive, the main thoroughfare of Kul-El displayed a vibrant street life. A small group of men and women sat in a semicircle playing barrel drums while a few played the sistrum. A few of the musicians sang out to the gods, their voices rising and falling in a melodious harmony as they sang praises to the blessed beings.

Merchants beckoned him over, genuine smiles lighting up their faces as they realized he could understand them. Many times, he was told that it was rare that a stranger came by who would they could talk to. Alexis humored them, engaging in light conversation as he checked out their wares. The precious stones and metals were intricately crafted, creating beautiful necklaces, earrings, and other bits of jewelry. On several occasions, Alexis thought he saw the deep red of a dragon blood stone catch the light, however, he couldn't be sure. Each time he did notice it, he asked the merchant who would quickly offer an explanation.

One story in particular intrigued him. An older woman, her hair wispy and white and her skin wrinkled like an old piece of papyrus, spoke with him about a few loose stones she carried along with the jewelry expertly constructed by her skilled fingers. Her soft voice barely sounded over the din of the street vendors, causing Alexis to lean over to hear her. She spoke an older dialect, one that he thought possibly originated from north of the palace. With people not living past their fourth decade in Ma'Alkin, many not living to their fifth even in the capitol of Kul-El, Alexis did not rush his conversation with her.

"The stones," her faint voice continued, "are said to be from the gods. We have one whom my people revere along with the Great Creator. A mighty dragon who offers us her protection as we prepare for our journey to Dū-aat."

"Dear mother, I have heard tales of Mehen. Would you please share more with me?"

"No, no, sweet child," she replied with a small shake of her head. "These are not of Mehen. These are of Kebechet."

Alexis made an exaggerated gasp of surprise, trying to hide the twinkle in his eye at the news. He'd hoped he'd hear something from one of the locals, and his patience had been rewarded.

"A second dragon?" he said in awe.

"Yes. The daughter of Anubis and Anput. She cares and protects us as our bodies are prepared for our journey to Dū-aat. She keeps us refreshed, our discarded bodies kept pure before the priests embalm them. Are you familiar with our customs?"

Alexis nodded, the tip of his tongue darting out to lick his lips in anticipation.

"Then you know that we preserve the body so the soul, or akh, may reunite. I'm sorry, that's not right. The body is like a home for the akh, and as long as the body is safe, the soul can return home. If the body is destroyed, the soul cannot return and becomes lost.

"Kebechet and the Great Creator both watch over us once we die. They protect us as we begin our next journey. To protect us in life as well, the Mother Goddess decided that they should offer a gift of themselves, imbued with their holy essence. The Mother created a stone of lavender chalcedony to hold all her wisdom. Kebechet, in an act of pure love, offered us her blood. The blood hardened, and these very stones that my people use to adorn our bodies, were made. This is why we use only the finest stones and gold to make our jewelry."

The woman waved her hand over the fine jewelry as it glittered despite them standing in the shade.

"Where did you hear these stories?" Alexis asked.

"My grandmother used to tell them when I was a little girl."

"Does longevity run in your family?" Alexis asked. Gently stroking the back of her hand, he added, "Grace and beauty obviously do, but to gain such wisdom does not come to those who have not lived long enough to experience it."

Her eyes twinkled as they crinkled into a smile. "And one is not born with such a silver tongue. Tell me, my son, what is your story. You look much too young to be so knowledgeable. Something tells me there is more to you than these old eyes can see."

"You flatter me, dear mother," Alexis said, taking her hand in both of his. Letting the honey drip from his voice, he brushed his lips against the back of her hand before continuing. "Alas, I am but a humble merchant. Though my master sends me out into the world to collect rare treasures, my passion lies in the people. There is always a story to be told, if you can find the right person to tell it."

The woman's smile disappeared and the wrinkles in her brow deepened as she furrowed it. Alexis felt a knot form in his stomach as the woman scrutinized him.

"My apologies, if I offended you, dear mother," he said as she slowly pulled her hand from his. "I only hoped to learn the history of your people before it is lost. I have heard rumors that the old ways are disappearing, and from my previous travels, I grew to love Ma'Alkin as a second home. I would hate to see her beauty lost forever."

Pulling one of the thinner bangles closer to him, Alexis let the tips of his fingers rest on the gorgeous blood-red stone placed within the gold. He felt a warmth from the stone, and something he couldn't quite put his finger on. Energy? Something about the stone felt alive. He felt the old woman's eyes boring into him intently as he considered the piece.

"This has so much history to it," Alexis finally said. "It would be a waste to return home empty handed."

"It is good," she replied. "If you look on the gold, you will see the Eye of Horus. I normally do not put the Eye of

Protection on my work, but this bangle demanded it. It is the best piece I ever made."

"Then I must have it," Alexis declared.

The woman cocked her head, studying him once more. Alexis felt the hair at the base of his neck prickle at her scrutiny. He almost sensed that she could see through his lies. She definitely got where she was in life on more than luck. After much consideration, the woman picked up the bangle and slipped it into a small, deep blue silk pouch. Alexis was surprised to see such a valuable commodity at a lowly merchant's stall.

"Normally I would sell this for fifteen gold," she began. Alexis balked at the kingly sum. "However, you have been most kind to this old woman. I also think that you will need some extra protection to help you get home. For you, my silver-tongued prince, I offer it for ten."

It was still a hefty price, and Alexis was running out of money. However, the piece drew him in. It was not just the fine craftsmanship, but the stone as well. Could there be any truth in her claims that the blood of Kebechet was imbued into these stones? And what of the Mother Goddess? The woman knew her stories, but the one about the chalcedony stone intrigued him. Perhaps that was what made Neith's necklace so special.

Reaching in to his pocket, Alexis withdrew a small leather pouch and pulled out ten gold coins from the already slim bag. Placing them one by one on the wooden table, he pulled out one more, a silver, and added it to the rest.

"You intrigue me, dear mother. If you would be so kind, would you add your blessing on to this lovely piece. If your words are true, I will indeed need protection on my journey."

"I'll do what I can, my son."

The woman brought the bangle close to her mouth and closed her eyes. She began murmuring a prayer in a dialect Alexis couldn't understand, but that sounded similar to the ones before her time. One he realized he may have to study before it was all over. When she finished, the woman dropped the bangle into the blue silk and pulled the strings tight. She then took out a length of papyrus rinds dyed black and tied the bag closed tight, handing it over with a knowing nod.

"Thank you, dear mother," Alexis said, cradling the pouch in both of his hands. "Your gift is truly invaluable."

"Mother Amunet knows. Take care, my son. May the Eye protect you on your journey."

It was over. The woman, Amunet, returned to the wares on her table, straightening the already perfectly laid trinkets. Alexis took the cue and tucked it into a larger leather pouch on his hip, tying one of the black papyrus rinds to a cord that he'd tied to his belt to keep his valuables secure. Most likely, he'd never see this old woman again.

Pity, Alexis mused. *I rather liked her.*

An idea struck him as he took a few steps away. Already, merchants attempted to attract his attention as Alexis began moving through the main thoroughfare.

"Dear mother?" Alexis called out over his shoulder as he walked away. The woman hummed in acknowledgement. "What is the name of the Great Creator?"

"Neith."

Alexis' breath caught in his throat. There truly was more to Amunet than met the eye. At least she would be spared when at the end of it all.

XXIX

T HE BACK ROOM WAS constantly bustling as girls went in and out of the darkened room. Low-burning candles sat on tables and in lanterns on the wall, providing a dim but manageable light to see by. There was no telling the time of day as people were always moving. It had been a long time since Evaline last saw Safira or Lateef. She hoped it would be a long time before she saw him again, even if he was her only source of information. Asenath had made several appearances over the hours, always shooting menacing glares at Evaline as she walked past. Evaline found herself trying to squeeze into the smallest crevice she could to hide from the woman. A few of the women would walk by, shooting her a curious glance, almost boring on pity. Most pretended she wasn't there, going about their business in relative silence.

On a few occasions, Evaline noted how Asenath would scold one of the younger girls, shrieking at them and even slapping them in the face so hard their hair flew. Through her observations, Evaline began to see Asenath as the one in charge, after Lateef. Evaline's stomach rumbled. How long had it been since she'd last eaten?

God, I wish I knew how much time has passed. Her stomach knotted. *I wish I knew what happened to Alexis.*

As if to answer her question, Lateef strode into the room. The younger girls shied away hoping to not be noticed. Evaline took note of their reactions and tried to mimic their movements, praying that she too remained unnoticed. Her heart jumped to her throat as she thought he glanced her way. In three long strides, he crossed the room until he was right in front of her. Grabbing her roughly, Evaline brought a feral grin to Lateef's lips as she whimpered despite her best efforts. Throwing her down onto one of the cushions, Lateef climbed on top of her, placing his hand over her mouth to stop her pleas as he undid the cord around his pants.

Evaline tried not to cry as she felt him force his way inside her. His body moved roughly, not in the tender way she and Alexis shared during their moment together. Her muffled cries became more high-pitched, tears rolling down her cheek as she felt her body tear with each thrust. In the background, Asenath's voice could be heard speaking animatedly. Evaline couldn't tell if it was to someone in particular or to the room as a whole. As her screams turned to sobs, Asenath let out a laugh. It felt like an eternity, but Lateef finally got off of her, his seed running down her legs, and left the room, closing the door with a heavy bang. Evaline lay on the cushion crying and alone. No one went over to help her.

Asenath approached another girl. The older woman said something to the younger, the tone almost sound like she was chastising the girl, before slapping her and walking off. Unable to muster up the energy to care, Evaline shakily got to her feet and tried to smooth out her dress, soft sobs still wracking her body. Every movement brought her more pain.

The door then opened and Safira finally entered, bumping into Asenath as the older woman exited with a sharp word. Through the curtain of tears, a small flicker of hope fluttered in Evaline's chest as she saw the familiar face. Even though they could not speak, Evaline felt a sense of comfort seeing her. Forgetting that she was still disheveled on the cushions, Evaline observed as Safira went over to the young girl. Stroking the girl's hair, Safira spoke softly to her, letting the girl cry on her shoulder.

It took but a few minutes before the young girl calmed down enough to answer Safira's questions. Safira continued to stroke the girl's hair, offering what sounded like reassurance to the girl. As the girl's hiccupping breathing slowed down, Safira kissed the girl on the top of her head. A couple of the other girls tentatively approached, apprehension evident by the stiffness of their body and their strained tones.

Safira replied to the others in the same soothing voice she did to the young girl. Responding to her instruction, the others encircled the younger girl, offering her a sip of water and rubbing her back as Safira stood up. Evaline thought she heard Safira thank the others, but couldn't be sure.

Evaline wished they would come and comfort her after the ordeal.

Safira then turned Evaline's direction and began speaking. Evaline looked around, trying to see who Safira was speaking to. Safira repeated her statement. Hearing what sounded like "Ehvahrleen" confirmed that she was the right person. The two went back to the corner Evaline had been hiding in before Lateef snatched her, Safira taking the lead. While the other girls were distracted, Evaline felt comfortable skulking out of sight with Safira.

However, Safira didn't share the same level of comfort. Her eyes darted about, several times before turning her attentions to Evaline. Safira began speaking, her voice pouring out in a rushed whisper. Evaline struggled to understand anything Safira said. She thought she heard Lateef a couple of times, but the language was so different that even then she couldn't be sure. Evaline all but gave up hope on getting anything useful from the conversation when Safira pressed a small folded piece of paper into her hand. Keeping Evaline's hand clenched in hers, Safira gave the hand a gentle shake before pulling Evaline in a tight embrace.

Struggling with all her might, Evaline heard Safira hiss, "Run." The message came out in a slow, deliberate voice.

Hope blossomed in Evaline's chest once she received the message. Clearly, Safira had snuck away once more if she was able to bring back this message.

Still locked in an embrace, Safira had one more message: "Hurry."

Breaking apart, Safira glanced to the group of women. Looking over her shoulder, Evaline saw a few of the woman no longer hovering over the Lateef's victim and now staring their direction. The hope that had erupted moments before quickly turned to panic.

Oh God, I hope they don't get suspicious, she worried.

To her surprise, Safira's hand gently caressed her cheek. Focusing on Safira once more, the young woman stared pointedly at Evaline before wrapping her finger under Evaline's chin and pulling her in for a kiss. Evaline nearly let out a gasp as Safira's tongue moved in lazy circles inside her mouth. She wanted to pull away, but she didn't want the situation to turn dangerous. Closing her eyes, she let Safira kiss her, not pulling away, but not reciprocating. As Safira pulled away, a number of questions flowed through her mind.

"Go," Safira repeated softly, making sure she locked eyes with Evaline.

Evaline nodded, forcing a smile on her face as though she enjoyed the kiss. She brought her hands to Safira's face and cupped the woman's heart-shaped face in both her hands. To her credit, Safira played along, letting the moment linger before breaking away completely and finding a cushion to sit on. The other girls no longer watched Safira or Evaline, having decided that there was nothing to see there. Evaline hoped that no one would try and press her. She didn't think she could handle any more surprises.

By now, the young girl had cried herself to sleep in one of the other girls' arms. A few others were lounging on cushions, either asleep or sprawled out. Others, including Safira, quietly chatted off to the side. A member of Safira's group disappeared outside for a moment, only to return with a small platter of dates and dried meat to share with the others. Evaline's stomach rumbled at the sight of food. Taking the opportunity to slip out unnoticed, Evaline made her way to the door as inconspicuously as possible.

How can I escape dressed like this? she worried. *Someone is going to notice me. God, how can I look any more obvious?*

Not wanting to draw attention to herself, Evaline sat on a nearby cushion, just far enough away from the others that she didn't seem like she wanted to engage with them. No one gave her a second glance. No one wanted to draw Lateef's attention. It felt like an eternity, but Evaline forced herself to sit on the cushion for a while. The light shone brighter in this portion of the room, but the room still remained dim. Pulling her knees to her chest, Evaline brought her hands to her thighs. Scanning the room, she looked to see if anyone was watching her as she slowly unfolded the paper Safira gave her.

Evaline's fingers trembled as she opened the strange paper. It was made from pressed reeds. If Lateef or Asenath ever saw her with it, she doubted she'd be able to destroy the message by eating it. Her ears strained for any sort of sudden exclamation or the door opening. To her relief, by the time she finished unfolding the paper she remained basically ignored by the others, including Safira. Glancing down at her lap, Evaline studied the message.

It was a crudely drawn map with a few square rooms. A crook and flail were marked in the center of a room, the gold and blue images obviously denoting something important as they stood out from the other images all drawn in black. Strange glyphs filled the page, all illegible to Evaline's ignorant eye. In the uppermost corner on the right, a small blue X was placed in one of the smaller rooms. She almost missed it since the dim light made the ink appear black, but it was there.

A loud thump followed almost immediately by a man's cry in the other room. Everyone in the room's attention was focused on the door, still as cats. A rapid flurry of thumps could be heard accompanied by desperate pleas and whimpering. A voice filled with rage shouted at the person begging for mercy, the thumps continuing at steady intervals. After several long minutes, a loud thud hit the floor and the thumping stopped. The angry voice returned to a normal volume, clearly spitting some curses at their victim.

A moment later, Asenath threw open the door, the light from the other room nearly blinding Evaline as her eyes struggled to adjust to the sudden appearance of light. A man on the ground, a spilled bag of coins splayed out around him, writhed on the ground, blood flowing from his mouth and nose. The room smelled heavily of beer and poppy, smoke wafting over from one room to the next. Evaline's eyes burned, and she struggled not to cough, not wanting to draw attention to herself. Raucous laughter rang out from Asenath as Lateef gave the man another kick before grabbing the loose coins from the ground and pocketing them.

Noticing Evaline, Asenath made her way over and grabbed Evaline by the hair, yanking her to the ground with what sounded like a gleeful scream. Evaline let out a cry as her hands flew to her head, trying to remove the woman's fingers from her hair. As soon as Evaline's hands touched Asenath's, the older woman spit out a tirade dripping with rage, slapping Evaline hard enough that she split Evaline's lip. Blood filled Evaline's mouth and dribbled down her chin. She whimpered in pain, spitting out the blood onto the floor and earning another slap. None of the other girls moved to help Evaline, their eyes glued on the door, waiting for Lateef.

"Shit! Fuck!"

The sound of someone cursing in Aceatian caught Evaline's attention. As Asenath yanked her head up once more, Evaline strained to listen to Lateef in hopes of hearing anything useful.

"Thief!" Lateef roared. "I should feed you to my slaves."

The man groaned on the ground, a rapid stream of Ma'Alkinian pouring from his bloodied mouth. Stars exploded in Evaline's mind as Asenath slammed her head into the ground. A cry of pain escaped Evaline as tears stung her eyes. Hearing Asenath's beratements and Evaline's yelp, Lateef finally turned to face the girls in the room. He shouted something and Evaline felt Asenath release her immediately. The woman stepped away, cowering under Lateef's fury. Evaline looked up as Lateef grabbed Asenath by the neck. She almost thought she saw his eyes flash red in the dim light as he growled at the older woman.

Asenath's face went pale, her eyes wide in fright as she clawed at his hand around her throat. She babbled out a panicked plea. Evaline almost felt sorry for the woman, but another mouthful of blood reminded her of how cruel she truly was. Spitting out the blood, Evaline tried stopping the bleeding with her cloak.

I hope he doesn't kill her. I wish I could've saved her.

Another tirade streamed from Lateef's mouth, spittle flying as he raged. He squeezed until Asenath almost passed out. Her eyes lulled in her head and her body went limp. Once her hand stopped scratching his and dropped to her side, he threw her into some of the barrels on the far side of the room. Turning on his heel, Lateef stormed out of the room, muttering to himself. Evaline perked up when she heard him mention Nefret.

The door slammed behind him, shaking the frame and eliciting yelps from the other girls in the room. More shouting from Lateef from another room. Feeling brave, Evaline made her way to the door and opened it a crack. Light filled the dim room, and the smell of smoke hit Evaline in the face and twisting her stomach. Angry voices and the sound of furniture hitting the walls sounded from the main room. On the floor in front of her, the fallen man had already been moved. Evaline didn't want to think of what happened to him.

A light touch on her shoulder startled Evaline. Safira's finger went to her lips as she listened, her face tense as she listened. Several painfully long minutes passed before the shouting finally died down and the last chair had been thrown. Safira moved to shut the door, but Evaline shook her head. Meeting her gaze, Safira gave Evaline's shoulder a squeeze.

"Akh," she whispered.

The word sounded familiar to Evaline. She racked her brain, trying to remember what it meant. Seeing her confusion, Safira said the word once more, slowly, hoping Evaline would understand. Evaline's mind raced as she struggled to recall the word. Safira's gaze turned down as she began to walk away dejected. With a gasp, Evaline finally found the word.

"Akh," Evaline whispered back. Her heart raced, not from terror – though she was afraid, but from the thrill. Finally, it was her chance to act.

XXX

THE WOODEN DOOR felt like it weighed a ton as Evaline leaned against it, her ear pressed flat against the grain, as she inched it open. The women in the room behind her were strangely quiet, but Evaline could feel all eyes boring onto her as she pushed. Even Asenath stood unnaturally silent behind her. Glancing back, Evaline saw it was because the older woman sat on a cushion in shock. Obviously, she did not receive Lateef's wrath often. Safira whispered words of encouragement, either that, or warning Evaline that she didn't have much time. Evaline chose to assume it was a mix of the two. More light filtered into the room as the closed door opened wider.

In another part of the building, Evaline thought she could hear people talking, but the shouting had died down.

She could also hear the sound of women moaning as they continued their duties. Evaline wished she could bring the women with her, but she knew she had to escape first. Pulling the hood of her cloak down low over her face, Evaline took a deep breath and slipped in to the anteroom.

Incense wafted into the room, the more delicate scent of sandalwood mingling in with the heavy scent of tobacco. She gagged, her empty stomach threatening to bring up what little it held as the smell of smoke smothered her. Her eyes adjusted quickly. Disoriented, Evaline tried to remember the way she came in. There were doors on every wall. Straight in front of her, she heard the sound of girls at work. To her left, she believed was the tavern's entrance. That left the back. Evaline wondered what lay to her right.

The pragmatic response won, and Evaline found herself pressed against the door leading to the front of the tavern. Somehow, smoke continued to leak through the thick wood, strangling her with its acrid aroma. Evaline's eyes burned as she held back the furious coughing fit that tickled her throat. On the other side, it was quiet. Unsure if the room was empty or the patrons were preoccupied, Evaline gathered her courage and opened the door.

Darkness enveloped her once more as the dim lights from the lanterns washed the room red. At first glance, it appeared empty. Taking her first few steps into the room, movement in the corner of her eye caught her attention. A group of men sat at a table, drinks piled high as they played cards. One of the men called out, repeating himself as

Evaline looked around. He meant her. Sauntering over, Evaline slipped onto one of the men's laps as they wrapped their arm around her and pulled her in.

Alcohol permeated from his breath as he said something she didn't understand. Another man at the table said something and the men broke out into laughter. The man holding her pulled down her hood, drawing an appreciative gasp from the group and leaving Evaline feeling exposed. He grabbed her face, bringing her close to him until she could smell the spices from his lunch underneath the heavy scent of alcohol. His tongue quickly found its way into her mouth, and Evaline recoiled, eliciting a round of laughter from the man's friends. He said something to her before forcing her mouth to his once more. His other hand grabbed her own and brought it to his groin. It was stiff under his pants.

If she could just get him alone, she might be able to slip outside and escape under the guise of performing services. While Evaline tried to formulate her plan, the man returned to his game with his friends, holding Evaline on his lap and moving her hand up and down over his stiff member. Every so often, he let out a breathy moan, pushing her hand down harder on top of him. As he let go of her to play a card, Evaline continued to rub, letting him think that she was submitting to his desires.

How do I lead him outside? she wondered.

Her heart raced, fearing he would do something to her at the table while the others watched, or worse. She had to keep him happy for now. Time passed and his moans got louder and more frequent. Evaline's mind wandered as she thought of different ways to get him to follow her outside. As his body began to twitch, she got an idea. Standing up, she grabbed his hand and motioned for him to follow her. Thanking whoever watched over her, Evaline led the man out the front door unbothered, an amused smile on his face and what must be catcalls from his friend.

Evaline squinted, shielding her eyes as she stumbled into the brightness, the sky a merciless blue without a cloud to be seen and the sun glaring overhead. She wasn't sure if it had been a day, or maybe two since she'd seen the open sky. Her chest expanded with a desperate breath, the clean air sharp against her lungs, stripping away the stale taste of tobacco smoke. The man babbled away behind her, but she pushed his words aside as she looked for a secluded place for her to hide. Evaline caught the silent judgement etched on their stares. The sight of the auburn-haired woman leading a scruffy looking drunk left no doubts to what was about to happen.

At long last, Evaline found what she was looking for: an empty side street. Leading her companion into the narrow street with her, Evaline positioned him until his back leaned against the building. Standing on her tiptoes, she kissed him, silencing whatever he was about to say. His hands roved over her body, his breathing coming in heavy and his body still stiff as he pressed her into his groin. His hands slipped under her dress and up her thigh. Evaline tensed, not wanting him to touch her. Instead, she pushed his hand back and wrapped her fingers around his.

His eyes were focused on her, his lips trying to find her neck, affording Evaline a chance to quickly scan her surroundings. The area was still empty. With a deep breath, Evaline steeled herself. Her knee swiftly met his groin, bringing a wail of pain from the man as he doubled over. No doubt the stream of words pouring forth from his mouth included curses. Taking the opportunity, Evaline ran down the alley before he drew too much attention.

Hopefully he didn't see which way I went, she thought as she turned a tight corner.

Her heart nearly stopped as she ran into someone. A strangled gasp escaped her lips, her eyes widening in fear. Glancing up, Evaline heaved a sigh of relief. In front of her, Alexis wrapped his cool arms around her. Unable to control herself, Evaline broke into sobs, her hands clutching at Alexis' chest. She was so exhausted, her adrenaline having finally run out after everything she'd experienced, that she didn't fight or question him as he led her through the increasingly narrow streets.

"I failed," she mumbled over and over.

Alexis made soothing sounds, trying to calm her as they moved quickly. His words were distracted, not fully acknowledging her trauma. After two more turns, they found themselves at a dead end. The backside of a mudbrick building loomed over her. Evaline thought she heard someone coming from the way she came. Panic set in and her already labored breathing quickened. A strangled gasp escaped her as she searched for an escape. Then she saw it – a door. Alexis must have already seen it because he pushed it open and shoved her inside.

The room was dark and wooden beams stood exposed. A large patch of sunlight from the hole in the ceiling afforded her a bit of light in the otherwise gloomy building. It was eerily quiet with only her racing heart beating in her ears. The silence didn't help her nerves. It only enhanced them.

Her adrenaline vanished and Evaline collapsed onto the floor in a sobbing heap. Her body ached, both from where she'd been slapped over the last day and from where Lateef had brutalized her. She lay there for several seconds before she felt Alexis' hand on her back.

"You didn't fail," he said softly. "People like Safira have a hard time leaving situations like that. You did your best to help her. Your sister would be proud."

Looking up, Evaline tried to blink away the tears. Shame burned her cheeks. She couldn't bring herself to meet Alexis' gaze.

"He- he…" Evaline stumbled over her words, unable to vocalize what had happened.

Alexis looked from her face down her body. His face hardened as he noticed a small trail of blood that had started to dry between her legs. Evaline followed his gaze and was surprised to see the blood. She broke into sobs once more, unable to look at proof of her violation.

"Don't worry," Alexis said through gritted teeth. "He will pay for what he's done."

"I'm sorry," she whispered.

Evaline felt Alexis pause, his hands no longer stroking her.

"Sorry for what?" he asked.

"I wanted to go home. I was going to leave you all here."

A soft, tired chuckle greeted Evaline after her admission. A flash of crimson marred the hazel eyes that still captivated her against her will. Giving herself a mental shake, Evaline forced herself to no longer let Alexis charm her. Her mind now clear, Evaline found his reaction unsettling.

"Of course," he said, pinching the bridge of his nose with a sigh. "Why would you help a prostitute?"

Meeting Evaline's gaze, Alexis maintained prolonged eye contact. His hazel eyes bored into her own, almost as though he studied her soul.

"I need you to listen to me," he said slowly. "Your life is in danger. I need you to trust me – for now. Stay put. I will come back for you. We can get out of her. Together. Alive. I just need you to trust me."

As she stared back at Alexis, Evaline felt that familiar tug in her chest whenever he spoke to her. His words were like a spell, mesmerizing Evaline and urging her to follow him to the ends of the world. She wanted to believe him. He would be her best chance to escape. However, part of Evaline cried out in protest. Alexis let her be ravaged by Lateef. It was a betrayal she hadn't begun to process.

But after this, maybe she would be free. Free to return to her family.

Amalie will have had her baby by then. What I wouldn't give to have her little one nuzzled up in my arms.

With a half-nod, Evaline sealed their agreement. Alexis gently grabbed her hands and gave them a squeeze.

"Thank you, ma chérie. I will make sure no one has tracked us here, so you'll be safe. I'll also have food brought over. I don't know how long this will take, but I will come back for you."

Alexis wrapped his arms lightly around Evaline's waist and pulled her in. She felt her body tense as he held her softly. Alexis must have noticed that there was something wrong when Evaline didn't melt into his body like she used to. His lips brushed her forehead before he released her. Turning on his heels, Alexis slipped out of the darkened room without another word.

Evaline found herself rooted to the spot, unable to break the phantom embrace that still held her. Her adrenaline pumped through her body, a raging conflict between her desire to feel his cool flesh against her own and the terror of being held by a man. She could still feel Lateef inside her, his own cool flesh on hers. After what felt like hours, Evaline's body collapsed onto the floor in a trembling heap. Her stomach clenched, wanting to void itself, but there was nothing there.

Laying on the ground, Evaline took deep breaths to try and collect herself.

I need to rest, she told herself.

Making herself a little nest in one of the corners, Evaline took off her cloak and took stock of her surroundings once more. It was a large building with many rooms spidering out in different directions. Many of them had parts of the ceiling caved in, creating dangerous rubble piles. Light filtered in through the cracks in the walls or the boarded-up windows. Evaline still hadn't figured out if it was a residential home or something else, but the more she moved around, she felt certain it used to be a home like the one she'd stayed at in the Eastern District.

Tables and other bits of furniture lay overturned on the dusty floor. Clay jars were shattered, bits of pottery sprayed everywhere. In one room, Evaline found a small reed doll, a splotch of red marring its little dress. Kneeling down, Evaline picked up the doll, running her thumb over the simple toy. Its stitched face stared up at her, a story hidden behind its eyes. Her eyes stung as tears prickled the corners. The doll reminded her of Elise. With the doll still in her hand, Evaline straightened up and was met with what looked like large scratches gouged into the wall. They traveled down the wall in a diagonal angle, as though whatever made these markings was trying to hit something.

Running her fingers through the claw marks, Evaline let out a gasp as she realized how deep they ran. If they had hit flesh, it would be devastating. Her feet carried her backwards, as if the scratches burned her. She happened to look down and noticed a dark stain at her feet. Crouching down, Evaline wiped the floor with her hand, moving the dust to the sides and creating a clearing. A dark puddle of dried blood stained the floorboards. Glancing around, she thought she saw several more puddles of various size scattered throughout the room. Heart pounding, Evaline stood and quickly exited the room.

Evaline explored more of the building, all of it in the same state of disarray as the room of death, as she came to call it. However, there weren't as many with the same level of carnage as the room of death. The scratches, she came to realize, also could be found in the hallways. She finally found a door in another part of the building, cracks splintering the wood, causing chunks to fall out. Pressing her eye to the door, she saw it led her to a part of Kul-El that she hadn't seen before. Merchants stood behind large stalls, gold sparkling in light. Fruits, nuts, and meat waited at other vendors' booths to be purchased. The mere sight of the food set her mouth watering and brought about another growl from her stomach, more insistent this time. She would get a bite to eat later.

For now, she needed to rest until the sun began to set. She didn't want to be out after dark, but she hoped that as the sun set, she could conceal herself enough to go out and make some distance away from Kul-El.

Loyalty be damned, Evaline told herself. *I need to get out of this place as soon as possible.*

***

Evaline jerked awake, having been startled with her head lolling to the side as she dozed. A trail of drool pooled on her chest, darkening her dress. The room was dark, the sun's rays no longer filtering in through the hole in the ceiling. A moment of panic gripped her as she shot to her feet. Racing to the door and smashing her face against it, Evaline heaved a sigh of relief. Dusk had not yet fully fallen. Donning her cloak once more, Evaline pulled the hood down low over her face and slipped out the door. After being inside the boarded apartment in the Eastern District, Lateef's brothel, and now her little hideaway, the heat struck Evaline with an intensity that made her pause for a moment. She didn't understand how she never noticed it earlier when she made her escape from Lateef's tavern.

Traveling through this less seedy part of Kul-El, Evaline found herself more at ease and able to enjoy the beauty of the city. Fewer stares accompanied her as people went about their business, allowing her time to casually explore the various merchants.

An old man called out to Evaline, beckoning her closer. Making sure her hood was up, she made her way to his stall. Bearing more wrinkles than Father Time himself, the man stood just below Evaline's shoulder. Though his hands shook as he showed off his wares of fruit and nuts, his voice remained steady. She tried to gently turn away but found it hard to say no to such a friendly looking face after all she'd seen.

"No, thank you," Evaline said in her broken Ma'Alkinian, waving her hands in front of her for emphasis.

The man cocked his head, a smile blossoming on his face as her stomach rumbled. He said something to her before holding out an apple, nodding as she eyed the fruit warily. Once she grabbed the apple, he busied himself with making a small pile of figs and tiger nuts. Evaline stared at the strange looking nuts, their earthy color and cone shaped appearance different from what she was used to back home. Again, he smiled at her, his hands splayed wide over the small mounds of food he offered her.

"Th-thank you," she muttered as she scooped the food and dropped it into a pocket on the inside of her cloak.

Her pocket now laden with food, Evaline made her way through the mainly empty streets. The crisp apple refreshed Evaline. She wandered aimlessly, trying to not draw attention to herself by appearing lost or confused. In her mind, Evaline pictured a confident merchant on a business venture in a foreign city. She needed to look like she belonged if she didn't want to wind up in Lateef's lair once more.

The streets all appeared the same, making it difficult for Evaline to get her bearings. Moving on to the nuts, Evaline started looking for a place to stay as the last rays of the sun started to slip below the horizon. She needed to find a safe place for the night. Tomorrow she would continue her search for a way out of Kul-El.

"Get ahold of yourself," Evaline whispered to herself. "You'll be home soon."

XXXI

Traveling with Abukhar and Hapu proved to be more trouble than it was worth. The now exiled pirate seemed to know everyone in the damned city, and they all seemed hellbent on calling out to him and his brother to have a little chat. Zahir stood off to the side. For the third time that day, Hapu regaled some acquaintance with an edited version of his last time at sea. For a man of the waters, he was certainly talkative, and despite his earlier displeasures at seeing the sparkle wiped from Ma'Alkin's crown jewel, Hapu maintained that it would make their trip more pleasant.

The first time it happened, Zahir made sure to warn the two that they were to, under no circumstance, mention him. To their credit, they listened to him. As the two returned to their meeting place, Zahir couldn't hide the scowl on his face.

"Come now," Hapu said, trying to smooth over Zahir's irritation after a particularly animated encounter. "It's been ages since I've been in the city. I haven't seen them in years."

"It seems you haven't seen many people in years," Zahir groused. "We are trying to *not* draw attention to ourselves, and here you are talking with every damned person in Kul-El. How are we to get into the palace if we stop all the time?"

"I can appreciate your concern, but that happened to be my younger cousin. He knows someone who is one of the guard, and I managed to find us a way in. It'll be harder to get an audience with the Pharaoh, but I believe it can be done."

Incredulity must have been written all over Zahir's face because Hapu and his brother broke into laughter. Those two actually managed to find a way to get them in.

"Well damn," Zahir replied, impressed. "Now all we need is for you to speak with the Pharaoh while I head to the library. This might actually be possible."

"At sea you quickly learn that most of life is about luck, with a bit of skill. Like the ocean, fate is always moving, always changing its course. If you find a bit of calm, you take advantage of it to push ahead as much as possible."

A smirk played on Zahir's lips as he observed the proud pirate. Abukhar commented on how it would be nice to grab a bite, and Hapu began babbling about how he remembered a place where they could get the best kebabs in Kul-El. Zahir allowed the two to lead the way, making sure to trail a way back out of habit. If anyone had been observing him the last few days, they would know he traveled with them.

Their course over the last three days had been circuitous, allowing the three to take an agonizingly slow pace, much to Zahir's annoyance. While the brothers grabbed snacks and small trinkets to bring home to their families, Zahir stayed to the shadows searching for those with loose lips. That was where Hapu and his brother came in handy. Whenever they found someone talkative, Zahir would join them, listening to their stories as he browsed their wares. So far, there hadn't been much luck. But as they gradually moved towards the palace, he hoped things would change – and today was that day.

The delicate aroma of spiced meat and onions proceeded the kebab shop. A slab of meat rested in the window, its juices dripping onto the sill. Years ago, it would have made his mouth water in longing, but now, he just ignored the heavenly smell. As the brothers ordered their meal, Zahir slipped into a chair in the corner of the room to wait. The pair paid for their food and made their way to him. The group sat in silence for a while as Hapu and his brother enjoyed their kebabs.

Zahir used this time to figure out their next steps. Hapu and Abukhar could not continue on with him once they reached the palace. However, he needed to come up with a convincing cover so the two could at least create enough of a diversion requesting an audience with the pharaoh. If by some stroke of luck they managed to get one through their connections, Zahir needed them to be ready. The royal library was too deep into the palace for him to sneak in so easily.

"So, an audience with the pharaoh?" Hapu said, wiping the meat juices from his chin with the back of his arm. "This is some big scam you're trying to pull."

The question took Zahir off-guard. He thought everything between them had been worked out. His eyes narrowed as he met the brothers' gazes.

"We served as your guides out of gratitude for you saving me, but I'm not stupid. You have something big going on, and I don't plan on separating without my due. I'm not going to put my neck on the line for nothing."

The smirk that played on Zahir's lips earlier that day became a smile, his eyes glinting red in the shadows. Things were getting interesting. Licking his lips, Zahir maintained his posture, not wanting to give the illusion that he was taken aback by the sudden shift in demeanor of the pirate and his brother. To his credit, Abukhar remained impassive as he watched the exchange between Zahir and Hapu.

"What do you want?" Zahir asked.

"Whatever you take, we want half."

A bold move from someone who didn't know the true stakes at play. Zahir raised his brows in amusement. Perhaps this would play right into his hands after all.

"How can I trust you won't betray me?" Zahir asked. As Hapu opened his mouth to speak, Zahir added, "Either through your own ineptitude or on purpose?"

The little comment had its desired effect. Hapu's eyes darkened as his previously cheerful demeanor soured instantly. Zahir almost regretted his choice of words. It wouldn't do to have the man acting overconfident just to prove him wrong.

"Don't you worry about me," Hapu said, regaining his composure.

The vampyre's brows raised once more. There was more behind those words than the pirate was letting on. He *needed* the money. Hapu's betrayal of his captain had marked him as untrustworthy, disloyal. No doubt he would be hard-pressed to get a position on another ship. Those who sailed the seas talked. And pirates had a bad reputation by those on land. No, Hapu would struggle finding a new way to make honest money.

"Say I give you your cut," Zahir began. "Can I trust your discretion? As you've guessed, I have big plans in the works and won't tolerate betrayal."

He leaned forward as he spoke, meeting both of Hapu and Abukhar's eyes. He made sure they showed the faintest hint of red, just enough to unsettle them. They needed to know that he was still in charge. Hapu's resolve faltered, but Abukhar held firm. Zahir noted that he would be more trouble than his brother.

"We are men of our word," Abukhar said. "My brother is a good man. Just hard on his luck. We'll not risk our own necks just to spite you."

Hapu nodded.

That was enough for Zahir. "I'm glad we have this understanding," he said. "It's always been my belief that only one person is needed to help deliver a message. I'd hate for one of you to become redundant."

Leaning back in his chair once more, he made a show of stretching. He cursed himself as he struggled to come up with a viable plan for when they spoke to the pharaoh. Why couldn't every human be as easy to manipulate as that damned Hasani? Then it hit him.

"The discontent in the smaller villages seems to be moving towards open hostility," Zahir said. "It might be because those ruthless seafarers are moving inland, stealing both property and women from the small villages where the Ma'Alkinian guard are stationed. If nothing is done, they could be motivated to take action."

"I have heard rumors," Abukhar said with a glint in his eye, "that there is a scoundrel, goes by the name of Hasani, who has been terrorizing the nearby homes. I wouldn't be surprised if he became more aggressive."

"I've heard bad things about him, too," Hapu agreed, his usual jovial demeanor returning. "I believe I even have a few people in other villages who could provide additional stories to our dear pharaoh. It's a shame things are getting so complicated. Our beloved leader has spent too much time away from his humblest citizens."

"And as a thank you for bringing him the message," Zahir said, "I would love to give you a little something for your troubles. If you don't mind taking time out of your busy schedules."

"Not a problem at all," Abukhar said raising an invisible glass as a toast and nodding his head. "All we want is to keep the people safe."

"Agreed," Zahir replied.

The brothers returned to their meal, chatting softly amongst themselves. Zahir leaned back in his chair once more. Everything was falling into place. His worries about the brothers were fading; if they got themselves killed, all the better. It would buy him more time. Now, the games began.

XXXII

THE OUTER WALL of the great palace gleamed in the sunlight. Zahir squinted, lifting a hand against the morning sun as it bounced off the white stone. The gardens spilled out before him, grass cut to knife-edge squares that framed the walls in angular precision. Rows of sycamore fig and palm trees stood like sentinels, their shadows twitching and stretching as the faint breeze teased the leaves. On the left, the river slid into the palace grounds through a narrow opening in the wall, its turquoise surface glittering like gemstones against the golden sand. Not a speck of dirt marred the marble paths. Not a blade of grass dared to grow out of line. Behind the palace, the royal tomb loomed over the unspoiled grounds. Gaps between the massive sandstone bricks made for a jagged outline, like a large maw rising up from the earth.

A thin trickle of guards circled the perimeter, their khopesh hanging loosely in their hands. There didn't seem to be too many walking about which concerned Zahir. Either the main force roamed the palace halls proper, or they were secreted in the underground tunnels. He hoped it wasn't the latter. That would make his search much more difficult.

Behind the large stone statues of Horus that lined the palace walkway, Zahir saw the woman who had been burned into his mind for the last two centuries. Dressed in a striking blue dress, her golden bangles shining in the sun, Nefret strode confidently towards the entrance of the palace. Trailing behind, a group of five men covered in deep brown cloaks, their flesh hidden from the sun's rays. A shiver ran down Zahir's spine as the priestess' head turned his way. He almost thought he saw a smirk pull up the corners of her mouth and her eyes sparkle as they darted his way. A moment later, the look was gone.

Zahir ducked behind the larger Hapu, earning him a questioning stare from the man. Zahir quickly tried to correct course and show an outward display of confidence by picking up his pace as though his movement had been on purpose. The damage had been done, however, and both Hapu and Abukhar shared a silent glance.

"The High Priestess must be meeting with the queen," Abukhar said, trying to distract from the awkwardness that now blanketed the three. "There's been talk in the villages that the queen has been struggling to produce an heir and has sought the guidance of the High Priestess in hopes of earning Hathor's favor."

"We should come back tomorrow," Zahir replied.

"No," Hapu pressed. "If the queen is busy, it might be easier to get an audience with the pharaoh."

"It is a bad idea," Zahir said more sternly. "The pharaoh will be distracted and there will be more guards inside, making my task more difficult." Hapu opened his mouth to speak, but Zahir silenced him with a glare. "If I can't get what I need, there will be no payment for you. One more day will not make a difference."

The pirate looked like he wanted to challenge Zahir, but chose not to. There was logic in his words, Zahir knew, and if it came down to it, he would have no qualms killing the duo in order to preserve his mission. It had been a while since he last fed after all. In the background he could hear Abukhar and Hapu talking to each other in whispers. He never would have believed that Abukhar would turn out to be the more pragmatic of the two.

"Just because we aren't going in today doesn't mean that we can't seek an audience with the pharaoh," Zahir said, trying to assuage some of Hapu's concerns. "I'll wait here and you two go and ask to speak to the pharaoh tomorrow. With your connection, it shouldn't be too hard to get an audience. Hopefully they are letting people in tomorrow."

The two slipped from the cover of the shadows and confidently made their way towards the palace. Zahir admired how they strode down the walkway, their backs straight as they disappeared into the building. Not knowing how long it would take, Zahir slithered from where he hid to take a leisurely stroll opposite the palace. It was time to feed. Unlike the main thoroughfare of Kul-El, the streets did not have the same crowds. More of the buildings were academic or guild master homes, places where they stayed away from the masses to enjoy the tranquility.

It would be easier to hide someone in the main streets amongst the worn-down houses, the body becoming one of many to disappear in the slums. This would be more of a challenge, and Zahir welcomed it. Spying a young servant boy maybe eight years of age, he dropped in step with the boy, maneuvering himself until he trailed silently behind.

***

The sun hit its midway point, and Zahir decided it was time for him to return to his original hiding spot and wait for the brothers to return. He wiped the dribble of blood that ran down his chin, the young blood leaving him feeling a little giddy. Zahir hated consuming children; not only did they remind him of his daughter, but they tasted much too sweet for his liking.

His hood hung low over his face, obscuring the sun and affording him a bit of cover as well. Not many cloaked themselves like he did, but it was not uncommon enough that he drew unwanted attention to himself, allowing him to move freely through the streets. He returned to the shadows of large sycamore fig tree before Hapu or Abukhar.

Thoughts of the two being captured buzzed faintly in the back of his mind. It wasn't likely they'd be apprehended, but there was always a chance that Nefret or one of her minions would be feeling a little hungry, and he didn't know how often they were given free range to hunt.

To his relief, he spotted the pair wandering over to where he was hiding. He noticed their even gait and how they smiled to each other – they must have been successful in obtaining an audience. If all went well, tomorrow would be the big day.

"It's done," Hapu said. Zahir couldn't help but pick up on the man's smug tone. "We will meet with the pharaoh at mid-day."

"He'll have a few advisors as well," Abukhar added. "Perhaps you should join us. This is getting out of our hands."

"You wanted to prove yourself and con me out of money," Zahir spat. "Now you come begging for my help? I thought you were more than capable of handling yourselves."

The contrast between the brothers' expressions spoke volumes. A cloud passed over Hapu's face, his mouth tightening until it was a thin, straight line. Abukhar, on the other hand, maintained a stoic visage, not giving away his emotions as easily.

He would be the better of the two during the audience, Zahir admitted to himself. *Damn.*

"But perhaps it would be better if I come after all. Together we can speak to the pharaoh, and afterwards you can spend time with your family in the capital. I won't forget our deal. I'll need your assistance returning to the coast and securing passage on a ship."

The relief on Hapu's face was almost palpable, confirming to Zahir that he made the right choice. He almost instructed the pirate to leave it to him and Abukhar. The risk that Hapu would give them away proved too great. How was it that a pirate was such a lousy liar?

"Who will speak?" Zahir asked.

"Abukhar," Hapu said as his brother raised his hand. "I haven't spent enough time in the villages to be able to provide a reliable narrative. I can only attest to the vile nature of Hasani."

That would do. Turning to leave, the two followed without a question. Zahir smiled to himself. He trained the two well. Maybe they would make it through the whole ordeal and he wouldn't have to kill them after all.

***

The sun beat down on Zahir as he traveled up the walkway towards the palace entrance. Even with his protective oil rubbed onto his flesh, he could feel the blistering heat from the sun. Between the burning sun and its infernal brightness nearly blinding him, Zahir was developing a headache. How his brethren could survive in this climate baffled him. Even when he lived in Kul-El, he never understood how he managed to endure her harsh weather. He tugged the hood further forward, shadow falling across his vision, though it meant his eyes caught only glimpses of Abukhar's boots ahead, the scuffed leather rising and falling with each step. Zahir fixed on them like a lifeline, forcing his feet to follow.

The patrol that morning had been as light as it had the day before. Did that mean that the bulk of the soldiers roamed the palace halls, or were they somewhere else? Perhaps they oversaw the efforts in constructing the pharaoh's tomb. No doubt the man-power required to construct such a feat heavily relied on the labor of prisoners and slaves.

"How long has the pyramid been under construction?" Zahir asked.

"I want to say they started it in the last two years," Abukhar replied. "Our great pharaoh only recently ascended to power, his father's death being most untimely."

"That is a shame," Zahir said. "May his ba rest for eternity in Dū-aat."

The false platitudes made Zahir's skin crawl.

"They are also constructing several smaller tombs for the children," Abukhar added, catching Zahir's attention.

"Smaller ones? Why?"

"The queen is struggling to produce an heir," Abukhar replied. "None of her children have made it past the age of five. She's had to send four of them to Dū-aat much too early." The normally stoic man's voice softened as he spoke of such misfortune.

"That is a shame," Zahir agreed. "May their ba rest for all eternity as well."

An image of his own daughter flashed in his mind. She was around five when he was reborn. He wondered if she lay in some unmarked grave somewhere or if she'd managed to find safety and become an old woman. His unbeating heart ached as he pictured her lying dead on the ground, her throat slashed and her chubby little arms splayed out in awkward angles. Shaking his head, Zahir dislodged his hood, blinding himself as he tried to push the unwanted image away. With a yelp of pain, he forced the cloth down over his face once more.

"All right?" Hapu asked.

A grunt of annoyance escaped Zahir. He didn't want to respond and draw more attention to himself. He noticed the guards turned to look at the three as they approached. At least he hadn't seen Nefret or her underlings.

"You said the High Priestess was helping treat the queen?" Zahir asked, driving the conversation away from himself. "Does she have that kind of power?"

"Hafor blesses those who believe," Hapu assured him. "I wouldn't doubt that the high priestess will help her bring forth an heir."

"If the queen does not provide one, there is rumor that the pharaoh has his eye on the princess of Hiba Al'qadasa. She's quite young, but I wouldn't be surprised if he took her as a consort."

A hint of disgust tinged Abukhar's voice. Though Zahir couldn't see the man's face, he wondered if Abukhar might truly be an ally in all of this. Perhaps they could pull at the threads here and see if they could bring chaos to Ma'Alkin. That might be fun.

Zahir felt the two slow down before he heard the gruff voice of the palace guard bark at them.

"Stop!" the man ordered. "State your business."

The three dropped their heads in respect to the pharaoh and his guard. Zahir could imagine the man watching them, his khopesh raised at the trio as they offered their necks to their king.

"We are but three humble villagers of Ma'Alkin," Abukhar said while maintaining his bow. "We received an audience with our beloved pharaoh yesterday, may the gods protect him for all eternity. We were told to come back to-day at mid-day and our beloved pharaoh will hear our plea."

"Please," Hapu added. "It is most urgent. A vile man threatens our small villages, and I fear that if we are not heard, more death and destruction will occur."

The earnestness in the pirate's voice surprised Zahir. Perhaps the man will be able to keep his composure in the face of otherwise certain death. A prolonged pause ensued, as the soldier waited to see if Zahir had anything to add. Zahir almost didn't say anything but thought better of it as he felt the soldier's gaze boring into him.

"Won't you please help us protect our people?"

The three straightened up, facing the guard once more. To his credit, the soldier lowered his khopesh and motioned for the three to follow him into the palace. Despite the palace halls being open to allow the sunlight to stream in, the shift from standing under the open sun to having the palace afford them a respite from its heat proved to be a huge relief to Zahir. Lowering his hood, he blinked several times, allowing his eyes to adjust. His head still ached, but at least his eyes no longer watered in pain and he could see.

The small group followed the soldier down the hall. Thick, white papyriform columns held up the roof, their intricate carvings on the body of the stone creating a beautiful accent to the smoothness of the mosaic floors and ceiling. Inside the palace, a large garden with a small pond under a sycamore in the center caught Zahir's eye. The casual display of wealth to such a grand scale intrigued him. When the Pharaoh Ahkash had lived, a river flowed through is palace. Now, the sacred waters had been diverted to create a frivolous pond. When would the arrogance of man subside? Their footsteps slapped against the mosaic that made up the floor. Images of fronds, the great river, and scenes of the gods decorated the palace. Each stone was pristine with not a speck of dust befouling it – an impressive display of wealth once more.

A golden arch with symbols of Toth framed a door that led to a darkened room. His heart leapt. He didn't expect to find the library so quickly. Glyphs filled the golden arch around the library's entrance, but they passed too quickly for Zahir to get a chance to read them. He forced himself to keep his expression neutral so as not to alert any of the guard inside the palace of his excitement. Making sure to memorize the path they took, Zahir continued on in silence.

After turning a few more corners, the group arrived at the door of the pharaoh's antechamber. Wadjet's watchful gaze hovered over the entrance, gold leaf gilding the papyriform columns that flanked the door like a pair of monoliths. Zahir felt a sense of foreboding wash over him as the group stood under the Eye. The soldier spoke to them, providing them with instructions on how to act while in the presence of the pharaoh. The words came out incoherent to Zahir's ears, their muted babblings lost to the vampyre as he took in his surroundings. Something felt off. With a final word to the trio, the guard led them into the antechamber and into the main hall where they would speak with the pharaoh.

Large columns lined the walls, creating an imposing walkway to the throne. The room was deathly silent as not even the palace servants uttered a sound. Zahir and his companions made their way towards a large golden throne. The closer they got, the more detail they could see was intricately carved into the massive chair. Sitting proudly atop the throne was the pharaoh. The ruler of Ma'Alkin did not strike Zahir as particularly imposing, his slim frame and gangly limbs acting in high contrast to his hawkish nose and piercing eyes. Zahir had only seen the pharaoh once years ago in passing as the vampyre searched for the entrance to Neith's tomb.

The tiles were cool pleasantly cool against Zahir's knees as he bowed low, pressing his forehead to the floor. The heat of Ma'Alkin was unbearable most days. From the corner of his eye, he could see the other two did not rise. Zahir waited. The weight of unseen eyes bore down. One of the pairs belonged to Nefret. Seconds stretched into minutes. At last, a soldier beside the throne ordered them to rise.

"What brings you to the halls of our holy pharaoh, Menkhe'n?" the soldier asked, his voice echoing in the silent room.

Taking his cue before the rest, Abukhar took a step forward and opened his arms in entreaty. The pharaoh watched the man, his face void of all emotion. Zahir observed Abukhar, impressed at the humble expression the man managed to pull up as he faced the ruler.

"Most beloved Pharaoh," Abukhar began. "For centuries my family has sung the praises of your holy line. We have thanked the gods for not only their bounty, but for bringing us one such as yourself to protect us and lead us into Ma'Alkin's most prosperous period. I am both honored and humbled to be in your shining presence this day.

"However, I come with worrisome news from my home. Those unscrupulous folk who sail the seas have brought a plight to our lands. There is one who goes by Hasani, and this scourge has stolen our crops, soiled our water, destroyed our villages, and worse yet, has defiled our women all in the name of his vile piracy. My brother and I have traveled far to beg you, our most beloved Pharaoh, please put a stop to these monsters."

It took a great deal of self-control to keep Zahir's brows from raising at Abukhar's impassioned speech. He didn't think the man had it in him to speak so eloquently. All the while, Hapu stood with hunched back, making him look small and meek in the face of the ruler of Ma'Alkin and his soldiers. Zahir made sure to soften his face and widen his eyes so as not to seem out of place amongst the other two.

"Please, beloved Pharaoh," Hapu began. "I have lost my job on the coast because of this man. His people have destroyed my fishing business and I can no longer provide for my family. My babies' cry because of their empty stomachs. My wife no longer eats, giving what meager meals we can scrape together to feed me and my little ones. We are all wasting away outside the jewel of Ma'Alkin's crown, Kul-El."

The pleas hung in their air, their sincerity ringing in every word. Zahir found himself surprised at the impact their entreaties held. If he hadn't been involved in creating the story, he would have believed that there truly was an issue plaguing the land. He knew the struggling villages, the small children wandering around with distended bellies and on the verge of succumbing to their hunger. Zahir knew those circumstances very well.

The pharaoh sat on his throne, his face a mask. As the silence stretched, Zahir hoped that Abukhar and Hapu would remain quiet. He didn't want the tension building up to destroy the imploration. After several long moments, a figure slipped out from the shadows and leaned over the pharaoh's shoulder, whispering into his ear. Zahir's breath caught in his throat, and it required every ounce of his resolve to keep his demeanor humble. He thanked the gods he no longer believed in that he didn't let out a gasp as he waited for Nefret to finish advising the pharaoh.

XXXIII

IT SEEMED LIKE AN ETERNITY before Nefret finally straightened up. Zahir observed her closely as her lips moved, tickling the pharaoh's ear as she whispered nonstop into it. He hoped she did not recognize him, but he doubted she would forget one of her own. Zahir held out on the off-chance that she didn't as it had been a long time since the two had been close together. By the time the high priestess finished her analysis and providing insight, the pharaoh shuffled in his throne, his chin now resting on his hands. When he spoke, his nasally voice echoed in the hall, drowning out the silence that permeated.

"You speak of disconcerting things," the Pharaoh Menkhe'n began. "However, none of what you speak is true. My advisor, the high priestess, has studied many things, and the gods have not spoken to her about such deplorable things."

"Please, my beloved Pharaoh," Abukhar begged. "You do not understand. There must be a mistake. I –"

"Are you saying that both our beloved Pharaoh *and* the gods are wrong?" Nefret's voice cut through the entreaty like a hot knife through fat. Her words bit at his rebuttal, silencing the man instantly.

"N-no, my lady," Hapu answered for his brother. "We were just saying that –"

"You were spreading lies," Nefret hissed.

Menkhe'n remained seated, a smug expression on his face as his priestess berated the three. Zahir felt his blood boil as he noted her haughty expression as she looked down upon the group. Their request fell on deaf ears, and if they wanted any chance at correcting this, he needed to speak up. Taking a step forward, Zahir bowed his head towards the man he wished only death.

"If it pleases, my most beloved Pharaoh," Zahir began, slowly raising his head until he met Menkhe'n's eye. Zahir made sure to deliberately speak to the pharaoh, ignoring Nefret and her influences behind the ruler. "Perhaps there has been a misunderstanding. It is possible for the message of the gods to be misinterpreted. A rare occurrence, but surely not unheard of."

To his satisfaction, the pharaoh leaned back in his chair. The silence that followed spoke volumes. He was listening. The small motion was almost overlooked. Abukhar and Hapu did not seem to notice the importance of the pharaoh's actions. The same could not be said about Nefret, however. The priestess glowered at the pharaoh from behind his back, her mouth tightening until her usually full lips drew into a thin line.

"By no means do I wish to impugn anyone, but I just hope to bring to light the travesties I have seen first-hand." Zahir began. Menkhe'n appeared to lean forward in his seat once more. "I am not from Kul-El. But I do travel here regularly. My family raises goats in Tel Amarna and we frequently bring them up and sell our meat in the bazaar. Our village hasn't been hit yet, but on my way to Kul-El, I saw the atrocities this man has wrought.

"Children roam the streets, their bellies bloated from hunger, the flesh hanging off their bones. I have a young daughter, and I fear this could be her future if we do not stop this."

Menkhe'n's hands now rested on his knees. His previous attempt at indifference now completely forgotten as he soaked in every word Zahir said. Two hundred years of mingling with the nobility had not been for naught. Zahir learned the dialect of the upper class, giving his words a sense of importance that a couple villagers from the outer cities couldn't convey. Hopefully, no one would question how a goat herder got to be so eloquent.

"And what would you have me do?" Menkhe'n asked, his eyes narrowing. "Send my soldiers out into the land to hunt for a pirate… On a wild chase to find someone who could be anywhere in Ma'Alkin?"

Taken aback by the pharaoh's angry tone, Zahir held up his hands in an attempt to appease the ruler. He had to act fast or else he may lose his opportunity.

"My beloved Pharaoh, something must be done…"

"Silence!" Menkhe'n roared, slamming his fist on the armrest of his throne. "The deaths of children, while sad, are not my concern."

"But my beloved," Zahir soothed, understanding where the pharaoh's anger came from. "The children of Ma'Alkin are yours. Imagine the delight of the gods if you were to save the children of our sacred land. I would dare say that it would earn you their favor. The Wadjet offers its protection to the pharaoh, and in return, he is to offer it to his people. Such is the power you wield, my beloved."

Menkhe'n leaned back in his throne once more. Through the shadows, Zahir could see the flurry of thoughts swirling in his mind. The pharaoh was conflicted, torn between the advice of his high priestess, his own internal conflict about his heir. Now was the time to let his words sink in. Zahir fought the urge to glance over at Nefret and check her reaction but failed. As his eyes roamed to hers, he saw a smile playing on her lips. Zahir felt a moment of panic grip him as the two locked gazes.

"You're right," Menkhe'n said after a lengthy silence. "It is my duty to protect my children with the gifts given to me by the gods. I can send word to my soldiers to keep an eye out for this Hasani. If he is a threat to those in the inlands, I can't imagine what damage he's wreaking on my coasts.

"Thank you for bringing me your concerns. You have done well to protect not only your families, but all of Ma'Alkin. May the gods bless you on your journey home."

A palpable relief washed over the three, most noticeably Hapu and his brother. A rivulet of sweat rolled down Abukhar's cheek, as he shared a celebratory glance with Hapu. Unlike his two companions, Zahir kept his eyes on the pharaoh and high priestess. Though their pleas succeeded and the pharaoh prepared to send some of Kul-El's soldiers out of the capital, something tickled the back of his mind.

A guard approached and ordered the three to follow him. Bowing to the pharaoh one final time, the three exited the hall in silence. The soundlessness of the audience chamber stifled the group once more. Not a soul let out so much as a cough as they walked past pillar after pillar. Only the sound of their feet hitting the smooth tile floor punctuated the uncomfortable quiet. In the antechamber, the soldiers flanking the doorway moved in front of it, preventing anyone from turning back.

The group continued on in silence. Zahir's mind raced, trying to figure out a way to slip away from the others to sneak into the library. He wondered if he would be able to leave the palace without any trouble now that he'd exposed his presence to Nefret.

As they left the antechamber and passed under the Wadjet Eye, Hapu let out a sigh of relief which quickly turned into a bark of laughter. Abukhar joined in, the guard cracking a smile as he elbowed Hapu. Zahir watched the three in bewilderment as the tension melted away.

"I can't believe we did it," Hapu breathed.

"Me neither," Abukhar added. "I thought we were done for."

"That priestess is really something. I don't think she was too happy." Hapu rubbed his face with his hands as he sped away from the audience chamber.

"She's a real viper," the guard replied. "You have to watch out for her."

"Thank you for pulling this off," Hapu said to Zahir, clapping the vampyre on the back. "If it weren't for you, we'd be dead."

Zahir hummed, still mulling everything over. While Hapu and the guard, the man who helped them earn their audience the day before, chatted casually to lighten the mood, Zahir prepared to break off from the group. He caught Abukhar's attention and gave a knowing look. The man nodded back, joining in the conversation. The group rounded several corners, the sun striking the garden in the center of the palace and shining off the little pond inside.

Flowers bent in the faint breeze, the leaves of the sycamore tree rustling over the golden sand.

The library neared, its gilded door frame coming into focus. Large paintings of Toth adorned both sides of the door, the glyphs carved into the gold leaf that circled the room's entrance. Straggling behind the group, Zahir slowed his gait, creating more distance between himself and the three. Ahead of him, Abukhar asked the guard a question, motioning with his hand behind his back for Zahir to break off. Without a word, Zahir slipped away from the ground and into the darkened room.

No light entered the library save for what little bit illuminated the hall he'd just come from. Keeping to the walls, Zahir continued forward, his vampire eyes allowing him to see into the darkest depths. The room was quite large, heading deep into the heart of the palace. His fingers traced along the shelves where countless scroll lay crammed into, the tightly wound papyrus feeling like leather to his touch. It seemed endless. At last, he managed to find a small space on a shelf where the scrolls were not nearly as dense, and in this section of the library he found a bit of candle sitting in a holder.

The little caverns on the walls that held the scrolls went from floor to ceiling and were all crammed full of rolled papyrus. A few tables were dotted in the middle of the room, burnt out oil lamps and opened scrolls sitting on the tables. A faint shadow danced on the wall from a lone oil lamp as he scanned the shelves looking for dates that would possibly help him identify which collection of parchment may be most helpful.

He went up and down the length of the room several times before he found a smaller shelf in the corner. There weren't as many rolled bits of papyrus in there, and the date carving was old and worn. He traced his fingers over the carvings as he did with all the others. Disappointed, he turned to walk away. None of the little scroll caverns had any information that would help him discern where he should even begin looking. There was too much to sift through and not enough time. He was about to leave when his fingers moved over another carving in the old wood. It wasn't very deep, but it was definitely added on purpose.

A faint serpentine creature was carved into the wood. Set or Mehen, he couldn't tell. But it was there. Excitement gripped him as he began pulling at the different scrolls, unfurling them to find the one he sought. His excitement turned to disappointment as the pile of rejected papyrus grew. The Scroll of Neith had to be there. All of his sources pointed to it being in the royal library.

"Damn!" he hissed as he rolled up the last one. "Where is it?"

The light on the wall went out, the oil-soaked linen having finally been consumed and he wasn't any closer to finding the scroll. Decades of talking to people, sifting through the folk tales and holy tales all over Ma'Alkin, all while staying to the shadows to avoid being noticed felt like a waste.

He wanted to scream and pound the wall, but he knew that had to wait. Nefret was still around.

Feeling the last remnants of hope within him deflate, Zahir realized that the library was probably a lost cause. As yet another potential source turned out to be a dead end, he decided it was time to leave. He'd stayed too long. Making his way out of the library, the sound of heavy footsteps approaching by the entrance gave him pause. Slipping further back into the shadows, Zahir tried to think of how long he'd been wandering around. The silhouette of the columns lining the halls and the trees in the garden ran down the mosaic floor, their elongated shape letting Zahir know that he'd spent much too much time in the library.

The footsteps passed by, the small collection of palace guards moving with a hurried step in the direction of the palace entrance, giving Zahir pause. If he could slip out between the papyriform columns he could avoid detection. Abukhar and Hapu could find their own way out of the palace.

"Hello my pet," a husky voice whispered into his ear.

Zahir's blood froze as a strong hand gripped his arm, the cool tip of a blade pressed between his shoulders. Silver. The dagger would be silver, the one bane of his people. With silver, he would have a hard time recovering from it, the cursed metal burning him once it penetrated his flesh. Or splintering bone if he were struck with her silver hammer. Nefret had plenty of toys to keep her monsters in line.

Nails, almost claw-like, dug into his skin as her hold tightened. The sickly-sweet aroma of the oils she rubbed over her body nauseated him as Zahir felt her close the distance between them until her soft body lightly pressed against his own. Memories of his rebirth came flooding back at that moment. Her scent, her delicately rough touch, and her voice all triggering the instant when his life was ripped away from him.

"I've missed you." He could hear the smile in her voice.

Zahir's body tensed and his arm twitched, as though he were going to try to twist out of her grip.

"Uh-uh," she warned, the sheer pleasure dripping from her tone. "Let's not do anything rash."

Her nails dug further into his arm. Zahir let out a grunt of pain as they turned into claws to move even deeper as she readjusted her grip. The tip of the blade got dangerously close to breaking flesh. Zahir could feel the burn from the effects of the silver spread through his spine. It must have actually pierced him.

"Why don't you come with me? I would love to know what you've been up to all these years."

"What do you want with me?" Zahir spat. "You have plenty of toys to play with."

"You've always intrigued me," she whispered, her lips tickling his ear. "Ever since I met you, you were not drawn to my vision. It held no allure to you. What is it you seek? I can give you everything – if you will let me."

His fingers morphed into claws as his fangs dropped down. Ignoring the pain, Zahir spun around, swiping his claws across Nefret's chest. The high priestess let out a yelp as she jumped back, bits of fabric from her dress ripping off as they got caught in his claws. Trails of blood ran down his arm from where she gouged him and Zahir licked them away. Her eyes flashed red in the wan light of the fading day, matching his own.

"I want no part of your games," he hissed.

Up until that point, Nefret had been hunched over in a half crouch, her body ready to spring away should he move to attack her once more. Her lip curled up in a snarl, her fangs exposed in the shadows. Now, she straightened up. Small dots of red beaded her chest where his claws managed to tear a bit of her flesh. Licking her own claws, she smirked at him as she cleaned off his blood. Slipping her dagger back into the sheath on her thigh under her dress, Nefret smoothed her hair, tucking a strand behind her ear.

"But I want you," she purred.

In the distance Zahir heard men shouting. Swiveling his head, Zahir checked the library entrance that now stood un-guarded behind him. In that instance, Nefret pounced. Her claws raked his ribs, drawing blood. A searing pain blos-somed as Zahir let out a growl, swiping at Nefret once more. The priestess danced out of the way, his claws only grabbing air. Nefret giggled as Zahir growled in frustration. Her body relaxed as she slipped into a defensive pose, her clawed hands up. More shouts echoed in the hallway, but Zahir ignored them. Springing into action, Zahir darted towards Nefret.

The two exchanged blows, their punches bringing out groans as they landed. Nefret danced around him, slicing his flesh with her claws and landing a few blows to his ribs. She also took a number of hits as well. A strike to the face split Zahir's lip and quickly filling his mouth with blood. As he spat out the blood, Zahir narrowed his eyes. The priestess proved to be frustratingly nimble and they moved through the library.

Switching to a more defensive posture, Zahir studied her body. His muscles ached from where her blows landed. A handful of cuts, mostly superficial caused small trails of blood to run down his body. He steadied his breathing as he observed Nefret closely. To her credit, Nefret mimicked his pose, her body ready to move at a moment's notice. The screams in the hall got louder, but Zahir blocked them out. If he lost focus, he would be in trouble.

The ground was slick under Zahir's feet as the lack of dust or dirt on the floor became even more evident. Shifting his weight, Zahir took a deep breath then attacked. Darting forward, Zahir feigned a strike to the shoulder. When Nefret moved to evade his attack, Zahir suddenly dropped, kicking his leg out and sweeping Nefret off her feet. The priestess let out a shriek as she dropped roughly to the ground. In an instant, Zahir was on top of her. His fingers wrapped around her throat, his knuckles turning white as he squeezed. Nefret's feet scrambled for purchase as she attempted to slip out from underneath him.

Zahir's blood pounded as he gazed at the panic on the priestess' face. Her full mouth was parted in a silent scream as she gasped for breath that would not come. His grip tightened as fear overtook him. Thoughts of Abukhar and Hapu being betrayed by their friend, leading to their capture, raced through is mind. Everything abruptly went black as an agonizing pain erupted at his temple. He dropped to the ground unconscious, a man standing behind him with a silver hammer clenched in his hand.

XXXIV

THE BLISTERING SUN caused Alexis' skin to sting. Angry red patches formed under the protective oil. Even it was no match for the Ma'Alkin sun. Rubbing his arm, Alexis forced himself to wait a little longer before making his move. Whips cracked as the foreman shouted orders to the slaves as they labored in the heat. Twenty or so strained against the ropes they pulled as they struggled to pull a large limestone towards the pyramid they were constructing. Massive stone statues of the gods lined the street, watching the efforts of the slaves.

The tip of the whip met the flesh of one of the slaves as they tugged against the ties, drawing a pained cry as the man dropped to his knees. The others in his group continued to pull on the ropes, ignoring the commotion around their stone. Most likely hoping that the ire of the foreman would not fall on them. The fallen man attempted to get to his feet to resume his work. The man with the whip shouted at the man, mocking him and his efforts.

The laborers were skin and bones, their ribs and pelvic bones protruding under the scant muscle they earned from their work. Alexis looked to see if the foreman was one of his kind, but couldn't be sure. He'd figured he'd better be extra cautious just in case. Pulling his attention from the construction of the pharaoh's final resting place, Alexis turned to the east.

A simple structure made from crumbling granite sat partially buried in the golden sands. A singular palm tree loomed over it, providing it with a modicum of shade. Nothing to afford the vampyre with any protection. Pulling his cloak low over his head, Alexis stuck his hand in his pocket and pulled out the bracelet he purchased from Mother Amunet. The gold sparkled in the sun, the Eye of Horus caught the light highlighting the carving in the metal. He slipped it onto his wrist, tucking the pouch back into his pocket before stepping into the open doorway. It was completely dark inside. A set of uneven stairs led down to the unknown depths. Checking his surroundings, Alexis tugged on his cloak once more and stepped into the granite structure.

The stale air hit him as he descended. Alexis wrinkled his nose in disgust at the putrid smell. His hand trailing the wall of the building as he walked. There was no railing or rope for him to grab onto, but he kept contact with the wall out of habit. A couple times he landed on a step, only to have a small chunk of it break away from under his foot. The sound of limestone striking limestone echoed into the cavernous room. After what felt like an eternity, the stairs leveled out. They wound deep into the earth making a sharp turn at one point as though he was being taken to another part of the structure.

A little way off, Alexis noticed a soft flickering inside the wall. Moving carefully to avoid triggering any traps in the pitch darkness, he inched his way towards the light. A small oil lamp sat in an alcove. Several pitchers of what smelled like oil sat next to it. Alexis' body tensed. Someone must come down here fairly often if they were leaving lit lamps and spare oil down here. A faint breeze startled him. It broke the stale air that he'd been breathing upon entering. It also confirmed to him that there was a second entrance. There was no way the wind would be this deep into the earth otherwise.

Taking the lamp from its spot, Alexis ventured further into the structure. The light flickered on the walls, his shadows taking on a sinister appearance. Glyphs were inscribed on the limestone walls, their message erased over time. Alexis took his time, examining the glyphs in hopes of deciphering the ancient texts. He noticed on several occasions that deep gouges marred a cluster of glyphs as though someone wanted to hide whatever was carved.

The text was difficult to read. Alexis found himself struggling to figure out one in every ten words. "Danger," "eternity," and "Dū-aat" popped up most frequently. There were also the names of a few gods, and the name of an ancient pharaoh, but Alexis wasn't able to read the name of the king. It was too faded during time. A sense of unease began to creep in.

"Where is Neith?" he murmured. "There's nothing here."

No mention of the goddess' name could be found. Tracing his fingers over the chunks of limestone cut out from the smoother section of the wall, Alexis closed his eyes as he tried to picture what had happened. A faint flicker coursed through him like a shock. Someone wanted to keep Neith's secrets within these walls. The wind blew through the passage, howling deeper in the tomb. Something beckoned him further.

Turning towards the entrance, Alexis paused. Evaline waited for him. His body twisted unconsciously, as though to leave.

I'm so close, he told himself. *She'll be safe for a little longer.*

The secret of creation, and with it, the secrets on how to become human once more, lay in the tomb. He had to find it. When he did, he could finally kill Estrie. Once he'd done that, he could undo the curse she'd placed on him and maybe live a quiet life with Evaline in Bord du Pétale.

XXXV

EVALINE'S STOMACH GROWLED AS she peeked through the window of an empty building. She'd managed to evade Lateef and his ilk; however, she hadn't eaten more than the apple and nuts she'd gotten from the kind merchant earlier. Coupled with her lack of sleep and the lingering effects of Alexis consuming her blood, and Evaline was getting weaker by the hour.

How long until I find my way out of here?

Kul-El lay in a valley, the sprawling sand dunes encircling the capital on all sides. With each passing hour, Evaline wondered if she'd ever find her way back to the coast. Pushing the uncertainty down, Evaline pressed on. With each step, her doubt bubbled closer to the forefront of her mind. The possibility of being trapped in Kul-El and forced into prostitution left Evaline feeling nauseous. It kept her going.

Now, she wandered through more residential looking streets. Evaline had no idea where she was supposed to go. She tried to follow the path of the sun, but the tall buildings made it difficult. There weren't many people walking around and her nerves were on high alert. A small crash resulted in Evaline letting out a yelp as she spun around. She cursed herself as a tabby ran out between from between a few barrels.

"Get yourself together," she hissed.

Though she tried to remain calm, something left her hackles up. The eerie sensation that someone was following Evaline. It had been that way for some time now. The feeling that someone was watching her, but being unable to see anyone kept Evaline on guard. Gathering her composure, Evaline continued her travels. No one peeked through windows or cracked doors. No one acknowledged her on the streets. The doll she'd picked up in the first house was clutched in her hand. Evaline found comfort in holding the little reed toy as she made her way through the city. The little doll would be a perfect gift to give her new niece or nephew upon her return – and gave Evaline a reason to keep pushing forward.

A light touch brushed against Evaline's arm as a soft voice croaked out something, possibly a question. Yanking her arm away, Evaline jumped, putting distance between herself and a frightened looking old woman. Blood rushed to Evaline's cheeks as she flushed a brilliant shade of red and stammered out an apology that she knew the woman would not understand. The woman took a few steps back from the babbling Evaline, confusion and fright etched into her heavily wrinkled face.

The woman said something in return, trying to put a kind look on her weathered face. More than one tooth was missing, the darkened hole in the woman's mouth evident as she spoke. Still, she maintained her distance from Evaline.

Taking a moment to soothe her nerves, Evaline studied the old woman. White hair that went down to her mid-back was tied in a loose tail. Her hands, which she used to try and help convey meaning with her words to Evaline, appeared gnarled like a tree trunk. Arthritis not only kept them curled in a perpetual claw but also gave her back a noticeable hump. She was unlike any person Evaline had ever seen in Ma'Alkin. In fact, Evaline didn't think she'd seen anyone near this woman's age apart from the kind merchant who fed her.

The woman inched forward, her claw-hand outstretched. Fighting the adrenaline that rushed through her, Evaline reached out and tentatively took the woman's hand. It was warm. She wasn't one of them. A smile crept over the woman's face and she turned, leading Evaline down a side street.

Evaline tensed, ready to pull herself free from the woman's grip, but the woman began babbling on in a cheerful manner, shooting Evaline her toothless grin on occasion as they wound through some side streets. The woman moved with a spritely step that Evaline didn't anticipate. Though she didn't struggle to keep up the pace, she couldn't help but feel like the woman might be leading her to a trap.

The woman led Evaline to a small alley blocked off by a mudbrick wall. A broken door exited into the alley. The woman disappeared into the home, beckoning Evaline to follow her with a crooked finger. Something inside Evaline told her to run, but instead she stood rooted to the spot. It didn't seem right. Popping her head out from the doorway, the woman beckoned her in. In her other hand, she held out a small clay cup of water, pointing inside the building as she spoke. Evaline could smell meat simmering in some sort of spice. Her mouth began to water, and her stomach rumbled at the scent. A wave of light-headedness rolled over her and Evaline's legs buckled.

I have to risk it, Evaline said to herself as her hunger took over. *If she's truly kind, perhaps she can help me get out of here.*

Taking a step forward, Evaline paused. Her body didn't want to go further, despite the hunger that ravished her. The primal fear that plagued her since she escaped Lateef and his brothel kept her adrenaline pumping and her nerves on edge. Evaline's stomach raged at her. If she was going to die, at least she would die with warm food in her belly.

Evaline forced herself to walk into the house after the elderly lady. Inside the home was surprisingly dark. It took only a few moments for her eyes to adjust, but Evaline couldn't push away the feeling of vulnerability that gripped her. Her muscles tensed, ready to run in case something went wrong. The smooth surface of the clay cup pressed into her hand was coupled with a gentle word from the old lady. A man's voice called out to the woman from another room. Evaline's blood ran cold, and she turned to flee. The clay cup in her hand fell to the ground with a crack, the water seeping into the floor.

The old woman grabbed Evaline's arm in her gnarled fingers, her eyes wide as she implored Evaline to stay. Unable to understand the woman, Evaline frantically pawed at the woman, swiping the aged hand off her. The man's voice called out once more, and he popped his head from around the corner. The door to the alley opened as Evaline finally managed to pry the old fingers off of her arm. The elderly woman stumbled backwards before losing her balance and falling. Hearing the shuffling steps draw neared, Evaline turned to leave.

"No, no, no," the man's voice cried out in Ma'Alkin. It was followed by a quick stream that Evaline could not understand.

Recognizing the word, Evaline glanced up. The familiar face of the kind old man from the Kul-El market raced to the old woman as fast as his wobbly legs could take him. He spoke to the elderly woman softly, helping her up and checking her for injuries as he pulled. The woman must have reassured him that she was fine because the man then turned his attentions back to Evaline. Holding up his hands to show they were empty, the man slowly crept towards her like he was approaching a stray.

Poised to flee, Evaline hesitated as the man beckoned her closer. Her body remained tense, adrenaline racing through her veins, but Evaline took a step back into the house. The man shut the door behind her before stooping to pick up the broken bits of clay.

"I'm sorry," Evaline said.

The man did not respond, returning his attentions to his wife instead. Guilt-ridden, Evaline followed him, slipping her arm around the older woman and helping her into the nearest chair. The old wooden legs creaked as the woman's body sank into the seat. The woman babbled away, patting Evaline's cheek in thanks. Her husband reappeared with two new cups of water for the women.

Evaline hesitated for a moment before taking a small sip. The cool water refreshed her almost immediately, the dust that caked her throat washing down with even that small gulp. The elderly couple did not pay her any mind, the old man fussing over his wife. Evaline's lips twitched up in a smile as she took another sip, both hands cupping the clay mug. It didn't take long before she finished the water as she watched the pair. The old man kissed his wife on the head and gave her a little pat on the cheek before returning to the other room.

"Wait!" Evaline called out.

The man paused, cocking his head as if he had a question for her.

"Thank you," she said. "I know you can't understand me, but thank you."

The old man's eyes twinkled at her like they had at the Kul-El market and he flashed her a crooked smile. He responded to her, his gentle voice reminding her of his kindness days before. She hoped that he and his wife meant well; she was too tired to run much more and her adrenaline vanished, leaving Evaline exhausted. A young girl walked by, asking him a question. Evaline pretended that the girl was his granddaughter visiting for a few days. When the girl spied Evaline, she darted behind her grandfather and stared at Evaline through wide, terrified eyes. He said something to her, but Evaline could barely hear it. Her head began to droop as sleep threatened to overtake her.

The girl inched out from behind her grandfather and said something, pointing to the reed doll in Evaline's hand. Slipping into the nearest chair, Evaline dropped the doll as her chin dropped to her chest. The last thing she saw was the little girl picking up the doll and hugging it tightly.

***

A painful thump to Evaline's head jarred her awake. Behind her, the chair she'd been sleeping in scooted away, dust marking its trail. The little girl peered around the corner, reed doll in hand to see Evaline laying on the floor in a heap. Her childish giggle filled the room and caused her grandmother to see what happened. Rubbing her temple, Evaline sheepishly tried to stammer out an explanation, aware of the pool of drool that built up on the front of her dress. The old woman crinkled her eyes as a toothless grin spread across her face. She helped Evaline up, leading her to another room where Evaline was hit with the tantalizing aroma of spiced meat and vegetables.

Her stomach growled angrily, clenching as if to accentuate her hunger. Grandmother guided Evaline into a chair at the table where Grandfather placed a bowl with beans in front of her. Kebabs rested on the rim of the bowl, the skewers barely visible between the chunks of goat and vegetables. Evaline tore into the meal like a ravenous wolf. Meat juices dripped down her chin, but she just wiped them off with the back of her hand. Grandfather and Grandmother sat at the table while the young girl ran off to another room.

As the meal continued, food magically appearing after finishing what was in front of her, Evaline found herself slowing down and savoring the rich flavors of the food. She must have gone through three sets of skewers and two bowls of beans before her stomach felt full to bursting. Setting the spoon down, she took a sip of water and leaned back in her chair. Grandmother cleared the table while Evaline relaxed.

"Thank you," Evaline said, hoping one of them would understand her.

Grandfather gave her a gentle smile before lighting his pipe. The heavy scent of the tobacco filled the room with a cloud of smoke. It was not the same acrid smell that nearly choked her at Lateef's hideout. This tobacco had a sweet scent that she couldn't quite place.

Grandmother hobbled over to another room and lit some of the oil lamps. She then sat down in a chair next to her husband and grabbed his hand while he puffed away on his pipe. The two sat in silence together while the young girl played with the reed doll.

Maybe someday I'll find love like this, Evaline thought with a smile.

The four sat in contented peace for an unknown period of time. The shadows on the wall lengthened as the sun moved closer to the horizon. Evaline found herself dozing off in her chair several times. It reminded her of cozy nights with her family. Mother would be sewing something, maybe knitting one of them a new sweater, and Father would read a book next to the hearth. Evaline hadn't really known her own grandparents too well, but she imagined this is what a weekend at their home would feel like.

Her eyes snapped open at the thought. The little girl had gone to another part of the house with the doll some time ago. Grandfather loaded up his pipe with a little more tobacco, his eyes closing in pleasure as he took another long puff. Grandmother leaned back in her chair as she slept. Turning back to Grandfather, the old man appeared quite relaxed. His eyes remained closed and his hands rested on his thigh.

I'll have to give Mama a big hug when I get home, Evaline thought as her eyes drooped once more. *Maybe I can offer to go to live with Amalie to help her with the baby. I miss her so much.*

Cracking open her eye, Evaline noticed that Grandfather had fallen asleep in his chair. His pipe dangled between his slightly parted lips, not quite tipping onto his chin, but getting dangerously close.

I can't put them in danger, she thought as she looked at the peaceful couple. *If I hurry, I can still cover a lot of ground. I think I can reach the edge of Kul-El by tomorrow.*

Slipping out of the chair, Evaline crept into the cooking area. She found a small cloth in a bowl that she whipped out. Filling the cloth with figs, melon, and whole wheat bread that she found in the cooking area, Evaline also managed to fit a few kebabs into her makeshift sack.

Water, she told herself.

Rummaging through the cooking area, Evaline found a bottle filled with beer. Dumping out the amber liquid, she refilled it with water from the little cistern by the window. She hated robbing these people who had been nothing but kind to her, but Evaline did not want to take any chances.

"I'm sorry," she whispered.

Carrying her sack and the bottle, Evaline made her way to the back door. The pair rested comfortably in their chairs, the pipe now having fallen on the floor. Tobacco leaves littered the ground, the burnt bits now smothered out. The little girl was nowhere to be found. Evaline hoped she slept in her room somewhere. Hopefully the doll would be enough to pay for what she was taking from this family.

Placing her hand on the latch, shame and fear hit her at the same time. She looked over at the slumbering couple, silently apologizing for her actions. Would they report her to the authorities? She hoped not. If the city soldiers began looking for her it would be all over. Slipping the latch free, Evaline gently pushed open the door.

"Hello, beautiful."

Standing in front of her, Lateef pushed her back into the home. The other door burst open in a roar of splinters and wood shards, startling the sleeping couple. In another room, the groggy voice of the young girl could be heard calling out to her grandparents.

"Imagine finding you again," Lateef smirked. "Did you miss me?"

The elderly man stood, stammering out a question. Behind him, a younger man, not much older than Evaline, pushed him back down in the chair with a bark. His wife sputtered out something, earning her a smack to the head. Grandmother yelped as she covered her head with her feeble arms. Her husband attempted to comfort her, only to be yanked back by the man.

"Leave them alone," Evaline gasped as Lateef grabbed her arm roughly.

A soft voice squeaked out something that caught Grandfather's attention. He said something to her, and she turned to head back to her room. Lateef then said something to his partner. The elderly couple brought their hands together, Evaline imagined begging for their granddaughter's safety, but Lateef ignored them.

"Please," Evaline begged. "They've done nothing wrong."

"Wrong," he hissed. His eyes glinted red in the low light. Evaline noticed how his teeth elongated into sharpened points. "They helped you."

Issuing a command to his partner, Lateef squeezed Evaline's arm, digging his nails into her flesh and causing her to cry out in pain. He pulled her in close and spun her around, wrapping his arms around her slim frame. His partner shot Evaline a wicked grin before slitting the throats of both the old man and woman. It happened so quickly that neither had time to react. Their bodies fell to the ground as blood poured from their wounds. Evaline shrieked in horror as she watched the blood pool around the now lifeless bodies.

"Don't hurt her!" she cried as she struggled against Lateef's hold. "Please! Take me. Leave her!"

She could hear Lateef chuckle in her ear, but he didn't say a word as his partner sauntered off in the direction where the little girl had gone. Tears streamed down Evaline's face as she fought against Lateef, but he was too strong. A tiny scream ripped the air, but was quickly silenced. A primordial shout echoed in the house as Evaline lost all feeling in her legs. She began cursing Lateef and his people, wishing death and pain upon them for all eternity. Lateef just watched her as she struggled in his arms, her body hanging limply. Her nails tore into his flesh, drawing small drops of blood.

"You're a feisty one," Lateef smirked. "I know what you need."

"I'll fucking kill you!" she snarled. "The last thing you'll see before you die is me."

A dark cloud crossed over Lateef's face. A muscle twitched in his temple, and he tightened his hold on her.

"I look forward to that day," he said softly, his tone deadly.

Falling to the floor with a thud, Evaline attempted to regain her footing. Her legs did not want to work, but she continued to fight. At last, she managed to make it to her feet. The younger man stood in the hallway, watching her vain struggle against Lateef. He asked Lateef a question, his head tilting as he spoke. Remembering her water, Evaline grabbed the bottle from the floor and smashed it against Lateef's head. His partner cried out in surprise, moving quickly to grab her. Lateef shouted a command, staying the man's actions. Holding the broken shards, Evaline jabbed at Lateef with the sharp edges.

A piece of the glass embedded itself into Lateef's arm. He winced in pain but did not make a sound. Lateef grabbed her hand and pulled out the jagged piece of glass from his flesh. Evaline trembled at his strength. Without another word, Lateef struck her on the head. Instantly, Evaline's world went black.

XXXVI

Darkness greeted Zahir as he opened his eyes. His head throbbed from the blow in the library. He raised his hand to touch the back of his head and found that he was shackled. The heavy cuffs sank into his wrists, limiting his movement. Zahir tried to readjust himself so he could try to sit up, but his vision swam, and he almost passed out. The pain in his head left him feeling nauseous and he slumped back over. Heavy gasps filled the blackened room. Zahir steeled himself to lift his arm, the cuffs cutting into his flesh and burning him. A bitter laugh scraped his lips.

"Silver. That bitch!"

Pushing through the pain, Zahir touched his face and the back of his head. A wet spot left his hair matted down.

His labored breathing was the only sound in his prison. Closing his eyes to try to help the nausea subside, Zahir relaxed onto the floor. His fingers traced small circles on the ground. Tiny grains of sand lay in the space between the smooth stones that made up the floor. His fingers pushed the sand around, following the shape of one of the rocks. They appeared to be as big as his hand with a few cracks spidering through, and not the delicate pieces of mosaic that he'd traversed earlier. So not everything in the palace was perfectly maintained.

A groan escaped Zahir as a particularly sharp throb spiked through his head. It felt as though someone squeezed his head in a vice. He wondered if his skull was cracked from the silver. There had been a lot of blood around the wound. The cool ground and smooth stones helped soothe Zahir's pain and the throbbing in his head gradually subsided. His body didn't ache as much as he thought it would, and he even managed to run his hand over parts of his body.

The wounds he'd received from Nefret in the library were not as bad as he first thought. His ribs no longer burned, but they did have a dull pain where her claws cut deep. The rest appeared to be more superficial. Taking a chance, Zahir wiggled his lower half of his body. Nothing. That gave him hope. Lifting his arms once more, not higher than his chest, Zahir was relieved when he didn't feel a wave of nausea hit him. Just his head. If he were careful, he could gather enough strength to escape. He just needed to break free of his shackles.

The cuffs around his wrist didn't allow for much room for movement. The chains also made it difficult as they were quite heavy, but Zahir still managed to inch them around different parts of his body. The links clinked together, echoing in the empty room, as he discovered he could lift his hands over his head after several agonizingly long minutes. If he could just get a little rest, he might be able to fight through the throbbing in his head and break free.

The creak of a door rang out in the room followed by footsteps on the worn stones alerted Zahir that someone was coming. It wasn't Nefret, the steps sounded too heavy. A small lamp hovered in the air, bobbing with every step. Feigning unconsciousness, Zahir let his body go limp and closed his eyes. The fetid stench of opium permeated the still air, making his eyes water.

"Wake up," a deep bass said gruffly. "I know you're faking it."

With a smirk, Zahir opened his eyes and brought his knees to his chest. He knew that voice anywhere and would not give Lateef the satisfaction of knowing that he was as injured as he was. Ignoring the pain in his head, Zahir managed to reposition himself to a sitting position, leaning his back against the wall. In the flickering light, the shadows illuminated his eyes. There was something in there that put Zahir on edge; a smugness that led him to believe that the corrupt man knew something important.

"What do you want?" Zahir drawled. "Can't you see I'm resting?"

Lateef chuckled. "How's your head?" A wicked gleam flashed across his face, visible even in the wan light.

Cocking his head to the side in mock consideration, Zahir paused, drawing out the silence. The glint on Lateef's face switched from arrogant to annoyed. The change happened surprisingly quick, even to Zahir. Pressing his luck, Zahir waited a few seconds longer as if he were pondering the answer.

"Did you hit me?" Zahir asked, changing the direction of the conversation. "That wasn't very nice."

"You fucking dog," Lateef spat. "You're not as powerful as you believe. The High Priestess decided to use better men after your failure."

"Who would've thought I could piss you off so easily?" Zahir replied. "Nefret must really have trained you well."

The large man's body twitched as though he wanted to strike Zahir but thought better of it. A vein throbbed in the man's temple, and he gnashed his teeth, but he managed to control himself. Instead, he took a step forward, squatting down so that he was eye-level with Zahir. The wicked look returned to his face, and he spat at Zahir's feet. There were no bars trapping Zahir, only the shackles on his wrist. Leaning in, Lateef slapped Zahir hard, splitting his lip and drawing a trail of blood that dribbled down his chin. Grabbing Zahir's face roughly in his hand, Lateef twisted Zahir's head side-to-side as he took in the injuries. Zahir's chains clinked as he raised his hand towards Lateef's.

"No," Lateef said softly, dangerously. "You have no power over me. You are weak. If only you accepted who you are, accepted Nefret's gift. You could have been so much more. Pity." Zahir's head snapped back and his body collapsed under the force of Lateef's strike. His mind swam at the sudden, harsh action. The smug expression returned. "See?"

A groan escaped Zahir's lips as he struggled to push himself up to the sitting position once more. A swift kick to his back with the bottom of Lateef's boot sent him sprawled out on the floor once more. Coughing from the blood filling his mouth and the trouble breathing, Lateef chuckled once more and left. His heavy gait quickly leaving the darkened room.

"By the way," Lateef called over his shoulder from the opposite side of the room. "We have your little mouse."

Zahir waited until the door closed before attempting to return to leaning against the wall. His breathing came out labored as he spat out the blood filling his mouth.

"Damn bastard," he muttered.

Bringing his hand to his injured side, he felt a warm liquid on his fingers. Lateef had reopened the wound, and it began bleeding once more.

"Damn."

His mind turned to Evaline. The way Lateef said it led him to believe that they hadn't killed her outright. They may have brought her to Nefret which was the same as a death sentence. Why hadn't Lateef kept her for one of his own?

"Bastard loves pissing me off," he muttered. "Joke's on him."

Raising his hand, Zahir unstoppered the cork from the little bottle he'd slipped off of Lateef. Hoping his intuition was correct, Zahir brought the bottle to his lips and downed its contents. The tangy taste of blood flowed down his throat. It wasn't a magic elixir that would heal him, but with all of the blood Zahir had lost, this little bit would help. A constant dull throb pulsed in his skull. When he shifted even slightly, the ache spiked, sharp, blinding jolts that threatened his head in two. He wasn't sure how much more he could take.

Staring at his hands in the utter darkness, Zahir wondered how he was going to break his shackles. The chains didn't feel as heavy now that he had a little snack. A true feeding would do him wonders. The chains clinked as he shook his hands up and down, searching for a weak spot. He didn't find anything, however.

He pulled on the chains until he met resistance. They were tethered to the floor. If he could only gain proper leverage, he might be able to pull them out of the ground. Running his hands along the floor, Zahir found the spots where the shackles went into the floor. There was a small spot between the worn stones where they were buried into the earth. The stakes were encircled by a group of stones.

"Damn," he muttered once more.

Zahir took a moment to compose himself and steel his nerves. Then with a sudden movement, he forced his left thumb into the palm of his hand, breaking the finger and giving himself enough room to slip his hand out from the cuff. He grunted in pain before attempting to reposition his thumb so it could heal properly until he had a chance to find a doctor. Straightening up, Zahir had to hunch over because the chains didn't go very high. This made it more difficult. Spreading his legs until he was in a wide stance, Zahir cradled his right in his left and pulled with all of his might. At the same time, he pushed himself up with his leg, yanking the stake clean out of the earth.

Checking the stake, Zahir was disappointed to find that it wasn't silver. He wouldn't have a weapon to use should the need arise. Placing it under his foot, Zahir pulled his arm once more. The chains snapped from the force of his movements, leaving only the cuff around his wrist. He'd deal with that later.

***

Peeking out from behind the door, Zahir slipped into a dank passageway. Oil lamps flickered every few feet, providing enough light for him to see by as he walked quietly. He controlled his step in an effort to minimize the noise as his feet hit the stone. There weren't a lot of doors in the passage giving Zahir a moment of panic. Would they keep Evaline up with the main prisoners? Part of him hoped that they would. It would be much better if they flayed her with the whip instead of leaving her to Nefret's devices.

Time stretched for an eternity as Zahir crept slowly through the passage. Every time he found a door, he pressed his ear to the wood, listening intently for any sign of life. Each time, no sound could be heard and he moved on. After what felt like a day, Zahir ran into the end of the passage. With nowhere to go, he turned around and inched his way back the way he came. The only bright spot he could find was the blood he'd consumed helped combat the pain from his head wound.

After another agonizingly slow journey, Zahir spotted a bright patch of light in the otherwise dim passage. It drowned out the light from the oil lamps that lined the walls and bathed the surrounding area in a warm glow. Cursing his luck, Zahir accepted that he would not find Evaline right now and vowed to come back after he'd had a chance to recover. As he neared the light, he noticed that it came from a stairwell. He'd found an exit.

Just as Zahir approached the bottom of the stairs, he heard the heavy footsteps of someone descending. He was too far from the nearest door to slip into a room, and even if he ran, the unknown held the possibility of being worse than what approached. Mustering up his strength, Zahir let his fangs drop and his claws grow. The element of surprise was his only chance. The rancid scent of opium proceeded Lateef and bringing a smile to Zahir's face. Slipping back into the shadows, he waited for the bastard to come closer.

As soon as Lateef's foot stepped onto the bottom step, Zahir sprung. Lateef let out a cry as Zahir latched onto him, sinking his teeth into the muscle between the neck and shoulder. Zahir tore at the muscle, hoping to render the arm useless. At the same time, he sunk his claws into the man's chest and neck, wrapping Lateef in a tight hug. Once the surprise wore off, Lateef reached over his shoulder and grabbed Zahir by the scruff of his neck. The corrupt man's strong hands dug into Zahir's back, tearing muscle and sinew. Zahir dragged his fangs through Lateef's muscle as he cried out in pain before being pried off by the larger man.

Blood poured from the wound on Lateef's shoulder and down his front. Drops landed on the floor, shining crimson in the warm light of the stairwell. Zahir struggled to remain upright, his side aching and head throbbing. His vision fuzzed as he fought to regain his breath.

"Is that all you got?" Lateef asked.

Drawing his arm back, he landed a punch to Zahir's sternum. Zahir screamed in pain as he felt a few of his ribs snap. His right leg buckled, bringing him to his knee. Taking advantage of Zahir's momentary weakness, Lateef pounced. The two exchanged punches, several of them resulting in grunts of pain from either side. While Lateef was powerful, Zahir had one advantage – he was nimble. Forcing himself to react, Zahir managed to slip between a few of the punches, causing Lateef's fist to slam against the stone of the passageway.

As their fight progressed, they moved deeper into the passageway. Their shadows moved in an intricate dance as they ducked and dodged blows. Zahir could feel his strength giving way as his vision swam once more. Drawing upon his dwindling energy, Zahir succeeded in dipping under a vicious swipe of Lateef's claws. He felt the air rustle his hair as the claws traveled through the air. Using the moment while Lateef was off-balance, Zahir launched himself forward, his claws raking the larger man's thigh and sinking his teeth into his pelvic region.

Zahir was rewarded with a shriek as he ripped the sinew of Lateef's thigh, effectively severing the man's hamstring in the process. Blows rained down on Zahir's head, striking the injured spot repeatedly. Blinking in and out of consciousness, Zahir pulled his hand from Lateef's thigh and raked his claws down the man's chest. He then bit Lateef's side, making sure to get as deep as he could next to the ribs. Lateef cried out in pain once more, halting his barrage as he grasped at Zahir's hands. With one final move, Zahir slammed his fist into Lateef's groin, caused the man to howl in pain as he doubled over.

Taking the opportunity to flee, Zahir hobbled over to the stairwell and began climbing. Each step was agony. His head throbbed, his vision spun, and he gasped for breath. Finally, he reached the top. A mosaiced floor lined with papyriform columns greeted him. The halls were bathed in the natural light of night, a small beam from the moon providing some illuminance. Blood dripped from his body as

Zahir staggered towards the closest column. He hoped he would be able to squeeze through the sides and escape into the darkness.

As he neared the pillar, a blow to the back of his head caused his vision to go black. Zahir dropped to the ground without so much as a grunt.

XXXVII

INCENSE HUNG HEAVY in the room as the candles flickered, bringing a wan light to the otherwise darkened room. Several men stood off to the side, chanting in low baritones. Evaline tried to lift her head but could barely get it up. Her vision swam, her head throbbing with a dull pain from Lateef's attack. How could she have not realized he was one of them. Evaline recalled his cold body on hers once more and cursed herself for not recognizing sooner. She could have saved the old couple by running away sooner.

Attempting to push herself up onto her elbow, Evaline quickly found her arms and legs were tied down. A strangled cry broke free from her lips as she looked down and saw herself bound to a worn stone slab in only a thin shift like she would wear under her normal dresses. Where embarrassment would normally bring shame to her face, her heart raced in fear as she pulled on the ropes that tightly bound her.

On the ground, a bloodied Zahir was propped up by silver chains. His head lolled to the side and is eyelids fluttered, as though he were going in and out of consciousness. Trickles of blood ran down his face and out the corner of his mouth. His hair was matted to the side of his head with dried blood and his shirt was stained as well. It didn't look good.

Four canopic jars and a collection of ushabti caught the flickering light. The little figures lined up in front of the jars. Both the jars and the figures were faded, the last remnants of their paint peeling away and leaving the clay of the jars exposed. Though she was tied, Evaline thought that she could make out the faces on the jars and figures. The detail was extraordinary. Nefret must have preserved them well for the small intricacies to still be visible.

"I see you're awake now, my sweet."

Evaline started as the husky voice announced the arrival of a beautiful woman. Her long, ebony hair flowed over her shoulders, delicate golden beads breaking small sections off from the rest of her hair. A crimson dress barely covered her perfect figure. On her chest, a scarab necklace rested, occasionally sparkling as it caught the flicker of one of the candles. In the background, the chanting got louder.

"How?" Evaline croaked. Her mouth was so dry, but she could still taste the blood.

"It pays to have eyes in the right places," the woman purred.

Noticing how Evaline's eyes darted from Zahir to herself, a smile spread across the woman's face. Her eyes sparkled.

"What did you do to Zahir?" Evaline asked, her voice rising in panic.

"Ah," she said softly. "It's so sweet how you worry for this traitor." Shooting a glare towards the bloodied man, the woman rearranged her face into a pleasant smile once more. "I'm Nefret," she added, touching her chest as she introduced herself.

Evaline felt a surge of panic shoot through her.

She's the one Alexis mentioned, Evaline realized. Her conversation with Alexis on the outskirts of the capital came flooding back to her from some corner of her mind. *The one who created the vampyres of Kul-El.*

Nefret glanced over at the barely conscious vampyre, his beaten body barely breathing. A small twinkle flashed on her face. The priestess asked a question to someone Evaline couldn't see. Lateef's name was mentioned several times as the two shared a quick conversation.

"It seems as though I should be asking Zahir," Nefret mused. "Seems he's driven away my dim-witted soldier."

From her position, Evaline noticed the dark look that crossed the priestess' face as she spoke of Lateef. It marred the beauty from her perfectly chiseled face. "No matter," Nefret continued. "I'll deal with that fool later. For now, I have more important matters to attend to."

The way Nefret said the last part sent shivers down Evaline's spine. She couldn't pinpoint what bothered her, but Nefret gave off an energy that truly frightened her. A thousand lifetimes shown in Nefret's eyes – the wisdom of the gods hid behind those beautiful lashes.

"I have lived many lives," Nefret said, her finger tracing Evaline's lips as she walked in front so Evaline no longer had to crane her neck. "I have seen more things than anyone could ever dream of. I have studied more than the most learned scholar. And," her eyes roved over Evaline's body, "I have been blessed to learn many tongues. It's been a while since I've had a woman before me."

"Stop," Zahir murmured, slurring his words as his head dropped. "Leave."

A light, bell-like chuckle erupted from Nefret's lips as she turned to the chained vampyre. She issued an instruction the soldiers guarding the door, and Evaline heard them marching out of the room, their sandals slapping the ground with each step. She wondered what Nefret told them. She didn't know how many people were in the room, but between the chanters, the priestess, and the semiconscious Zahir, Evaline didn't think anyone else remained.

What was going to happen that the priestess didn't want the soldiers seeing?

A tingle on her thigh turned Evaline's attention to the priestess. Nefret traced her fingers along the inside of Evaline's thighs, causing more tingling and bringing a flush to her cheeks. Evaline tried to move her legs, but found she was bound too tightly to move more than an inch.

"Stop," Evaline begged, her voice quivering. "Please, just let me go."

Nefret licked her lips, her hand slipping up under the shift. Before Evaline could say anything, Nefret began an incantation. A silver dagger, previously unnoticed, was brought to Nefret's chest as she closed her eyes in concentration. Together, Nefret and the group of men raised their voices in a fervent cry to some unknown entity. Evaline felt chills coarse through her as her vision slowly faded to black around the periphery.

What is she doing?

Evaline's heart hammered in her chest so loud that she almost thought the others could hear it as well. The way their chanting picked up as soon as she heard it echoing in her head had her nearly convinced. A heavy thump sounded somewhere behind her, and Evaline almost imagined that she heard a low growl near her ear. Nefret's red-stained lips parted, revealing her white fangs. Seeing the priestess in her true form caused Evaline's heart to skip a beat. Nefret leaned over Evaline, her breasts rubbing against Evaline's, and pressed her finger to Evaline's lips.

"Hush now, my sweet. It will all be over soon."

"Why are you doing this?" Evaline asked, tears beginning to run down her cheeks.

"Because," Nefret said. "This is the only way to save you. But first, you must show that you are strong enough for the gift."

Meeting Evaline's gaze, something flashed in the priestess' eyes. For the briefest of moments, Evaline almost thought that the woman was human. Though fleeting, Evaline saw the young nineteen-year-old girl hidden inside the ageless woman.

"You remind me of myself," she muttered, her voice softer and her eyes no longer cruel. "When I was your age, I too had to go through these indignations at the hand of the pharaoh's jackals. We all must prove our strength if we're to destroy those bastards." In almost a whisper, Nefret added, "They stole my Essam."

The sparkle of tears rimming Nefret's eyes in the flickering light caught Evaline by surprise and pulled at the strings of her heart. She could see the pain behind the mask of indifference that had been carved from so much pain. A moment later, that young girl hiding inside Nefret from countless centuries before disappeared and were replaced with the cold, powerful woman Evaline first met.

Black tendrils clouded Evaline's periphery as the chanting voices became one. The flames of the candles flickered in some unseen breeze. Another low growl sounded near Evaline's head. Craning her neck, she couldn't see anything. To her surprise, her fear did not grow as curiosity got the better of her. Nefret gave a passionate cry, catching Evaline's attention once more, the priestess' eyes closing as she clutched the dagger to her chest.

And then there was silence.

It hung heavy in the air, suffocating Evaline as she found herself struggling for breath. Her heart's frantic pounding echoed in the room. Anticipation filled Nefret's face, as though she could hear Evaline's heart as well. The priestess' teeth shone in the darkness as though something answered her call.

Running her fingers under the shift once more, Nefret found Evaline's sensitive spot. Her fingers played on the outside for a moment before slipping inside. Goose flesh prickled on Evaline's skin as the priestess' touch electrified her in a way she did not want. Her fingers moved with a purpose, searching for the proper spot. Evaline found herself aroused, her body reacting to the unwanted touch. Nefret then bent over and kissed Evaline deeply.

Soft moans escaped Evaline as Nefret's fingers found what they searched for. Evaline tried to stop, but she couldn't help it. Soft chanting could be heard in the background along with the still echoing beat of her heart. As the beating grew louder, Nefret stopped kissing Evaline. Instead, she turned her attention to below the shift. Evaline's body bucked up as Nefret's tongue flicked inside. The two women began moaning as the priestess pleasured both of them. Evaline's body clenched rapidly in response to the violation and her body's juices leaked from her, staining the inside of her legs. Nefret's tongue lapped up the inside of her thighs before returning to where it had just been. Throughout it all, the beating grew louder, and the chanting stopped. Evaline thought she heard shuffling between her gasps, but all she could think of what was about to happen. Nefret had said it would all be over soon.

Suddenly, everything stopped. Nefret let out a primordial shriek as the sound of her body slamming into the wall broke the rhythmic beating that echoed in the room. Evaline let out a shuddering gasp as she felt fingers working at untying the ropes that bound her. By the time she was free, the figure was gone. Sitting up, Evaline saw two bodies tangled together in the darkness. The glint of claws and fangs sparkled in the light of the flames as they moved faster than Evaline could even see.

As she slid off the stone dais and her feet touched the cold stone floor, Evaline tried to find something to hold for protection. The silver dagger Nefret planned to use in whatever unholy ritual they were engaged in lay forgotten on the ground. Slowly, so as not to draw the attention of the raging figures, Evaline grabbed the dagger and crept towards the door behind her, still in a crouch. Alexis' body slammed into the stone where Evaline had just been, blood running from his mouth and his shirt torn in several places.

With a shriek, Evaline dived out of the way, tumbling to the ground as Alexis' hand pushed her. Nefret's clawed hands pounded into the stone dais, cracking the ancient stone from the force of her strike. The priestess' hair flew out behind her as she attacked. The vampyress' eyes blazed red as she let out a growl of frustration at having missed her target.

Evaline pushed herself up, her palm pressed against her temple. The floor tilted beneath her, her vision swimming until she caught her balance on shaky legs. When her hand came away wet, Evaline blinked down at the smear of red across her palm. Her heart froze. Standing not more than a few feet away from her, Nefret had her gaze locked in on Evaline. The priestess' perfectly sculpted features were marred with deep gauges and blood. Her red dress was tattered from Alexis' strikes. Yet she wasn't bothered by any of it. Her full lips broke into a feral smile, her elongated canines catching the light from the lamps in an ominous way. Nefret was a predator on the hunt.

Stalking forward, Evaline's heart hammered in her chest, her mind shouting at her legs to move, and her body remaining perfectly rooted to the spot. Nefret licked her lips, her tongue sliding over her fangs. Evaline trembled as she frantically tried to unlock her body. Tears poured down her face as she stared death in the face. A blur slammed into the priestess as she prepared to pounce.

A stream of curses spewed forth from Nefret's mouth as she scrambled to her feet. Standing in front of Evaline, Alexis hunched over, breathing heavily as he faced the priestess. Behind Nefret, Zahir struggled to push himself up into a kneeling position. Agony lined his face as he inched his way off the ground. Nefret shot the injured vampyre an amused glance before kicking him in the ribs. Zahir let out a strangled cry as he collapsed to the ground.

"Stay down, my pet," Nefret purred, her sweet voice a stark contrast to her dark appearance. "I'll deal with you later."

The priestess then turned her attention back to Alexis. A smirk curled her lips as she took in the battered vampyre. She clicked her tongue in mock pity, her face returning to its usual composure as her body tensed to attacked.

"You're Estrie's?" Despite the question, there was no mistaking the acknowledgement of possession in the statement.

Alexis' body went rigid at the priestess' words. His eyes narrowed as he glowered at her, his clawed hands twitching as though he wanted to throttle her. Questions raced into Evaline's mind as she attempted to figure out the twisted dynamics she'd managed to get herself pulled into. The silver dagger dropped to the ground with a clatter, the sound somehow muted in the intense silence.

"Shame really," Nefret continued. "I'll have to return you to her a lifeless corpse. You could have had so much if you didn't get dragged down by my little pet here." Her head tilted towards the still struggling Zahir who coughed up blood as he pushed himself up. His muscles shook from his exertions. "No matter. The gods have made their decree."

With a screech, Nefret launched into an attack on Alexis. Dipping down, Alexis rolled onto his back, pushing with his legs as Nefret's body crossed over his and kicking her into the air. A pained moan escaped the attacking priestess as his shoes struck her chest and sent her flying. Alexis rolled over his shoulder and landed on his feet in a crouch. Nefret landed on the ground in a heap. Before she could move, Alexis raced over and clamped down on her neck, his claws digging into her chest. Nefret shrieked in pain as his fangs ripped into her flesh.

"Get off!" she screamed.

Her hands flailed wildly as she slashed at Alexis. Blood sprayed through the room staining the walls as she ripped Alexis' flesh like a wild cat. Nefret found his face and raked her claws from top to chin. Alexis cried out as her claws went over his eyes, his fangs releasing Nefret's neck. Blood poured from his face, his eyes closed in pain. Using the break in his attack to her advantage, the priestess spun around and slammed Alexis into the cracked stone dais.

His hands released from her chest at the force of the strike. Quicker than Evaline could follow, Nefret's claws wrapped around Alexis' neck. His eyes snapped open. His body was shredded by Nefret's attacks, drawing a wild smile back onto her face. The priestess' lips brushed against

Alexis' cheek as she licked the blood from his face. A soft groan escaped her tongue darted around the corner of his mouth.

"You know, my husband was killed on this same table right before Estrie found me," she said slowly. "They tore his essence from his body and placed them in canopic jars without properly honoring the gods – leaving me to search for him over many lifetimes. They stole my Essam from me, just like I will steal you from Estrie." Forcing Alexis' head up, Nefret added, "And then I'll do the same to your two friends."

Evaline scooted backwards in terror. Alexis let out a gurgle as Nefret squeezed her nails into his neck, her fingers looking to tear the muscles within. He stared at her with panicked eyes, his body struggling against the priestess' misleading strength. Alexis swiped at her hand, his claws making gauges in her flesh, which Nefret ignored. Evaline tried to push the image out of her mind, hoping that it was all a bad dream as she let out small, panicked gasps. Blood ran down Nefret's neck and onto Alexis.

The blood pooled onto the dais in a dark puddle before slowly dripping onto the floor. Alexis' eyes fluttered as he began to lose consciousness from blood loss. His body went limp, and his hands dropped from the one choking him. A dark shadow crossed Evaline's line of sight as she bumped into the wall.

"Oh God," she whispered. Her mind yelled at her to get up and her legs scrambled beneath her in a vain attempt to finally comply. Alexis' eyes closed. "I'm sorry," she muttered.

Nefret's teeth gleamed in the flickering light, the oil lamps slowly burning out as the clothes were consumed. She licked her lips once more, cleaning Alexis' blood from her teeth. The shadows intensified as more lamps went out. Nefret's shriek echoed in the room, squeezing Evaline's heart in terror. A heavy thump hit the ground as Evaline passed out, but not before she heard Nefret let out a heart-wrenching cry as the sound of clay jars shattered on the ground.

"Essam!"

XXXVIII

A SOFT HAND RUBBED Evaline's face as she regained consciousness. Her eyes fluttered as her blurry surroundings came into focus. The spot where her head hit the wall earlier ached, creating a continuous dull throbbing. A groan escaped her lips as she tried to move away from whoever touched her, causing her head to pound. Someone shushed her as they tried to keep her from moving. She couldn't understand at first, but as everything became clearer, she saw Zahir's bloodied face looming over her.

"Hold still," he muttered. "It's all right now."

"What happened?" she croaked out.

Her hand went to her head as she pushed herself up in his arms. This time, Zahir didn't try to stop her. The room was barely illuminated as the last of the oil lamps fought valiantly to remain lit. It was deathly silent with only Zahir's labored breathing breaking the tension. Blood caked his flesh and clothes, staining everything a muddy brown. As her eyes adjusted to the almost nonexistent light, Evaline saw two bodies on the floor.

"No!" she gasped, her feet slipping as she stepped in a puddle of blood that had dripped onto the floor. "Oh God, no!"

Zahir made no effort to stop her as she stumbled over to his fallen friend. Deep puncture wounds in Alexis' neck showed the depth of Nefret's evil. The scratches on his face were not as deep as Evaline first feared, but they were enough to draw a significant amount of blood. The facial wounds ran together until they met up with the blood that poured from his mouth. Everything was dry at this point and the blood lost its appearance of liquidness as it dried on his flesh. Under his torn clothes, Nefret's claws gauged him as deep as any sword could.

Next to him, Nefret's body laid sprawled out. No care was taken in how she was placed, almost as though she were shoved off the dais without a second thought. Evaline nudged the fallen priestess with her foot, noting how Alexis managed to do some serious damage to Nefret during their fight. Claw marks and fang punctures marred the priestess' beautiful body. Her crimson dress was tattered and her ebony hair disheveled. The spot on her neck where Alexis had bitten her was torn open, bits of muscle and other tissue exposed.

"The dagger," Zahir managed to get out between shuddering gasps.

Glancing to the spot where she'd fallen during the battle, Evaline found the silver dagger she'd picked up for protection. She studied the fine craftsmanship on the blade and hilt. The dark leather was soft and of high quality, while the blade itself was emblazoned with markings that didn't look like any of the few glyphs Evaline recognized. They left her feeling disconcerted, as though there were still an evil attached to the weapon. Walking over to Zahir, she handed the weapon over to him.

Nefret looked barely older than Evaline. Her full lips and soft face belied her age. Unconscious, Evaline found her beautiful, and almost sympathetic.

Out of the corner of her eye, Zahir's sudden movement as he plunged the blade into Nefret's chest caught Evaline off-guard. She let out a small shriek as the dagger sunk into the priestess' soft chest where her heart lay underneath. The blade glowed briefly, and a faint sizzling sound could be heard. Nefret's body twitched violently as the silver mixed with her blood. Like a fountain, the blood flowed from the priestess' chest and onto the dais, staining everything the same unsettling black as the blood that left her body. Evaline jumped back at the sight of the unnatural display.

Zahir held tightly onto the dagger until the blood stopped pouring from Nefret's body. Time passed at a crawl, Evaline no longer able to look at the darkness the flowed from the young woman until finally, Zahir grunted. She turned to face him and was met with him cleaning off the blade.

"Alexis," Evaline muttered.

Dashing over to his prone body, Evaline ran her fingers through his bangs, moving them to the side. Blood ran from his mouth and onto his chest. A long scratch down the side of his face bled freely. Evaline couldn't bring herself to look at the wounds on his chest again, but she felt how his blood soaked his shirt.

"Why isn't he breathing?" Evaline asked.

She felt Zahir stumble over to her. Out of the corner of her eye, she watched as he leaned over her, staring at his friend. She thought she saw a glimmer of moisture rim his eye.

"We don't need to," he replied.

"So, how do we? Is he?" She couldn't finish the question.

"We have to leave," Zahir said, ignoring the question.

Evaline's head shot up. "We can't leave him," she said simply.

A thousand protests came and died on Evaline's lips. *I can't leave him,* she told herself over and over. Yet, Evaline knew that if she were to return home, she would have to.

But why did it hurt so much? Alexis brought her into danger time and again, but somehow, Evaline found herself oddly attached to him. A sob caught in Evaline's throat, her eyes burning as her nose tingled. She didn't dare speak because she knew her voice would crack. Instead, she nodded with a sniffle. Evaline followed Zahir to the door.

I have to go home, she told herself.

The tension that filled the room during the ritual still hung in the air, not as heavy, but there were still remnants. The thumping and sounds of something scraping on the stones had disappeared sometime during their battle with Nefret. She hoped that whatever they were trying to unleash would not hurt him.

"Thank you for everything," she whispered, her voice cracking from emotion. Pressing her index and middle finger to her lips and blew a kiss. Then, she turned and the pair walked out the door.

***

It felt like they had been in the room for hours and day should have risen. To Evaline's dismay, it was still night. The moon hung low in the sky as they managed to slip through the palace doors, evading the guard and Nefret's personal soldiers. Their journey through the palace took an agonizingly long time as they had to stop many times as someone walked past. Not long after leaving the ritual room, they found the charred bodies of Abukhar and Hapu on the floor of a room. Their torn and bloodied clothing told the story of their desperate attempt to fend off their attackers. The way their mouths hung open in silent screams were testament to the torture they endured. It was just as difficult to block out as Alexis and Nefret. Ma'Alkin had turned into a place of excruciating death.

The sand crunched under their feet as they sprinted towards the nearest building. Evaline found herself checking over her shoulder several times. The feeling that someone watched their flight sent shivers down her spine. Instead of heading towards the main streets of Kul-El, Zahir turned them north, towards the construction site behind the palace.

"Lateef and his people are still out there," he'd explained. "We only have one chance to enter the tomb. By morning, the palace and all holy sites will be swarming, both with the pharaoh's soldiers and my kind. The Menes won't be able to help us if we're caught."

The chilly air brought goose flesh to Evaline's skin. She rubbed her arms as they continued through the tomb construction site. Unable to quickly find anything in the palace, Evaline was still dressed in only her shift. They would need to find clothes before they left. The sand crunched under their feet. In the moonlight, the imposing statues that stared down at them seemed more sinister. Their eyes bore onto the pair as if they prepared to render divine judgement onto them.

The light of the oil lamp was nearly extinguished by the time they found a small granite structure. Bits of granite rock lay scattered around, the pieces of the tomb a witness to the passage of time. As they stood on the precipice of the entrance, Evaline felt a gust of wind pull at her from inside.

"That doesn't make sense," she said.

"What?"

"The way the air pulled at me. From inside. How?"

"Get behind me," Zahir instructed.

"We're going in?" Evaline gasped.

A grunt was Zahir's only reply as he began the steep descent.

***

As Evaline's foot rested on the smooth floor at the bottom of the stairwell, she noticed that the stale musty air that smothered her as she descended had cleared up. Just before the light of the oil lamp flickered out, she noticed a torch on the wall. A small breeze blew out the lamp in Zahir's hand and Evaline let out a wail that echoed in the underground passageway. Zahir shushed her. Evaline heard what sounded like clacking rocks and was startled to see a flame burst forth and onto the torch. Zahir slipped the rocks into his pocket and motioned for her to follow him.

"Stay close," he warned. "There will be traps down here to stop looters and desecrators."

"Like what?" she whispered.

"I don't know," he admitted.

Evaline clung to Zahir as they slowly made their way through the passage. Several times, he would hold out his hand to stop her as he strained to listen to anything. Evaline held her breath each time, hoping to hear whatever his sharp ears could pick up.

"How are you able to see so well in this darkness?" Evaline asked.

"No clue."

She wanted to mention something Alexis told her, but the thought of his name made her freeze and the lump return to her throat. The image of his mangled and bloodied body lying on the stone floor squeezed the air from her lungs. Evaline gripped Zahir's arm as they proceeded forward. The chill from outside returned in some small measure despite them being in a fully enclosed passageway. The stale air completely cleared out, replaced with fresh air so deep below the earth.

"There must be another way in," Evaline muttered.

"Huh?" Zahir's head leaned towards her as he continued forward.

"The air. It's changed."

Zahir stopped and took a deep breath. "You're right."

Light from the torch danced on the wall, elongating their shadows as they traversed the passageway. They hadn't found a single trap yet, and their absence left Evaline feeling uncomfortable. Were the builders trying to lure people into a false sense of security before springing death upon the unsuspecting? The tunnel twisted and turned nearly as much as the stairwell, almost as though it were trying to disorient travelers.

Finally, they came upon a room that was different from the rest. Two large statues made from sandstone flanked a gaping hole in the middle of the wall. The doors were already open. The sand on the ground was disturbed, as though someone had to move quickly to avoid something. A fire burned in a small pool on the wall, the shadows casting eerie shapes against their own.

"He disarmed everything," Zahir muttered.

"What?"

"That's why we haven't run into anything. Alexis... Alexis cleared the passage for us."

Glancing around, Evaline saw a discarded spear butt and tip on the floor next to the scuff marks in the sand. What else had they missed as they made their way through the passage?

"Is it safe to go in?" Evaline asked.

"I think so. Wait here."

Standing alone in the room in only her shift left Evaline shivering in anticipation. They were about to meet a goddess, and here she was in her underclothes. Not only that, but she was completely alone. What if there were more traps about that both Alexis and Zahir had missed? She didn't have their reflexes to keep her safe. A short time later, Zahir's head popped out from the imposing entranceway and announced the all clear. Behind him, she thought she saw the room glitter in the torch light.

As Evaline walked into the room, her breath caught in her throat. Everything inside was covered in gold. Zahir had lit a few of the wall torches to give them some extra light. Glyphs were carved into the walls, the adjoining images depicting a beautiful woman dressed in red. room. Evaline expected to find gifts and other worldly goods littered about the place, but all she saw was a simple stone slab in the middle. Her eyes roved over the glyphs, trying to decipher the strange symbols. How she wished she could read them. Her attention was drawn to a symbol of a woman. Normally, the glyphs she saw showed the people kneeling or standing in a simple pose, but this one showed the woman with the sun in front of her.

"Zahir," she called out. "What does this mean?"

Zahir came over and stared at the image. His face scrunched up as though he were struggling to remember something. Eventually he shook his head.

"I don't know. It's an ancient text that's different from what I learned. The language is dead. I can only get a few clues. Follow me."

He led her to the simple stone slab in the middle of the room. On the front, the face of a beautiful woman was carved into the stone itself. Gold leaf draped down part of the top slab like the beginning of the beaded collar that adorned most other women.

"She's beautiful," Evaline breathed.

A golden bracelet sparkled on the ground. While Zahir studied the stone coffin, she bent down and picked it up. An Eye was carved into the bangle, a piece of brilliant red stone, just like the one in the necklace Amalie gave her, was embedded in the gold as well. Ancient script was also written inside. When she held the bracelet, she felt a sense of peace.

"Was this Alexis?" she asked, holding up the bangle.

"No idea. Help me push."

The two leaned against the top slab and pushed with their shoulders. Grunts filled the room, along with the sound of stone scraping stone. Slowly, the top inched off from the bottom until there was enough space for them to see into it. Holding the torch up high, Zahir let out a curse. It was empty.

"How?" Evaline asked.

Zahir stared into the empty tomb. Evaline tried to figure out who would have made it this far only to steal the body.

Who would want to steal a corpse. Was there even enough left?

"Let's go," Zahir finally said.

"Go where?" Evaline asked.

"We need to catch a ship."

Moving towards the doorway, Zahir blew out the torches that lined the wall, leaving his as the only source of light.

"What's going on?" Evaline asked, jogging to catch up.

"Things have changed," Zahir replied. "Neith has left her final resting place. We need to find her."

"It was never about a necklace, was it?" Evaline asked.

Zahir only grunted in response.

He doesn't know, Evaline realized. *Their goals were similar enough, but different. He wanted vengeance from Nefret, and Alexis wanted vengeance from Estrie. The necklace was Alexis' means to achieve his objective.*

Feeling herself deflate a little, Evaline found that focusing on her final moments with Alexis provided a measure of comfort she did not imagine. So, she concentrated on that. She didn't remember his mangled body, instead, she pictured the two of them together. Their bodies becoming one, and his gentle hands holding her. He would be her strength as she fled Ma'Alkin with Zahir.

Alexis had come back for her in the end. He wanted to take her to safety. Maybe they could have lived a happy life together. Evaline could only wonder. Keeping pace with Zahir, Evaline shed one final tear, slipping the bangle she'd snatched from the outside of the coffin as they left onto her wrist.

Good-bye, Amalie, she whispered to herself. *May the gods allow me to find my way back home to you once more.*

*****

About the Author

K.N. Nguyen is a fantasy author and founder of DragonScript. Growing up, she often found herself immersed in some imaginary world, conquering enemy nations, and saving the day. As time went on, her love for horrible puns and nerd culture pulled her out of these worlds and brought her back to reality.

It wasn't until she started working at her office job that she felt the itch to begin writing. Since 2015, she's been bringing her stories to life, one-by-one, and following her passion by delving into new mythologies.

A native of Sacramento, California, K.N. Nguyen spends her time singing karaoke, playing taiko, enjoying rhythm dancing games, and traveling with her friends and family when she isn't writing.

ALSO BY K.N. NGUYEN

THE FALLEN SERIES

King's Blood

Oath Blood

God's Blood

Nightmare Blood

DRAGON SCRIPT

Dragon Script

Lost Chapter

OTHER WORKS

A Song of Strength

Last Chance

Kuchisake-Onna

www.ingramcontent.com/pod-product-compliance
Lightning Source LLC
Chambersburg PA
CBHW072006190726
48293CB00001B/183